FINDING LOVE ON SUNSHINE ISLAND

THE SUNSHINE ISLAND SERIES – BOOK ONE

GEORGINA TROY

Boldwood

Hardback ISBN 978-1-80426-028-9

Ebook ISBN 978-1-80426-026-5

Kindle ISBN 978-1-80426-027-2

Audio CD ISBN 978-1-80426-034-0

MP3 CD ISBN 978-1-80426-031-9

Digital audio download ISBN 978-1-80426-025-8

Boldwood Books Ltd
23 Bowerdean Street
London SW6 3TN
www.boldwoodbooks.com

I am dedicating this book to Gerald (Gerry) and Joan Honeycombe, who came to the island as honeymooners in 1957, and to all those honeymooners who chose to spend that special time in their lives in Jersey, Channel Islands.

AUTHOR'S NOTE

Jersey was known as the Honeymoon Island from the forties through to the sixties, although in this book Piper likes to think of it as the Sunshine Island.

1

A NEW SEASON AT THE BLUE HAVEN

Piper Le Brocq smoothed down the bedcover and straightened the guest welcome pack on the chest of drawers next to the circular tray displaying cups, saucers, a glass jar filled with chunks of Jersey fudge, and a tiny milk urn. She stepped back to take in the full effect of the room, satisfied that their second-best bedroom overlooking Gorey Harbour was exactly as her mother would expect it to be.

She bent to sniff the fresh floral arrangement she had collected earlier from Harbour Blooms along the pier. It was in prime position for Mr and Mrs Chapman to notice as soon as she showed them to their room. *How amazing must it be to have spent sixty years of your life with someone, and still like them enough to want to return to stay in the same bedroom where you spent your honeymoon all those years before?*

Noticing a couple of fingerprints on the window, she pulled the duster hanging from her back pocket and wiped them away. Unable to resist gazing out to her favourite view, she took a moment to sit on the window seat and looked at the vista. It was high tide and the small sailing boats, and a couple of fishing boats moored in the harbour, floated a few feet below the pier.

The late afternoon sun warmed Piper's face and she closed her eyes, listening to the carefree laughter drifting up from the visitors strolling along eating ice creams. She loved it here and couldn't imagine ever wanting to live anywhere else.

Hearing her mother's voice, she followed it down to a bench at the edge of the harbour wall, across the narrow road, which was lined with Victorian cottages, small shops, hotels, restaurants and cafés. Her mother, Helen, was chatting to Dave, her 'man friend', as she insisted on calling him. Piper wasn't sure what was wrong with calling someone your boyfriend, but her mother insisted that at fifty-one she was far too old to be using titles like that for someone she only occasionally agreed to accompany out for a meal.

As a taxi drew up outside their front door, Piper pulled the window open and leaned out to see if it was dropping off their newest guests. A passenger opened the door but looked far too young to be Mr Chapman. She watched as the tall, broad-shouldered, dark-haired man stepped out, thanking the taxi driver as he walked to the boot of the car and lifted out a large red rucksack. He stepped back as the car pulled away and, seeming to sense that he was being watched, glanced up to where Piper was peering down at him.

'Bugger,' she groaned, immediately pulling back into the room and knocking the back of her head against the window frame. She winced, and her orange duster floated out down to the pavement below. She rubbed her head and was contemplating what to do next when she heard the front door open and someone – presumably the taxi passenger – walk into the house.

She caught sight of herself in the mirror and grimaced. Her long, dark, curly hair was messier than usual. She hadn't expected anyone this early, so her hair was still unbrushed and not in its usual ponytail. As her mother was outside, she had no choice but to go downstairs and greet their new guest. She quickly ran her fingers through her tangly hair and hooked as much as she could behind her ears.

'Hi,' he said as she descended the stairs to the hallway wishing she wasn't so flustered; it was hardly the professional welcome her mother expected her to make. 'I'm Alex Cooper.' His voice was deep and confident. 'I've booked a room here for four days.'

'Yes, of course,' she said, noticing the duster in his hand. 'If you'll come into the front room, I'll sign you in.'

His eyes followed her gaze. 'I think this is yours. You dropped it out of the window just now.'

Embarrassed by her clumsiness, she stepped forward and took it from him, remembering to smile.

'If you'll come this way,' she said, leading him into the reception area. 'Your room is ready for you.' She sat at the computer, checked his details and took a few more. 'Have you been to Jersey before?' she asked, trying to sound professional.

He set his rucksack by his feet. 'I've been to the

island a few times, but only when I was young. My grandparents used to bring me and my sister during the summer holidays, but we usually stayed out in St Brelade's Bay.'

Piper was aware that visitors tended to favour one area over another, often returning to the same place, rather than stay somewhere different. 'And you didn't want to go there this time?' she asked without thinking.

'Why?' His blue eyes twinkled in amusement. 'Would you rather I did?'

'No!' she replied, picturing her mother's horror if she could hear her. 'I mean, mostly people choose to go back to the place they know, to reminisce, that sort of thing.'

'I don't remember much about it, to be honest.'

She picked up his room key, remembering how her mother expected her to greet guests for the first time. 'I'd like to wish you a warm welcome to the sunshine island.'

His eyes widened in surprise. 'I'm sorry, what?'

Piper cringed, glad she had already turned her back to him. Although her mother insisted on the welcome, sometimes, like this time, it embarrassed her.

'Jersey was known as the honeymoon island back in the forties, fifties and sixties,' she explained. 'It was a big deal to come here for your honeymoon.' She wished she hadn't mentioned honeymoons. 'Although it's also supposed to be the sunniest place in the British Isles, so I like to refer to it as the sunshine island.' *Why was she wittering on?* 'What I should be saying is, welcome to Blue Haven Guest House.'

'Right. Thanks.'

'If you follow me, I'll take you up to your room. You're in number two. It's a lovely room right at the front of the house. Shall we go now, and you can settle in?'

She led the way up the first flight of stairs. Recalling his mention of earlier visits to the island and the hint of sadness in his tone, Piper sensed there was more to his return than a quiet few days away.

She reached the bedroom door and opened it, standing aside to let him enter.

He stepped in and looked around. 'This is lovely and bright,' he said, lowering his rucksack to the painted floorboards by the chest of drawers before walking over to the open window. She watched him silently take in the view of the harbour and Grouville's golden arc of sand stretching out across the bay. 'I might not want to leave,' he said, almost to himself.

'Well, feel free to extend your stay here. Although, if you did, I would have to move you as a couple of return visitors have booked in here from Monday for two weeks and always request this room.'

He kept staring out of the window as she spoke and seemed lost in thought. 'You're lucky having this view to look at every day.' He turned to face her. 'I'm presuming you live here. Or nearabouts?'

'I live upstairs in a tiny flat in the eaves with my mum, Helen.' She cringed, hearing herself sound like some sort of modern-day Cinderella. 'Um, it's her B&B now really. You'll meet her soon no doubt. She's got ash-blonde hair and wears glasses. She took it over from my gran a few years ago. Gran lives in the cottage next door, further down Gorey Pier.' *Why was she blabbering on like this?*

'I don't blame her for not going far. I wouldn't want to move away from somewhere like this.' He took off his leather jacket and folded it before draping it across the back of the chair near the drawers. 'Have you always lived here?'

'I have.' Piper forced herself not to stare at his muscular arms and the way his T-shirt moulded to his torso. *Get a grip, woman.* She was used to guests asking her these sorts of questions and didn't mind at all. She cleared her throat. 'My gran came here in her late twenties with my mum after she and Grandad divorced, but I've always lived on the pier. I love it here.'

Through the window, she recognised her mother's voice, calling to Casey Norman and Tara Spencer. Piper's friends ran the Smoke and Mirrors stall at The Cabbage Patch, next to where Piper sold her mosaics when she wasn't helping out at the Blue Haven. 'Casey!' Helen shouted. 'Tell your mum I'll catch up with her later. She's making a Victoria sponge for my guests, and I said I'd collect it.'

'I can drop it off if you like?' Casey called back.

Alex turned to watch the goings-on down below. 'I think I already love this place,' he said quietly. She wasn't certain if he was addressing her or talking to himself.

'It's certainly got its own character and characters.' Piper laughed. 'Most of them have good hearts too.'

'Hey, Helen,' bellowed a deep voice with a thick Jersey accent Piper recognised as one of the farmers who regularly dropped off produce for the small restaurant and café a few doors along from the guest house. 'Got some tasty maincrop spuds, aubergines and butternuts if you want them, ma love?'

'You're all right thanks, Len. I've still got some from the last batch you brought me. Possibly next week.'

'Right you are then.'

Alex turned to face Piper once more. 'I have a feeling I'm going to enjoy my stay here.'

'I hope it doesn't get too noisy with all the chatter,' she said. 'As well as the locals who live and work around here, we get quite a few holidaymakers at this time of year.'

'I'm sure it won't bother me at all.'

She was relieved to hear it. 'Where have you come from if you don't mind me asking?'

'London,' he said. 'Not far from Hammersmith,

so this might be noisy to you but it's extremely quiet to me.'

She really should get going before her mother wondered where she was, but she was fascinated by Alex and couldn't help wanting to discover more about him.

His stomach rumbled noisily, and he rested a hand on it giving her an apologetic smile. 'Sorry. I haven't eaten anything since leaving home after breakfast this morning.'

Remembering her manners, Piper shook her head. 'Please don't worry. I should have told you about the meals here. Obviously you get breakfast and that's served between eight and nine-thirty each morning, but Mum is fairly easy-going if you need to catch an early flight or something like that.'

'Sounds great.'

'There's the café along from here where you can find really tasty meals for your lunch and supper. In fact, there are several cafés, and also a great fish and chip shop if you walk into the village.' She indicated the general direction he should take. 'It's about fifteen minutes away. Turn right just before the village green and keep walking. There's a post office, chemist and plenty of other shops. Gorey village is really pretty.'

'It sounds like I'll be well catered for.'

She smiled. 'Most people are happy with what's on offer.' Turning to leave, about to close the door, Piper realised she was still holding his room key and placed it on the chest of drawers. 'If you have any issues with the television, kettle or anything else, ring downstairs and either Mum or I will come and help you. The Wi-Fi password is written on the card next to the tea tray. Oh, and the bathroom is down the hall to your right.'

'Thanks.'

Piper closed the door behind her and returned downstairs where she found her mother making a cup of tea in the kitchen.

Helen narrowed her eyes thoughtfully. 'You've been an awfully long time settling that new guest into his room. Was everything all right?'

'Yes, Mum.' Piper took a mug and placed it on the worktop next to her mother's. 'Can I have one of those too,' she asked. 'I'm parched.'

'Probably all that chatting you've been doing,' her mother teased.

Piper grinned. 'I'm not the one who's been gossiping. I saw you, on the bench, chatting away to your "man friend". And anyway, you always tell me to try to make the guests welcome.'

Her mother popped a tea bag into Piper's mug and poured hot water onto it. 'I do.' She gave the steaming liquid a bit of a stir. 'What's he like? Alex something-or-other, isn't it?'

Piper nodded, not realising she was smiling as she thought of him. 'He's quite nice. I think he's hungry, so I told him where to go to find food. I'm fairly sure he'll be down for breakfast in the morning.' She took her mug and poured in milk before removing the tea bag. 'He seems to like his room.'

'That's good.' Helen picked up her mug and Piper followed her through to the dining room where they sat at one of the smaller tables.

She loved this time of day, when everything had been done and the two of them had a chance to sit and chat.

'I wonder why he's here,' Piper said.

'Who?' Her mum raised her eyebrows. 'The new guest?' Piper nodded. 'He probably needs a few days away from wherever he lives. And what better place to do it.'

Piper agreed, but they usually welcomed couples for long weekends, or friends getting away to visit the sights rather than single men. Never mind. She would probably find out at some point. Alex seemed friendly enough.

After finishing their teas, Piper set the tables ready for morning. She was looking forward to setting off to The Cabbage Patch. She loved the large barn in Trinity where she and other artisans ran their concessions. Before she had a chance to leave, the front door opened and she heard voices as new people arrived.

'That'll probably be Mr and Mrs Chapman,' Helen said, folding tablecloths ready for ironing. 'Will you look after them, love?'

'Sure.' Piper grabbed a hairband from her pocket and quickly scraped her hair back into a semi-neat ponytail as she hurried through to greet their guests.

'Mr and Mrs Chapman?' she asked, smiling.

'That's us,' the husband confirmed. She noticed they were holding hands, their free hands gripping the handles of their cases. 'Please call us Eric and Patty, dear.'

'Thank you. And I'm Piper.' She took their details and picked up their room key. 'You're our honeymooners. We're extremely excited you've chosen to come and spend your sixtieth wedding anniversary with us.'

They gazed at each other with such love that Piper unwittingly sighed. 'It's lovely to have you back. We've put you in Room Four, as you requested. If you want to follow me, I'll show you up.' She reached out to take Patty's case. 'Please, let me take that for you.'

'I don't mind carrying both cases,' Eric said, attempting to take it from her.

'It's fine, honestly. I'm used to it.' Piper led the way, taking it slowly, aware that when the couple had come on their honeymoon they had been six decades younger and might not find the two flights of stairs as easy this time round. 'If you decide after a few days that you would rather swap rooms for one below, I'm sure we can arrange that. The gentleman in there is only here for a short visit.' She heard them whisper something to each other as they reached the second floor and stopped outside number four. 'Well, here we are.' Piper unlocked the door and pushed it wide open, stepping back to let them enter.

Patty gasped and rushed forwards to the flowers. 'These are from you, aren't they, Eric? Only you would buy me red roses and orange tiger lilies.'

It was obvious they had already forgotten Piper was there. They might be seventy-nine and eighty years old, but the young newlyweds they had once been shone in their faces as Eric stepped forward and took Patty in his arms.

Not wishing to intrude on their privacy, Piper placed the suitcase inside the room and set the key on the bedcover, before closing the door quietly behind her.

As she returned downstairs, she thought about the saying 'true love never dies'. She might have agreed with that sentiment once, but in her experience, true love only pretended to exist. It warmed her heart to witness this couple still so clearly in love with each other and gave her hope that, one day, she might experience something similar.

2

The following morning, Piper woke a few minutes after seven. She always left her curtains slightly open to wake slowly as the sun rose and lit up the bay in front of the harbour. On warm spring days like this, she slept with the window open and could already hear noise and chatter coming from the pier as the fishermen set out in their boats. The locals were leaving for work, or opening up businesses ready for the day, while the seagulls noisily made their presence known.

Piper got up and looked out of the window, happy to discover that it would be another warm sunny day. She had two rooms to clean and freshly make up once the current guests had left. They had spoken to her mother about arranging a taxi to collect them at ten o'clock to take them to the airport. The next guests, arriving by ferry from France, weren't due to dock in St Helier until two that afternoon, leaving her plenty of time.

After a quick shower, she cleaned her teeth, then dressed in her uniform of black linen shorts and a white T-shirt that she believed complemented her more athletic figure. Piper wished she had a shapelier figure like her mum and Gran, but took after her father with her looks and there was little she could do about it. She brushed her hair back and tied it in a high ponytail to keep it out of her face while she was working. Her mum was always immaculate and liked her to be neat and tidy. She had initially expected Piper to wear a black skirt and blouse, but Piper had persuaded her that nobody would mind how she dressed as long as she looked presentable. Her mother finally relented when Piper said she wouldn't be able to help out as there would not be time to change before driving to Trinity to The Cabbage Patch for her *actual* job selling her mosaics.

Piper hurried downstairs, surprised to find her

mother already in the kitchen. 'I thought you might still be asleep, Mum.'

Helen lifted the red-and-white-striped apron she used to protect her clothes from the brass hook on the wall and slipped it over her head, tying the strings neatly behind her back. 'I couldn't sleep. Didn't you find it hot and a bit stuffy last night?'

'It wasn't too bad with my window open, but I agree it's a little warm for April. More like July.'

'I love the spring but have to admit I prefer it a bit cooler. The winter can't come soon enough for me.'

'I don't think I'd go that far, Mum.' Piper laughed. 'It's always hotter in the flat. Try leaving your bedroom door and the bathroom door open and let the breeze from the bathroom window blow through.'

'I might try that tonight.' Her mother pursed her lips. 'You're so clever sometimes. It makes me wonder where you get it from.'

Piper laughed. 'Well, it was either you, or Dad. Which reminds me, I haven't heard from him for a while.'

'When was the last time you spoke to him?'

'A couple of weeks ago, but he and Pam were

going on holiday for ten days, somewhere in Cyprus, so they're not back yet.'

She didn't mention her father too often, aware there was still some antagonism between him and her mother despite them divorcing twenty-two years ago when Piper was five and her father remarrying less than a year later. The antagonism was mostly on her father's side, which Piper thought a little unfair. After all, if he was as happy with Pam as he kept professing to be, he wouldn't give her mother a second thought. Piper didn't know the full story about why their marriage hadn't worked and wasn't keen to find out.

'We have a house full,' her mother said, interrupting her thoughts. 'You'd better check we have enough orange juice in the fridge and get out some cafetières. At least two tables will want coffee. I think the rest will be asking for tea.'

They set to work in the small kitchen, their movements like a rehearsed ballet, each knowing their steps and what was needed to ensure that breakfasts were served perfectly and on time.

'I can hear a few of the guests coming down,'

Piper said, grabbing several menus and her notepad and pen. 'I'll start taking orders.'

She greeted the couple and their daughters who were leaving at ten, stepping back to let them pass by and enter the dining room before attending to Mr and Mrs Chapman.

'Good morning, Mr and Mrs Chapman,' she said, handing each of them a menu and waiting for them to decide what they'd like to eat and drink.

'It's Eric and Patty, remember?' Eric let go of his wife's hand across the table they'd chosen at the back of the room. 'Is it all right, us sitting here?'

'Yes, of course it is,' Piper grinned.

'We sat at a table right here on our honeymoon,' Patty explained. 'Although, I can't imagine it would be this actual table.'

Piper recalled how her mother had upgraded the furniture after taking over the guest house ten years ago. 'No, it won't be, but the view will be the same.'

'Oh yes, that's true.' Eric took his wife's hand again gently in his and beamed at her.

Alex came in and gave Piper a smile. 'You can take the table by the window, if you like,' she said, handing him a menu. 'I won't be long.'

She concentrated on the Chapmans but couldn't ignore the atmosphere that seemed to have entered the room with Alex, making her jittery. *Get a grip.* She was irritated with herself. It wasn't like her to react this way to a man.

'I'll have the full fried breakfast with tea and orange juice, please,' said Eric, his wife's forehead creasing into a frown as she studied the menu.

'White or brown toast?'

'White for me, I think.'

Mrs Chapman widened her eyes at Piper. 'I've finally made up my mind,' she said. 'I'll have the veggie fried breakfast please.'

'Drinks and toast?'

'The same as my husband, please,' she replied after a little thought.

Piper thanked them and took their menus before walking over to Alex. 'I hope you slept well last night?'

'I did, thanks. That bed is so comfortable. I wouldn't mind spending an entire day lying there and staring out of the window, but that would be a waste.'

Piper held back from making a flirty comment.

'That's what we like to hear,' she said, pushing all thoughts of Alex reclining in the king-sized bed to one side. 'And have you decided what you'd like to eat this morning?'

'I'll have what he's just ordered.' He indicated Eric with a nod of his head.

Piper jotted down his order. She took his menu and left to speak to the family at the next table, aware of Alex's gaze on her.

'Here are the orders so far, Mum,' Piper said as she entered the kitchen and placed the notes on the stainless-steel worktop and began making the drinks. 'Everyone seems very hungry this morning.'

Her mother opened a large pack of bacon and began setting rashers and sausages in a pan. 'Is our new guest downstairs?'

'He is, and he said how comfortable the bed was.'

'Good.'

Piper glanced at her mother, happy to see her smiling as she worked. Helen had always loved cooking for people and Piper thought it was a shame she'd only had one child, and although her mother occasionally went out on dates with a 'man friend', they mostly kept their lives separate. She was certain her mother would have loved a large family despite her assertion that one child was enough and always pictured her in a farmhouse kitchen preparing meals for others. At least here, her mother enjoyed feeding their guests and making their stay on the island a truly wonderful time.

After breakfast, Piper was helping the family of four carry out their cases to the waiting taxi when Alex came down the stairs.

'Here, let me take those from you,' he said, taking the two cases she had been struggling to carry along the passage.

Piper watched him go outside, laughing and talking to the parents. Piper joined them and stood with Alex to wave them off.

'What are your plans today?' she said to him after they'd gone. 'Any ideas?'

He pulled a booklet from his pocket that she recognised from the display stand at the airport; a small magazine about Jersey and what was on that month. He opened it to a pocket-size map and peered down at it.

'I need to find a farmstead in Trinity. My grandfather is on an artists' retreat there and I'm hoping to surprise him by paying him a visit.'

'How lovely.' So that was why he had come for a long weekend. 'Do you know how to get there?'

'I'm guessing I need to catch a couple of buses to get to a place called The Cabbage Patch by the looks of things. He said there's a large barn and some out-buildings and that's where his retreat is being held. Apparently he's staying in a room in the main house while he's there.' He frowned as he studied the booklet. 'I think I need to catch one bus from here to the main station in St Helier and then another to Trinity.'

'We know The Cabbage Patch well, don't we, Piper?' Helen said, stepping outside to join them. 'You'll need the number thirteen bus from here for Trinity. But—' She checked her watch. '—You've missed it by a couple of minutes and the next one isn't for a while yet. Piper can drive you up there now if you're ready. It'll only take her a few minutes by car.'

Before Piper could argue that she was busy, her

mother produced the key to Piper's Mini. 'I heard you talking,' she said by way of an explanation as she and pressed the key into Piper's palm. 'Go on.'

Piper glanced at her mother, confused. It wasn't like Helen to offer her services to someone, especially when they were busy.

'Actually, I am ready.' Alex looked from Helen to Piper. 'If you're sure you don't mind.'

She wouldn't have minded if it was one of the days she worked at The Cabbage Patch with Casey and Tara. Piper thought of the two cousins who were such fun to be around. They looked nothing alike, Casey with her dark-brown hair and hazel eyes and Tara several inches taller, her dyed auburn hair accentuating her piercing blue-green eyes. Piper's mother looked rather pleased with herself for some reason. 'Not at all,' Piper said. 'I'll be back as soon as I can, Mum.'

'That's fine. You can pop into the shop in St Martin on your way back. I fancy a couple of their freshly baked baguettes. And buy the big ones, mind, not the skinny ones. I don't like those.'

'Will do.' Piper noticed Alex trying not to smile.

'The car is this way,' she said, leading him out of the guest house and along the pier. 'I usually try to park closer, but there were no spaces by the time I came home yesterday afternoon.'

'The harbour looks completely different when the tide is lower.' Alex stopped for a second and Piper did the same. 'When's the best time of day for this view, would you say?'

'I'd say it's around sunset.' She began walking again and Alex caught up with her. 'We're on the east of the island here and the sun rises behind us – or, rather, it's hidden from us by Mont Orgueil Castle.' She pointed ahead at the medieval castle standing proudly on its high granite mound above the pier. 'If you look out of your bedroom window tonight at around five-ish, you'll see the most incredible view. At least, I think it's incredible. I often sit at my bedroom window to watch the sun go down. The colours across the bay and over the sea are amazing.'

'It sounds magical.'

'It is.' She smiled. 'I walk on the beach most days.'

'I'm sure I would, too, if I lived this close to one.'

They reached her Mini and Piper pressed her keys to unlock the doors. 'I love it,' she said. 'It's where I find most of my sea glass for my work.'

'Sea glass? What's that?'

'Essentially, it's glass that's been washed up from the sea.'

Alex laughed as he folded himself into the passenger seat. 'I suppose that makes sense. You said you use it for your work. I'm sorry, I assumed you worked at the Blue Haven.'

'I help Mum out there, yes.' Piper strapped herself in and started the ignition. 'But I also have a stall at The Cabbage Patch.'

'Where we're going now?'

'That's right.' She slowed to let a couple of cars pass before turning the Mini and driving up the hill. 'One and the same.'

'But didn't you tell your mum you wouldn't be long?'

She understood his confusion. 'I did. I'm not working up there today. It's one of my days off.'

'Oh. Hell, I'm sorry.'

'What for?'

'Taking you out of your way. Especially on your day off.'

Piper laughed. 'It's fine, honestly. I love being up there, so it's not a problem.'

'Do you mind me asking what you sell, or do you make something?'

Piper slowed down behind a cyclist. 'Mosaic is my choice of art. I find unloved objects, like old mirrors, small tables, that sort of thing and make them as beautiful as I can, and I sell them. When I'm not there, my friends, Casey and Tara, keep an eye on my stall and take care of any customers. When they need extra help, I pitch in with them.'

'And what do they do?'

'They make deliciously scented candles and soap. If you want to buy gifts to take home, you could check out their wares.'

'I'll do that.'

She overtook a bike and continued driving until she had to slow down behind the bus that Alex had initially hoped to catch.

'Mine?' he pointed, grinning.

'It is.'

The bus stopped and they waited for several passengers to get off and a few more to get on.

'You were talking about walking on the beach,' he said. 'I'm determined to make the most of this glorious weather and have a walk this evening before the sun goes down.'

'Do, it's so relaxing, especially if you take off your shoes and let the sand get between your toes.'

He looked sideways at her, obviously unsure whether she was teasing him.

'Of course, if you want to see the sun setting you'll need to go to St Ouen's Bay. That is another sight that you shouldn't miss while you're here.'

As they neared Trinity, she pointed out the parish school she had attended when she was small, waving to friends as they passed. A short distance later they caught up with a coach, indicating to turn left. 'That's Jersey Zoo,' she explained as the coach turned into the car park. 'That's another place you must visit if you have the time.'

'Ahh, the zoo called Durrell for a while?' he asked. 'They do a lot for conservation, don't they?' Piper nodded. 'I used to love Gerald Durrell's books when I was young.' He gave a brief laugh. 'I was sure I'd end up following in his footsteps.'

Intrigued by his comment, Piper turned down a country lane. 'And did you?'

He shook his head. 'No, sadly not.'

'What do you do if you don't mind me asking?'

'I'm an app designer.' She wasn't exactly sure what that entailed, but before she could ask he explained, 'I basically create programmes for the apps on people's phones.'

'Like games?'

'Yes, but I'm mostly working on social networking apps at the moment.'

'It sounds interesting.' Piper wasn't actually sure it did. As someone who didn't often bother with her phone or have much of a social media presence, she wasn't that well informed about what apps people used. 'And do you like it?'

'Most of the time I do.'

She slowed as they caught up with a tractor and trailer and looked at him. 'It seems like the traffic is against us this morning.' She lowered her window and rested her elbow on the frame. 'Do you work for yourself then?'

He shook his head. 'I did for a few years, but not now.'

'Why not? Didn't you like it?'

He grinned at her, pushing his dark hair off his forehead. He looked good in dark jeans, and a plain white T-shirt that enhanced his golden tan. 'You like asking a lot of questions, don't you? But then I guess I've been doing the same.'

Yes, but he was a guest, and she should at least be trying to make a good impression. She realised she was being very nosey. 'Sorry. Gran says I'm too inquisitive for my own good sometimes, but I'm fascinated by people, especially those who come to stay with us.'

'That's nice.'

She sensed he was avoiding answering her question and wondered why he no longer worked for himself. Was he someone who had chosen to change his lifestyle and reduce his daily stress? If so, she admired him for having the courage to make such a decision. Reducing her stress had been why she now worked part-time in the guest house so she could run her stall up at The Cabbage Patch.

'That must be it,' he said, pointing at an elaborately painted sign on one side of a granite entrance leading to a farmhouse.

'It certainly is.' She drove slowly up the drive, passing the large farmhouse, and into a yard surrounded on three sides by a huge barn and various small outbuildings. 'I wonder where you'll find your grandfather?'

'I'm not sure, but I should probably leave you to get back to your job. I don't want your mother being angry with me for keeping you out too long and refusing to cook me one of her delicious breakfasts tomorrow morning.'

'You're a wise man,' she teased as he stepped out of the car.

Piper was about to put the car into reverse when an older man she vaguely recognised as having looked at her mosaics a couple of days ago hurried out of the barn and waved at her. She leaned her head out of the window. 'Is everything all right?'

'Alex?' the grey-haired man called. He was sporting a golden tan and looked too young to be a grandfather. 'What are you doing here?'

'I wanted to visit you.' Alex crossed the yard and

gave his grandfather a bear hug. 'You're looking really well, and you've caught the sun.'

'I have, my boy.' His grandfather laughed. 'We've been painting in the wildflower meadows at the back of this place whenever the weather isn't too hot or dull.'

'Fliss will be pleased to learn you're enjoying yourself.'

'Ahh, so that's it. You're both checking up on me.'

Piper had no idea who Fliss was but felt pleased that Alex's grandfather was enjoying himself on the retreat. She thought of her mother's close friends – the elderly Ecobichon sisters – who owned the property. They had struggled financially for a couple of years until someone had suggested that they could make money renting out the large barn on their farm to stallholders looking for somewhere to sell their handcrafted pieces, calling it The Cabbage Patch. Soon after, the sisters had also begun earning an income from renting out bedrooms in their large farmhouse and the smaller outbuildings to artists running courses and artist retreats as well as similar endeavours.

She was happy for them to have finally found

their footing with their business. Piper knew how close they had come to not making it, and made a mental note to pass on Alex's comments about how much his grandfather was enjoying his artist's retreat at The Cabbage Patch, because she knew it meant a lot to the sisters that everyone associated with the place was happy with what they were doing.

She began reversing, intending to turn the car. Alex seemed happy enough for her to leave and she didn't like to interrupt the surprise reunion. She was relieved that Alex's grandfather appeared to be delighted by his unexpected appearance rather than put out. As she glanced in her rear-view mirror, she noticed the older man looking in her direction. 'Who's this young lady?' he asked, loud enough for her to hear.

Not wishing to be rude, Piper pulled on the handbrake and got out of the car. 'I'm Piper Le Brocq,' she said with a smile. 'Alex is staying at my mum's guest house for a couple of days and needed a lift up here.'

His grandfather came over, hand outstretched. 'That's very kind of you, Miss Le Brocq.' His bushy eyebrows knitted together. 'Don't I recognise you from somewhere?'

She nodded. 'We spoke briefly the other day, in the barn.'

'So we did!' He returned her smile, eyes crinkling. 'You're the one who makes those incredible mosaics.'

'Thank you.'

'Well, I'm happy to meet you properly. I'm Colin Cooper.' He looked at Alex, who was watching their exchange and smiling. 'Thank you for bringing my grandson up here to see me.'

'It was my pleasure,' she said, turning back to the car.

'Thanks again, Piper,' Alex called as he was pulled into another bear hug by the older man.

She drove away smiling. It was wonderful to see them happy in each other's company, but she couldn't help wondering why Alex was concerned about his grandfather to the extent that he'd come to the island. Colin Cooper seemed happy and relaxed, but she knew from her own experience that putting on a brave face was exactly what people did if they didn't want others to discover their vulnerabilities.

* * *

Twenty minutes later, having stopped to buy the baguettes for her mother and a Twix for herself, Piper was pleased to see a car pulling out of a parking space almost in front of the guest house. She waited for the driver to leave, then parked and took her shopping inside.

'I'm back,' she called as she entered the kitchen to put down the bread and place her chocolate in the fridge. She found her mother in the small office at the back of the house, where she worked during the day.

'You were gone for ages. I thought you'd forgotten you were supposed to be working here today. Did you remember to get the bread?'

'I did. It's on the side.'

'Good girl. If you want to go and clean the bedrooms that were vacated this morning, I'll get back to replying to emails.' She looked up from what she was doing. 'We've had four more bookings this morning already. That advert you set up online is bringing in so many new visitors, I'm going to have to be careful not to double-book and upset our regulars.'

Piper thought of the return guests whose visits had kept them going when times were leaner, or during the winter months. She understood her mother's wish to ensure they were catered for whenever possible.

'Did you drop Alex Cooper off with his grandfather?'

'Yes.' Piper bent to pick up a stray paperclip that must have fallen from her mother's pine desk. 'Why did you suggest I take him, anyway? And don't say it's because you wanted me to buy the bread because we both know I could have bought that from the Co-op down the road.'

Her mother stopped typing and looked up at her, a half-smile on her face. 'I just think he's a pleasant young man and that you don't spend enough time away from here, that's all.'

Piper wasn't convinced. She understood her mother well enough to be certain she had been up to something and then it occurred to her. 'You were trying to matchmake,' she corrected. 'Well, you can stop wasting your time.'

'You don't like him?'

Piper wasn't in the mood to discuss how she felt

about Alex or any other man for that matter. 'He's perfectly nice, but you know I'm not interested in dating again, Mum.'

Her mother pursed her lips, looking at her over a pair of glasses, her ash-blonde hair newly washed, smart in her black top and skirt. Not for the first time, Piper thought how much younger she looked than her fifty-one years. 'You're going to have to find a way to move on from him one day, darling.'

Piper narrowed her eyes. 'We've had this conversation many times,' she said, weary from having to remind her mother. 'I'm aware you only have my best interests at heart, but I'm not looking for any romance, Mum. Please try to understand.'

Helen reached out and took Piper's hand. 'I do understand, darling. Probably more than you realise, which is why you shouldn't shut yourself away here. What about your friends? You don't even bother with them any more.'

'Mum.' Piper gave a warning groan. 'Can we leave it, please?'

'Fine, I'll do as you ask. For now.'

Piper walked over to the airing cupboard and took out two sets of bed linen for the rooms she needed to make up. She loved her mother more than anyone, but wished she would take Piper's word that she was happy spending her days working and her evenings in her room, reading, or walking along the beach. She didn't need a man to make her life complete.

3

'Helen? Piper? Are you out the back?'

'I'm here, Gran.' Piper lay the paperback she had been reading on the concrete floor of their small backyard where she had been relaxing during her lunch break. She stood to greet her gran. Piper knew that after decades running the Blue Haven her grandmother must get a little bored sometimes, now that she no longer had as much to do each day.

'Phew, it's warm today, isn't it?' Her gran stepped out of the office carrying a small shopping bag. She walked over to the circular metal table they kept outside, and Piper put up the sunshade to keep cool.

'Would you like me to fetch you something cold to drink?'

'No, thank you, sweetheart. I had one before leaving home.'

'So, what have you been doing today, Gran?' Piper asked, happy to spend time with the woman who had always meant so much to her. 'I hope you haven't been overdoing it with your wild swimming?'

'You should come with us and try it.' Her gran wagged a finger at Piper and stared at her for a moment. She seemed to be making up her mind about something and a sense of dread began to build in Piper's chest. 'In fact, I'm not going to take no for an answer any longer. Tomorrow you can drive me down to Rozel and come swimming with me and the girls.'

'The girls' were a group of friends who met each morning regardless of the weather to swim from the beach to the pier and back again, sometimes twice, before sharing a flask of tea.

Piper scowled. 'You know I don't really enjoy swimming and I hate cold water. I don't mind taking you there but *I'm not* going in with you.'

'I think it's a great idea,' her mother said, joining them outside.

Piper suspected her mother had been the one to come up with the idea. 'Mum, no. It's not happening.' She sat back down on her sunbed and picked up her book ready to hide behind it.

'Rubbish,' her mother argued. 'It'll do you the world of good.'

'It will, sweetheart,' her grandmother said. 'Anyway, how can you say you don't like doing something if you've never tried it?'

She had a point, but in this instance, Piper was certain. 'Gran, cold water and me simply don't go together. Maybe later in the season when the sea has had time to heat up a bit?' Aware that she wasn't going to get any peace, she closed her book and stood. Maybe they would leave her alone to read in her bedroom.

'And where do you think you're going?' Helen asked.

'My room.'

'Helen, leave the girl alone,' her gran said, cheering Piper up slightly. 'I'm sure she's happy to come with me tomorrow.' She looked at Piper. 'I'll be ready for you to drive me there at nine forty-five. And, before you tell me you're too busy, I've already checked with your mother and she tells me that there are no new arrivals, or departures, for you to have to worry about.'

So, they had been conspiring together. Piper frowned at them both. Sometimes it was easier to give in, especially when they had the same intention. 'Fine.' She sighed heavily. 'I'll do it. But I'm only agreeing once and that's it.'

'If you insist.' Her grandmother looked pleased with herself.

Piper left the two women to congratulate each other on succeeding in their mission to get her out and wild swimming, even though the last place she would want to be the following morning was on a beach in a swimming costume. She walked upstairs to her bedroom, trying to recall the last time she had worn a one-piece. Or even if she still possessed one. She dropped her book onto her bed and opened her chest of drawers, looking for something appropriate. As she pulled out one piece of underwear after the other, she began to suspect she might have to buy a new costume, but the thought of spending money on something she had no intention of wearing twice upset her.

'Yes!' she cheered at last, finding a pink and black costume that had seen better days. In fact, as she pulled gently at one of the leg holes, it looked as if the elastic might be about to perish. It didn't matter. She would be in and out of the water in minutes and back in her clothes before she had time to get cold.

* * *

That evening, when the weather was a little cooler, Piper decided to forgo her usual beach walk and take a stroll along the pier and up to the castle green. She loved it up there, standing in front of the castle above the tiny bay where Rock Hudson and Yvonne De Carlo had filmed *Sea Devil* in 1953. To her left was a view of the pier and the harbour was down below on her right. The sound of laughter drifted up from the restaurant on the other side of the road. Piper gazed at the tables filled with locals and holidaymakers enjoying the beautiful evening as the sun lowered, casting shades of gold, orange and pink across Grouville Bay and the sea.

Piper bent down to take off her sandals, relishing the coolness of the grass between her toes. The only thing she missed having at home was a lawn. But then, why would she need one when there was this beautiful space high above the guest house?

As she walked on, someone called out her name. She turned round, but couldn't see who it was. She stopped to gaze at the setting sun and jumped when Alex appeared at her side.

'Sorry, I didn't mean to frighten you,' he said, slightly breathless. 'Grandad and I spotted you from the restaurant and wondered if you'd like to join us for something to eat, or for a drink?'

She looked back over at the tables and spotted Alex's grandfather waving at her. Piper waved back. 'I don't want to intrude on your evening,' she said, aware that they only had a few evenings to spend with each other. 'But that's kind of you both.' When she realised he was waiting, she added: 'and I'm not really dressed for a restaurant.' She indicated the navy shorts and pale-blue top she had changed into after work.

'You look perfectly fine to me,' he argued. 'Just come for a drink if you're not interested in eating anything. Grandad wants to thank you properly for dropping me off at The Cabbage Patch.'

Piper shrugged. 'I'd better put these back on then.' She dropped her sandals and slipped her feet into them. 'Did you have a fun day together?'

'We did,' he said as they made their way to the restaurant. 'And you were right, The Cabbage Patch is great. Grandad loves it there and says there's always something to do. In fact, he'll probably come back over the next couple of months.'

'I'm so pleased.' Piper loved to hear great feedback for The Cabbage Patch.

They reached the steps to the terrace where Alex's grandfather sat waiting for them. The place was packed with no spare seats apart from the two on either side of Mr Cooper. Alex stood back to let Piper go up first.

'Hello, Mr Cooper,' she said, smiling at the man who looked so much like Alex.

'I'm glad my grandson managed to persuade you to come and join us,' he said. 'I hope you've agreed to eat something?'

She hadn't been going to, but her stomach gave a noisy growl and she grimaced with embarrassment.

'I think that answers any indecision you might have had.' Smiling, Alex pulled out the chair next to his. 'Come and take a seat.'

'I'd love to.' She sat down and smiled her thanks at him. 'But I won't have too much in case Mum has made something for me to reheat later.'

A waitress came over and took their drinks order. 'Would you like a few more minutes to decide what you'd like to eat?' she asked, handing Piper a menu.

'Yes, please,' Mr Cooper said. Once the waitress had left their table, he added, 'Have you always lived on the island, Piper?'

'Yes, I was born here. My mum and gran weren't though, they're both from England and came over when Mum was little.'

'Clever ladies. I wish we'd kept coming back here on holiday.'

'Grandma didn't want to though, did she?' Alex asked. He smiled at Piper. 'I wish she had, then I could have grown up here too.'

Piper knew how lucky she was to live on such a beautiful island, but it had drawbacks. 'I loved it here when I was small but couldn't wait to leave by the time I was eighteen. I expected life to be far more exciting on the mainland and was desperate to find out for myself.'

'And did you?' Alex looked at her thoughtfully. 'Leave the island, I mean?'

She nodded. 'I studied History of Art at Kingston University. I loved it there and made some good friends.'

'But you came back, so you must have missed the place.'

Piper wished it had been that simple. She pushed away memories of her ex, Rick, who had come with her to the island after they'd graduated. She had thought herself lucky to have met 'The One' during her first week at university, spending three years together before he announced that he wanted to live in Jersey with her – until their relationship went pear-shaped and she'd had to live with the consequences.

'That's right,' she said to Alex, preferring to keep things light. People didn't need to know what she had been through, especially a guest and his grandfather.

Alex gave her a strange look that so quickly disappeared that she thought she might have imagined it. He indicated the waitress and lowered his voice.

'We'd better choose what we want before she reaches our table.'

They ordered their food and chatted a little more. As Piper ate her chicken Caesar salad, she watched Alex and his grandfather swapping anecdotes and laughing. They seemed to get along famously and were clearly fond of each other – like Piper and her grandmother. It warmed her heart to watch them enjoying each other's company, but despite enjoying the food and the perfect view from the restaurant, she felt as though she was imposing. Perhaps she should have refused their invitation.

'Piper?'

She realised Alex was speaking to her and finished chewing her food before swallowing. 'Sorry, I was miles away.'

'I thought as much.' He glanced at her food. 'Is that as good as my steak and chips?'

'Probably better.' She laughed, making a point of stabbing another forkful of salad and a chunk of chicken. 'Mmm, this is delicious.' She popped the food into her mouth and closed her eyes for a second. 'Yes, perfect.'

Alex and Colin laughed.

'You're selling it well,' Alex said. 'Although this steak is cooked to perfection.'

After their plates had been cleared away and they had refused pudding, they sat drinking coffees.

'This view is spectacular,' Colin said. 'I remember coming here once with your gran during our honeymoon, Alex.' He sighed. 'Not to the restaurant. I don't know if there was one here then, but to the castle. We stopped to take snaps of each other on the castle green. It was a magical day.'

'I didn't realise when I booked.' Alex frowned. 'I wouldn't have brought you here if I'd know it would bring back memories.'

Piper wasn't sure what to say, so focused on her cappuccino.

'I'm happy to look back on those times,' Colin said. 'They were very special and even if I do sometimes get upset when I miss my Jeanie, I still like to look back on our precious times together here.'

'Good. I'm glad you're all right.'

'I'm fine, Alex.' Colin's voice was gentle.

Piper looked from one to the other. 'You have a lovely relationship,' she said. 'I hope you don't mind me saying so, but it reminds me of the times I spend with my gran.'

'I don't mind at all,' Colin said. 'It makes me happy to discover you have a close relationship with your grandmother. Everyone should be lucky enough to enjoy those closest to them.'

He was right. 'It's probably time I left now,' she said, feeling a little awkward. She put her hand in her bag to get out her debit card, but Alex stopped her.

'No, this is our treat.' When she started to protest, he added, 'To say thank you for taking me to see Grandad earlier.'

He clearly wasn't going to let her argue, so Piper reluctantly relented. Standing, she addressed Colin. 'It was lovely to meet you again. I hope the rest of your stay here is as lovely as the beginning has been.'

He reached out to take her hand and wrapped it in both of his. 'Thank you. I'm sure it will be.'

As Alex stood, she said, 'Thanks again, Alex. I might see you later when you get back to the guest house. If not, I hope you have another good night's sleep.'

'Let me walk you down,' he said, stepping away from the table. 'I won't be long, Grandad.'

'I'm perfectly capable of walking down the hill to the pier,' she said lightly. 'It'll take me a couple of minutes.'

'But...'

She shook her head. 'Really, I'm fine. This is Gorey. Probably the most dangerous crime you'll witness here is a seagull attempting to pinch someone's ice cream.' She was tickled by his amusement. 'Bye, then.'

She mouthed her thanks at the waitress and walked down the steps from the terrace. Crossing the narrow road, Piper looked back to see Colin and Alex watching her. She gave a brief wave before walking towards the steep lane that would take her down to the pier.

Reaching the bottom, she waved at Eric and Patty sitting outside the Dolphin pub enjoying their drinks in the warm evening. Pete, a friend she had known all her life, asked her if she wanted to join them. She was tempted. On evenings like these, when the sun shone until late and the temperature didn't lower enough to warrant wearing a jacket, she could have happily sat outside, enjoying a drink with her friends, but she was tired and had work the next day.

'Thanks, but I'm on my way home. Maybe another time.'

Her entire world was now centred around this pier, and she loved it. Arriving home, she opened the pale-blue front door to the guest house. How different her life had turned out to how she had hoped it would be when she'd left to go to university.

4

Piper woke the following morning, recalled her grandmother's insistence that she join her friends for wild swimming, and groaned. The thought of getting neck deep into cold, salty water was not something she relished, but she knew her grandmother well enough to be certain she had little choice in the matter.

After another five-minute snooze, Piper threw back her duvet and got out of bed. She was relieved it was another glorious spring day that would help her warm up after her swim. It gave her a little boost as she rummaged around in her chest of drawers to find her swimming costume. She held up the pink and black item she had found yesterday and decided again that it would have to do.

Showered and dressed, with her costume rolled into one of their beach towels, Piper joined her mother and, surprisingly, found her grandmother was also in the dining room.

'Gran?' She couldn't hide her amusement. 'Are you here to check that I don't eat too big a breakfast before we go to Rozel?'

Her grandmother didn't seem impressed to have been caught out. 'Well, I know how you young ones can eat when you're hungry and we won't have time to digest a big meal.'

Piper caught her mum grinning at her from the doorway before slipping back to the kitchen. 'Can I tell Mum what you'd like to eat before the guests start arriving?'

'I'll have some scrambled egg on one slice of white toast, I think. And my usual tea, please.'

Piper ordered the same for herself and while her mother was scrambling eggs, made some tea and carried it back to the dining room. She loved rare mornings like this, when she and Gran ate together before any of the guests were up. Mostly, she grabbed a slice of toast and jam and sat out in the backyard to eat, or grabbed a bowl of cereal in the tiny kitchenette she and her mum shared in their attic flat.

After their meal, she cleared away their plates, wiped down the table and set it up for the guests to use.

'I'll pop home and wait for you there,' Gran said on her way out. 'Come to mine at nine-thirty. I don't want to miss the other swimmers. If I start after they do, people will think I'm slower than them.'

Piper wasn't sure why Gran would worry what others might presume, especially people watching rather than swimming. Who were they to criticise?

'I'll be there,' she said, kissing her gran's soft cheek before picking up some menus, her notepad and pen and setting off back to the dining room to take orders. 'I've got to be at The Cabbage Patch by ten-thirty today.'

Gran narrowed her eyes. 'That won't leave you much time for swimming.'

Piper tried her best to appear innocent of any exaggeration. She had no intention of admitting that her lack of time that morning had been the reason she had given in and agreed to accompany Gran.

'Nine-thirty on the dot.' Gran tapped the glass face of her small gold watch.

'You won't wear that while you're swimming, I hope,' Piper said, worried it wasn't waterproof.

'I usually take it off but forgot this morning.'

Probably to check what time she got out of bed, Piper thought, amused.

* * *

They arrived at Rozel Harbour a short while later. Although it was still early, Piper was unimpressed to discover that the pier and the small beach were already busy and there was nowhere to park.

'I'll get out here,' Gran said, as Piper slowed the car. 'I'll wait for you on the beach. I can see the others have already arrived and I don't want to keep them waiting. Hurry up now.'

Piper would have loved to return home with a bacon roll from her favourite little café, The Hungry Man, but there was no getting out of the swim now she had come this far. She turned the car around, drove back along the pier and up the hill until she found a parking space, before grabbing her things and hurrying down the hill to meet her gran.

Arriving on the beach, Piper realised that the older ladies had thought to wear their costumes under their clothes, whereas she now had to change awkwardly under a towel.

She struggled to hold it, pushing down her shorts and knickers before holding her costume in one hand and just about managed to get one foot in before almost toppling over. Gran grabbed Piper's arm to steady her and was helped by another friend, neither of whom bothered to hide their amusement at Piper's clumsiness.

'You should wear it under your clothes next time,' Gran's friend said.

'You think there'll be a next time?' Piper was certain there wouldn't be. 'Thanks for the help, though.' She took a deep breath and rolled up her clothes, hid them in her towel, and followed the group of ten or so women towards the edge of the sea.

'Piper, didn't you have anything a bit newer?' Gran whispered as Piper stepped ankle-deep into the freezing sea.

'No.'

'When was the last time you swam?'

'I've no idea,' she said, not sure how she would manage to force herself to keep going deeper into the cold sea, her teeth already starting to chatter. 'Not that it matters. I can't imagine I'll be doing this again in a hurry.'

'We'll see,' Gran said, giving her a knowing look that Piper ignored, striding into the water and waving for Piper to follow.

Piper took a deep breath. The sooner she got the swim over and done with, the sooner she could dry off and get warm once more.

Her gran looked over her shoulder. 'Do hurry up,' she called. 'You're supposed to be the young, fit one here and you're piddling about in the shallows.'

A couple sitting on the sand as their children played turned their attention to Piper, then spoke to each other in low voices, failing to hide their amusement.

'Here goes nothing,' Piper said, taking a deep breath and bending her knees so the water reached her neck. She gasped, shocked by the cold as it hit her chest. Not wanting to be a source of entertainment to onlookers, watching from the comfort of the warm sand, she pushed forward and began to swim.

'That's it,' one of the ladies said, turning to swim on her back. Piper recognised her as Peggy Carré, one of Gran's oldest friends. 'You'll soon get used to the cold and start enjoying yourself.'

Piper doubted it but attempted a grin. She no longer minded the cold. She was more concerned about running out of breath. There was still a long way to go, past the pier as the frontrunners in the group were now doing, and then she had to find enough puff to get back to the beach. She would never do this again, she promised herself. There had to be easier ways to get fit.

By the time Piper reached the end of the pier, she'd surprised herself by breaking through the pain barrier she had heard others mention when doing sports. She turned around, relieved to be facing the beach rather than swimming away from it.

'You see, you can do it,' Gran said.

Piper was surprised to see her there, treading water. 'I thought you would have gone back by now.' Her gran was clearly much fitter than she had assumed.

Gran closed her eyes briefly. 'I'm not about to leave you out here alone, silly girl. At least, not until I'm sure you can swim out and back safely.'

Grateful not to be out swimming alone, Piper pushed herself to keep going.

'Enjoying it yet?' Gran said beside her, silver-grey hair sleek against her scalp.

'Not yet, but I might look back on this experience a little more fondly once it's over.'

Gran laughed. 'I felt the same way the first time I did it but now I love the challenge, though it's much easier than it was. I enjoy the sense of achievement and the camaraderie, sitting with my friends, drinking a cup of tea after we're finished.'

Piper understood where Gran was coming from. 'It's a great way to keep fit,' she admitted. She really should start doing more exercise herself, she decided.

'We seem to have quite the audience.'

Piper looked at the beach and saw some holiday-makers watching and felt a sense of pride. It gave her the incentive to push herself a little faster to finish.

'I've tried to persuade Helen to come down. I think it would do her good, don't you?'

'Mum isn't much of a swimmer though,' Piper said, out of breath.

'She used to be very good indeed. Got her silver swimming badge at school, she did.'

Piper was surprised. 'Ask her then,' she said. Her arms were beginning to ache, and she noticed her gran's attention had wandered.

Following her gaze, Piper spotted two men by the white railings halfway along the pier, watching the swimming. She hadn't had this much attention in a long time. It amused her that they were watching someone decades younger than the rest of the group finish her swim way behind the others. She suspected they could tell that Gran was taking the exercise in her stride and keeping an eye on her, too.

Her gran slowed down and the next thing Piper knew she was on her feet in fairly shallow water. Delighted to have finally finished the seemingly endless swim, she lowered her feet and relished the sand underneath them. Standing, she opened her mouth to say something to Gran when she noticed shock register on her face.

'What?'

'How old is that swimsuit of yours? It's practically see-through!'

Piper gasped and glanced down, desperate to cover her modesty.

'Duck down in the water and I'll fetch your towel.' Without waiting for Piper to reply, she marched to where the others were sitting, now dressed and enjoying cups of tea from flasks.

Lowering herself into the water, Piper heard a murmur from her grandmother and could tell the women were trying not to appear as if they were looking at her.

Her gran hurried back to the water's edge. 'If you're quick no one will see,' she said, holding out a towel and wrapping it around Piper once she reached her. 'You really have to buy yourself a new costume,' she said with a chuckle. 'That one isn't decent.'

'I didn't know that, did I?' Relieved that no one she knew had seen her humiliation, Piper followed her gran up to the group of ladies and Peggy patted an empty space on her towel. 'Here, lovey. Sit down and have some of this. It'll warm you up nicely.'

Piper hoped it was tea or coffee and not one of

the alcoholic concoctions her grandmother and her friends sometimes tried out and enjoyed telling Piper about. She took the plastic cup from Peggy. It looked like tea and when she took a tentative sip, she was glad to discover that it was. 'Lovely, thank you.'

'How did you find your first foray into wild swimming, Piper?' one of the other women, whose name she couldn't recall, asked.

'The temperature of the sea was a bit of a shock, if I'm honest,' she said, holding the cup between her hands to warm them. 'And I didn't imagine I'd keep going for so long.'

'I sense a "but" coming.'

Piper laughed. 'It wasn't as bad as I had imagined,' she admitted. Then, seeing the delight on her gran's face, she raised a hand to stop her getting too excited. 'However, that doesn't mean I intend ever doing it again, Gran.'

'We'll see about that,' Peggy said with a laugh. 'Your grandmother isn't known for giving up easily on anything.'

Piper knew her grandmother's determination only too well. 'Gran, do you hear me?' she teased, her smile vanishing when she saw her grandmother's expression. 'What's the—'

'Hi,' said a voice she recognised. 'I hope you don't mind us disturbing you for a moment.'

Piper turned, shading her eyes against the sun as she looked up to see Alex. 'Oh, it's you,' she said, feeling ridiculous for stating the obvious. She checked that her towel was firmly tucked in place. 'So, you've found Rozel.' She saw his grandfather standing behind him and got to her feet. 'Hi, Mr Cooper. Are you having an enjoyable morning?'

But Colin Cooper didn't seem to hear her. She was about to ask him again when she realised that he was staring directly at Gran, who seemed transfixed by him.

'Gran? Is everything all right?'

'Hello, Margery,' Colin said, his voice quiet. 'I didn't expect to see you here.'

'Aren't you going to introduce us to your friend?' Peggy asked, giving Piper a nudge. 'Who is this mysterious man?'

'His name is Colin Cooper,' Piper said, trying to figure out why her grandmother was acting so strangely. 'He's on holiday. I had no idea he knew Gran though.'

Piper was grateful when Alex spoke. 'I didn't realise you knew Piper's gran, Grandad.'

'I can't believe I've met your granddaughter, Margery.' Colin shook his head. 'This is incredible.'

Peggy put her cup down on her towel and stood. 'If no one is going to make introductions, then I'll start.' Pressing a palm to her chest, she said, 'I'm Peggy Carré and I gather you're Mr Colin Cooper.'

Tearing his gaze from Piper's grandmother, he took her hand and shook it. 'That's correct,' he said. 'This is my grandson, Alex. He's staying at Piper's guest house for a few days while I'm here on an artist's retreat. I haven't seen Margery here for. . .' He thought for a moment, his eyes widening. 'It must be, what?'

'Decades,' Margery said, her voice strained. 'Helen would have been very young back then.'

Piper watched as Mr Cooper's mouth opened and closed again. He seemed staggered to realise that so much time had gone by. 'That long? Are you certain?'

'Helen and I came to live here in the seventies when she was seven.'

Piper stared at her grandmother, aware that something was wrong. She'd never seen such a haunted expression on her usually animated face.

'We were so young then, weren't we?' Colin said, a hint of sadness in his voice.

'We were,' Margery said. 'And we thought we knew everything.'

Piper heard the pointed note to her gran's comment and wondered what it meant. She decided it was best left until they were alone together to ask her.

Unsure what to say, she glanced at Alex who gave her an almost imperceptible shrug. He clearly had no idea what had happened between their grandparents.

Margery stood, and picking up her towel gave it a good shake as the atmosphere seemed to thicken all around them. 'It's about time we made a move, Piper,' she said. 'Your mother will be expecting you and I don't want you to keep her waiting.'

Piper knew it was their cue to leave. 'OK,' she said, securing her towel and slipping her sandy feet into her sandals. She would have preferred to change before leaving the beach, but could tell there wasn't time for that. Anyway, she reasoned, she did not relish having to change in front of Alex and his grandfather.

'Bye, Mr Cooper, it was nice seeing you again.' She turned to Alex. 'I'll see you at the guest house at some point.'

They nodded silently and Piper felt their gaze as she and Gran walked away, along the warm sand towards the granite slipway and off the beach.

When they were far enough away to be certain no one could hear her, Piper spoke. 'Are you all right, Gran?'

'I will be as soon as we're out of here, lovey.' She mumbled something to herself. 'When we get to the end of this road I'll wait while you fetch the car, there's a good girl.'

'Yes, of course.'

As she ran up the hill, Piper couldn't push away the expression on her gran's face when she'd spotted Mr Cooper. He had obviously meant something to her in the past, but what?

5

'Is that the first time you've seen him since leaving Harrogate?' Helen asked, placing a cup of strong tea in front of her mother and sitting next to her.

Having taken her grandmother straight home to her cottage and calling her mother to join them, Piper sat opposite them, relieved to be inside the cool front room. 'He seemed to be as stunned as you were to see him.'

'Fetch your gran a couple of biscuits,' Helen said. 'Check if she has some of those Lemon Puffs she likes, they're nice and sweet and I think she needs them for the shock.'

'I am here, you know,' Gran snapped.

Glad her fight had returned, Piper hurried into the small galley kitchen at the back of the property and grabbed the biscuit tin. She pulled off the lid, relieved to find several Lemon Puffs inside. After placing a handful on a plate, she returned to the living room.

'I know that, Mum,' Helen was saying. She rested a hand on her mother's arm. 'We're only looking out for you. We don't mean to be thoughtless.'

Margery's expression softened, and she picked up her teacup. 'I know you are.' She took a sip and then placed the cup back on its saucer. 'He looked so old.'

'He would if you haven't seen him for more than half a century, Gran.'

'I suppose so.' She grimaced, her hands flying to her cheeks. 'I must appear pretty ancient to him then, mustn't I?'

Piper and her mother swapped anxious glances. Piper didn't want to answer the question and was relieved when her mother spoke first.

'If you think you look older, imagine how I must look,' she said with a grin. 'I was only seven when I left England. I don't have plaits and knee-high socks on now.'

Piper was horrified to see her gran had taken the light-hearted comment the wrong way.

'You've met him?'

'No, not yet,' Helen said.

'What do you mean, "not yet"?'

Piper thought quickly. 'I suppose he knows where Alex is staying, Gran. He might turn up here, wanting to catch up some more.'

Her gran picked up one of the biscuits and ate it slowly, deep in thought. 'Well,' she said as soon as she had finished eating. 'If he comes here to speak to me, I'll tell him to bugger off.'

'Gran!' 'Mum!' Piper and Helen exclaimed in unison.

'Mum, you can't be mean to him. He hasn't done anything wrong.' Helen narrowed her eyes when Margery didn't speak. 'Has he?'

'Look,' Gran said. 'I'm sure the pair of you have better things to do than sit here questioning me. I'm fine now that I have a cup of tea and something to nibble on, so why don't you both go back to the guest house?'

Helen didn't seem very happy at the prospect of

leaving. 'I'm not sure. You've clearly had a big shock and that can be dangerous.'

Margery stood and made for the front door. Piper and her mum watched as she opened it and waved for them to leave. 'I'm absolutely fine,' she said. Then, spotting a friend outside on the pier, she called out, 'Sandy, come and have a natter over a cup of tea if you're not busy!'

Piper heard the woman accept the offer. Realising there was little option but to leave Gran to it, she stood and walked into the hallway to give her a quick hug. 'Call if you need anything, won't you?'

'The only thing I need is for your mum to stop fretting about me.'

Helen sighed behind Piper. 'It's all right, Mum. We're going.'

* * *

They arrived home and closed the front door behind them, and Helen turned to Piper. 'Did your grandmother say anything about him on the way home?'

Piper shook her head. 'Nothing. Have you any idea what he might have done?' She hoped it wasn't something bad. She would have to ask Alex to leave if it was going to make things difficult for her gran. Piper would prefer not to, especially as he seemed as surprised by Colin and Margery's unexpected reunion as they had been.

'Look,' her mother said. 'There's no point in us worrying unnecessarily. Your gran always bounces back from things and will probably be back to her old self once she's had a long chat with Sandy. There's no point in both of us being here.' She smiled. 'Why don't you pop to Harbour Blooms and ask Nancy for some fresh flowers for the communal areas. I would do it myself but I've got paperwork that I need to get out of the way.'

Piper knew her mother's answer to most problems was to find a way to keep busy and was happy to go on the errand for her. 'Will do. Did you have any particular flowers in mind?'

'Not really. Just pick anything you think I'd like.'

She left the house and walked along the pier until she reached the pink door that led into the florist's. She walked inside and breathed in the cool, calming scent of spring flowers. 'I love coming here,' she said, smiling at Nancy, the owner of Harbour

Blooms. She was tying string round an elaborate bunch of roses, peonies and greenery. 'Someone is in for a treat.'

'It's for a birthday,' Nancy said, picking up her mobile and taking a few photos of the arrangement from above.

Piper watched as she typed something into her phone and gave a satisfied smile before slipping her phone into her jeans' pocket. 'There. Today's Instagram post done.'

'Anyone I know?' Piper asked, wishing for once that she had someone who might arrange for such a splendid bouquet to be sent to her.

'Sorry?'

'The arrangement. I was just wondering if the recipient was someone local.'

Nancy snipped the end of the string still attached to a large, neat roll, put the scissors onto the worktop and tapped the side of her nose. 'Now that would be telling, wouldn't it?'

'I suppose it would.' Piper walked over to a group of metal buckets, one of which contained roses in a deep-pink shade. She bent to breathe in their deliciously fragrant scent. 'Mmm... they smell glorious.'

Nancy looked over. 'They do, don't they? Those are called Louise Odier and they're a personal favourite of mine.' She finished working on the bouquet and placed it to one side. 'What can I do for you today, Piper?'

'Mum would like some cut flowers for the dining room and living room, please.'

'No problem.' Nancy walked around the counter to the main shop floor. It was only a small area, with buckets grouped around the walls and underneath the shop window. 'I've got some beautiful gerberas. They last a while, or what about tulips? They're not too big and would look pretty in your place. I always feel they bring sunshine inside, don't you?'

'I do.' Piper loved flowers and wished they had space to grow more, but the couple of tubs in their yard were already overflowing with blooms in all shades, planted by her mother. 'Thanks, Nancy.'

'Hi there, Piper. Did you manage to get out of swimming this morning?' Vicki, Nancy's assistant, had known Piper most of her life and gave her a knowing wink. Piper had never been very sporty, and she wasn't surprised her friend had expected her to pull out.

'Actually, I went,' Piper said, pleased when her friend's mouth dropped open in surprise.

'Blimey, that's got to be a first.'

Nancy walked back to the counter, having chosen some tulips ready for wrapping. 'Will you stop teasing our customers, Vicki?' She rolled her eyes and gave Piper a nod. 'Good for you for going. It might do Vicki good to join you one morning and give her something to think about other than her wedding.'

'Oh yes,' Piper said. 'I'd forgotten about that. When is it again?' She'd been hearing about the wedding since Vicki and her boyfriend, Dan, had got engaged before he'd left for university, while Vicki stayed behind to help Nancy set up Harbour Blooms.

'Hah!' Nancy laughed, finishing wrapping the flowers with a flourish and handing them to Piper. 'You're lucky. I never get the opportunity to forget that Vicki is hoping to one day have the wedding of the century.' She put her arm around Vicki's narrow shoulders and gave her a hug. 'And we'll certainly all look forward to it.'

'I know I am,' Piper said truthfully. 'That is, if I'm invited.' She hoped she would be. Piper couldn't recall the last time she had been to a wedding and Vicki had mentioned wanting to book the castle for the ceremony.

'Yes, you're definitely on the guest list. So are your mum and gran. In fact, I'll be inviting most of the residents from the pier. Well, those who've lived here for years, that is. I'm not bothering with those I don't know, obviously.'

'I can't wait,' Piper said. 'Have you set a date?'

Vicki shook her head. 'We can't yet. Something to do with Dan's job, but as soon as we have, I'll let you know.'

'Great. I'll look forward to it.'

Nancy handed an invoice for the flowers to Piper. 'Here you go, just so your mum knows how much you've spent.'

'Thanks.'

'Shall I put these on her account for you?'

'Yes, please.'

* * *

Piper left the shop and stepped outside. It was busy again but that was to be expected, even mid-season.

The weather didn't stop visitors enjoying the cafés, pubs and restaurants, or the other businesses along the pier.

'Piper!'

She turned at the sound of Alex's voice and noticed that he was holding a wriggling dog in his arms. 'Hi,' she said as he caught up with her. 'I see you've made a friend.'

Alex laughed and moved his head back to avoid a lick. 'I found him on the pier and wasn't sure who he belonged to.'

'This is Seamus,' she said, stroking the dog's fluffy head. 'He belongs to Jax, who is probably nearby somewhere.' She could see Alex's face reddening slightly and remembered how heavy Seamus was. 'You can put him down. He won't run off.'

'You're sure?'

'Yes,' she laughed. 'He knows that I usually have a treat for him. We can take him to the guest house for now.'

Alex bent down and lowered the dog carefully onto the pavement. 'What is he? I thought at first that he might be a Schnauzer cross.'

'No one can work out for certain,' she said. 'I think he has Corgi in him somewhere.'

They both looked down and studied the black and grey dog that now had his front paws resting against Alex's lower legs. Alex ruffled the dog's fur.

'His legs are a bit too short for a Schnauzer and look at that tail,' she said, pointing at it moving rapidly from side to side. 'And the way his bottom wags as well. Have you ever seen anything quite so, um... waggy?' She realised what she was saying and blushed. 'If you know what I mean?'

Alex laughed. 'I think so.' He reached down and stroked the dog's back. 'Is that what you are, Seamus? What do you think?'

Piper watched Alex interacting with the happy little dog, and smiled.

'Your grandad not with you?' she asked.

'No, he had a few classes to attend at the retreat.'

They began walking back to the guest house with Seamus leading the way. 'I think he was taken aback by seeing your gran after so many years.'

'Did he say anything about her?' Piper asked, intrigued to find out more.

Alex shook his head, looking disappointed.

'Nothing, apart from that he knew her when they were much younger. Which I'd already gathered after what they said on the beach.'

'You don't think they were...' She hesitated. 'Dating?'

Alex shrugged. 'Who knows, but whatever it was, they still have feelings one way or the other.'

He was right. Piper wished she knew exactly what they were, and what had happened between them. 'Gran always said that she wasn't interested in being with a man after she divorced my grandfather,' she said. 'I always had the impression that she left home to marry him, so I'm not sure where Mr Cooper comes into the equation.'

'Neither do I.'

They reached the guest house and Alex held open the door for Piper as she carried the flowers inside. 'They're very springlike,' he said with a smile. 'Are they for your mum?'

'She buys in fresh flowers every week,' Piper explained. 'Says it brightens the guests' days to have something colourful on display if the weather's dull.'

'They will certainly do that.'

At that moment, her mother came through from the kitchen. Piper could tell by the book in her hand and sunglasses on her head that she had been reading outside and making the most of the sunshine.

'Hello, Alex. I see you've met Seamus.' She looked at the flowers in Piper's hands. 'They're beautiful. Great choice, darling.'

'Nancy was the one who suggested them.'

'She knows her flowers, does Nancy. Let's take them through to the kitchen and put them in water. I'll fill the table display vases later.' Helen took the bouquet and Piper followed her into the kitchen. Alex paused in the doorway. 'Why don't you two sit in the yard and I'll find a treat for this little chap and bring you both a cool drink?'

Piper glanced at her mother, shocked. She never invited guests to sit in their backyard. It was their own private area.

'That would be very welcome if you don't mind,' Alex said. 'I'll just go and freshen up, if that's all right?'

'You take as long as you need,' Helen said.

As soon as he'd gone, Piper pushed the kitchen

door closed and lowered her voice. 'What are you doing?'

'What do you mean?' her mother asked, gazing at her innocently.

'You've always told me I mustn't invite guests back here, never mind to the yard.'

Her mother snipped off the string holding the paper around the flowers. 'I thought it was a kind gesture. It's so warm, and the poor boy's probably been traipsing all over the island with his grandfather.'

Piper wasn't fooled. She leaned against the worktop and looked at her mother. 'Are you trying to matchmake?' Her mother had a tendency to read situations wrong, and Piper had no intention of getting caught up in any awkward situations. It was bad enough that Gran and Mr Cooper had some history that seemed to be making things uncomfortable. 'Or are you hoping Alex will tell us more about Gran and his grandad? Because if that's the case, you're wasting your time.'

'You don't know that.' Her mother nudged past Piper to fill a glass vase with water from the tap.

'I do, actually. I asked Alex outside and he told

me that Mr Cooper has said about as much as Gran did, so we're not going to find any information out from him.'

Her mother frowned. 'Blast.'

So that had been her mother's plan. 'I'm as disappointed as you,' Piper said, taking an extra gravy bone from the tin her mother always kept on a small corner shelf for Seamus and waiting for him to sit before feeding it to him. Knowing Gran, she would keep the answers to herself for ever. 'We'll just have to hope that Mr Cooper is more forthcoming with his take on what happened between them.'

She heard the tapping sound the copper pipes made when one of the showers was being used and presumed it must be Alex. The other guests were probably all out enjoying the beach or one of the many attractions on the island.

'Never mind,' Helen said, putting the vase and flowers to one side. 'It will be pleasant to spend a little time getting to know Alex. He seems such a nice young man.'

Piper groaned. 'Seriously, Mum?'

'Oh, do stop being such a misery,' Helen said, tapping Piper's arm. 'Go and check there are a couple of beers for him in the fridge and put some crisps in a bowl. We can at least try to act like we're welcoming him to the island.'

* * *

'That's a great shower you have up there,' Alex said a few minutes later, walking out to join them. His damp hair was neatly combed back off his face, already drying in the heat, dark curls giving him an angelic appearance.

'Take a seat,' Helen said, lifting Seamus off the chair that he had only just settled down on and placing him on the floor. 'A bottle of beer all right for you?'

'That would be perfect. Thank you.'

Piper watched him sit and, crossing her legs, leaned back in her chair with a glass of cool lemonade. 'Help yourself to crisps.'

He nodded his thanks. 'This is the life,' he said, glancing around and not seeming to mind when Seamus leaped up onto his lap and made himself comfortable

'I'm glad you're happy to be staying here.' Piper

returned his smile. 'Most people are, but it's always good to hear positive feedback.'

'You have a great place. The view is incredible.' He took the bottle and glass Helen was holding out and began pouring. 'I was saying to Piper what a great place you have here.'

'That's kind of you,' Helen said. 'I took over the running of the place when my mother retired a few years ago. Before that I used to help out, so I knew how things worked.'

Alex looked at Piper. 'So, you haven't been working here long. I assumed—'

Helen gave a little gasp and Alex looked startled.

'Mum, it's fine,' Piper said quickly, to stop her digging them into a hole. Her mother and Gran both became flustered when people asked personal questions. There were certain subjects they preferred to keep secret about their own pasts. Although Piper didn't really have much in the way of secrets to worry about, she knew her mother always worried that any reference to Piper's break-up with her ex, Rick, might cause her upset. It worried her that her mother's reaction to his question had made Alex think they were odd in any way. Piper wasn't really ready to discuss her disastrous love life with Rick with someone she barely knew, but thought she should say something.

'I was planning to go travelling with my ex, Rick, but about eighteen months ago, he announced that he had other ideas. He fell in love with someone else,' she explained, doing her best to keep her voice light, 'and instead of going travelling I stayed here and helped Mum with the guest house.'

Alex stared at her with an embarrassed look on his face. 'I'm so sorry. I didn't mean to bring up difficult memories.'

'It's fine,' Piper said, relieved to have rescued the moment from her mother's over-reaction. She raised her drink. 'Never mind all that. Let's celebrate this glorious weather.'

Alex raised his bottle in a toast. 'Cheers to that.'

He was smiling, but Piper didn't miss the intrigued glint in his eyes. She liked him but didn't know him nearly well enough to confide in him.

After a while, Helen stood. 'Are you meeting your grandfather for dinner tonight?'

Alex nodded and looked at his watch. 'I said I'd get the bus into town and meet him there. We're going to St Brelade's Bay for something to eat if you'd like to join us.'

Helen shook her head. 'That's kind of you, but I'm cooking for Mum tonight.'

'Piper?' Alex had turned to look at her.

'Yes?'

'Would you like to join us this evening?'

Worried that three might be a crowd, she said, 'Thanks, but I won't if that's OK. It's kind of you to invite me though.'

'If you're worried you'll be in the way, you won't be. Gramps loved meeting you yesterday and was the one who suggested I ask you to join us tonight.'

'He did?' She wasn't sure why he would do such a thing. 'But you're here for such a short time. It doesn't seem fair for me to tag along.'

'Better stop what you're doing, you've got company,' bellowed a deep, familiar voice as footsteps came through the kitchen. 'There you are.'

They all turned to look at the man in the doorway and Seamus sat up, ears pricked.

'Why can't you ever simply say "hello"?' Piper laughed, happy to see her cousin, Jax, stepping into the yard. He was in his usual state of messiness with his unruly hair sun-bleached from spending so much time taking locals, school children and visitors out on foraging excursions and boat trips. His grey T-shirt looked almost threadbare, and his shorts had seen better days. She wasn't sure how long his sandals would last either.

He smiled at Alex. 'I see Seamus has found a new pal.'

'I found him outside,' Alex said, stroking the dog's head with his free hand. 'He's yours?'

'He is.' Jax smiled. 'When he feels like it.'

Alex laughed, groaning as Seamus launched himself off his lap and raced towards Jax, tail wagging frantically as he turned in circles in front of him.

Jax put the bucket he was carrying down onto the floor and opened his arms. The excited dog leaped up into them and began licking his face.

'I do wish you wouldn't let him do that,' Helen grumbled. 'Anyway, what have you got there?' Helen asked, reaching for the bucket.

'Just a few bits.'

Piper saw Alex studying Jax and introduced him properly. 'His mum, Sheila, has the hairdressing salon along the pier. She's my mum's best friend and my dad's sister,' she explained. 'Among other things, Jax teaches people how and where to forage for food on the island.'

Alex's eyes widened in appreciation. 'That's fascinating. Have you been out foraging today?' he asked, turning his attention to the bucket.

Jax put his dog down and took the bucket back from Helen. 'No, these are mussels from my dad,' he said. 'He asked me to drop them off. Thought you'd like to make that Moules Marinière you two are so fond of.'

'Delicious.' Helen smiled. 'Please thank him for me, lovey.'

'Will do, Aunty Helen.' He leaned forward as she reached up and kissed his unshaven cheek.

'I've been out with a family group today, which was why I couldn't follow this one when he ran off,' Jax explained to Alex. 'We were low water fishing and I showed them which seaweeds are edible.'

Alex looked interested. 'Would you take me out sometime? I'd love to learn about that sort of thing.'

'Sure, mate,' Jax said, shooting a smile at Piper. 'I like this bloke of yours.'

Piper closed her eyes and stifled a groan. 'Alex is a guest here, Jax.' She sighed. 'I must apologise for my cousin,' she said to Alex. 'He forgets his manners sometimes.' She turned her attention back to Jax, who was enjoying embarrassing her.

'Take no notice of us, mate. We're more like brother and sister than cousins.'

'They are,' Helen said, giving Alex a knowing smile. 'They bicker a lot of the time. It's because they're both only children and grew up together, although,' – she wagged a finger between Piper and Jax – 'that's no excuse for acting like badly behaved children at the age of twenty-six.'

'Twenty-seven,' Piper and Jax argued in unison.

'Oh, I can't keep up with it all,' Helen grumbled.

'Sorry, Mum,' Piper said, more embarrassed at being told off than she had been by Jax's teasing.

'Sorry, Aunty Helen.'

'Don't call me that,' she said, getting up and carrying the bucket of mussels through to the kitchen. 'It makes me feel old.'

Piper wanted to change the subject. 'Can you take Alex out while he's here then, Jax?'

'It depends when. I'm a bit booked up for the

next few days, but I should have a day free next week.'

Alex's shoulders slumped slightly. Piper could tell he was disappointed. 'He's only here until Monday,' she explained, hoping her cousin would find a way to accommodate him.

'I'd love to help but it's a busy time of year and I really can't fit you in until then. Sorry.'

'Hey, it's fine,' Alex said. 'How about next time I'm here?'

'Sure. I'd like that. Let me have your dates and I'll set something up.'

Next time? Piper liked the idea of seeing Alex again.

6

Half an hour later, after Jax and Seamus had left, Alex finished his drink and got to his feet. 'I'd better get that bus into town.' He grinned down at Piper. 'Are you certain you don't want to join us? You're really very welcome.'

She shook her head. 'No, but thank you. I've got a few things I should be catching up on,' she fibbed. 'But thanks again for the invitation.' She walked him through the kitchen.

'You're going now?' Helen stopped cleaning the mussels for a moment. 'I hope you have a lovely evening. Your grandfather's more than welcome to come for breakfast before you leave, if you'd like to ask him.'

Piper's mouth dropped open in surprise. She was relieved to be standing behind Alex so he didn't see her reaction. Why was her mother being so friendly to this guest in particular? He was very pleasant and, she had to admit, rather handsome, but that didn't explain her mother's behaviour. Helen had always insisted their guests weren't allowed access to the private areas of the guest house and never invited non-guests to eat there. It didn't make sense.

'You're seeing Alex out?' Helen asked.

'Yes.' Piper narrowed her eyes at her mother as Alex continued into the hallway. 'I don't know what you're doing,' she whispered. 'But I wish you'd stop it. It's unnerving me.'

Her mother raised an eyebrow but didn't reply.

Piper caught up with Alex as he reached the front door. 'I didn't realise you were planning on coming back to the island.'

Alex stared at her for a second before replying, 'I've enjoyed it here more than I expected,' he said, opening the door. 'It occurred to me that as Grandad is staying for another two weeks it would be fun to come over again and take him out to explore a few more places.'

Piper tried to hide her delight at this unexpected news. 'Have you told him?'

'Not yet. I'm going to tell him tonight.'

She had been about to ask him when he was thinking of returning but realised there was a more subtle way of finding out. 'Would you like me to check if we have a vacancy for your preferred dates?'

'Would you?' He smiled. 'That'd be great.'

Piper realised she was being a little presumptuous. 'Unless you were planning on staying somewhere different,' she said, her cheeks heating slightly.

He laughed. 'No. I've loved it here.'

'You have a few minutes before your bus, so why don't I check now?'

They went back inside and into the front room. Piper logged onto the computer and was disappointed to see that all the rooms were almost fully booked for the next two weeks and beyond. 'There are no clear stretches of availability,' she said, unable to hide her disappointment. 'That's a shame. I can recommend another guest house if you'd like?'

Alex considered her offer. 'Do you have any rooms free at all, during the week?'

'Let me see.' She looked and spotted a vacancy. 'We have one room available for three days next week, but it's not the one you have now, I'm afraid.'

'That's OK. I don't mind. It's not as if I spend all day in my room, is it?'

'True.' She remembered how he had raved about the view from the window. 'This one is at the back of the building though. You won't have a sea view but will be looking out to where the castle green slopes down. Are you sure you don't mind?'

He shook his head. 'Not at all.' He checked his watch again. 'I have to run, but if you can book me in right away that would be brilliant.'

'Great,' she said, delighted. 'I'll do that now. Have fun tonight, and please say "hi" to your grandfather for me.'

'Will do.'

She watched him leave and sighed happily. He was coming back. She was surprised at how excited she felt. It was ridiculous. It wasn't as if there was anything between them. He was pleasant and kind, but she would have to make sure she didn't get carried away. It was so long since she had felt anything for anyone. She had been certain that she would never feel this depth of attraction for any man after Rick's betrayal, but she had to be careful. She didn't want to get hurt again.

Piper completed Alex's booking and closed the computer, deciding to take a stroll along the beach. There was often sea glass to be found on the sand, after a high tide, and she was too wide awake to sleep without walking for a while.

She left the house and walked along the pier then down the road towards Gorey village. She loved the view of the castle from here. It was always an imposing and beautiful sight, but on evenings like this, with lights glowing from the restaurants and houses, the castle looked like an elaborate cake on top of a pretty village scene, like something from a fairy-tale picture book.

Taking off her shoes, she picked them up and carried them in one hand as she began to walk. Within moments she came across her first piece of sea glass. It was yellow; one of the rarest colours. With a gasp, she picked it up and brushed sand from the surface, delighted to have found her first piece in that beautiful, delicate shade. It felt like a good omen.

7

The following morning Alex hadn't come down to breakfast at his usual time. As she took two orders through to her mother in the kitchen, Piper wondered whether he was having a lie-in.

The front door opened as she walked into the hall on her way to the dining room and Alex and his grandfather walked in.

'Good morning, Mr Cooper,' she said. 'It's lovely to see you again.'

'As it is you,' he said, smiling. 'And please call me Colin.'

'Hi, Piper,' Alex said. 'We decided to take your

mother up on her kind offer of breakfast for Grandpa. That's all right, isn't it?'

'Of course it is.' She gave them a reassuring smile. 'Please come through to the dining room.' She showed them to a table by the window and handed over a couple of menus. 'Can I fetch you something to drink? Tea, coffee or juice? We have orange, mango and apple today.'

She wrote down their drinks order and left them to decide what they wanted to eat. Back in the kitchen she told her mother that Alex had brought his grandfather over.

'I'll introduce myself as soon as I've finished cooking,' Helen said, looking delighted at the news.

'What is it with you?' Piper asked as she made Mr Cooper's coffee. 'I don't understand.'

'Nothing.' Her mother pointed at the half-made drinks. 'You'd better finish those and serve them before they get cold.'

Piper suspected her mother was hiding something and resolved to find out what it was.

As she tidied one of the tables after the guests had finished their breakfast and left the dining room,

Helen entered and walked over to Alex and Colin's table.

'How was your food?'

Alex looked up and placed his cutlery onto his plate. 'Good morning, Helen,' he said, smiling. 'This is my grandfather, Colin Cooper. Grandad, this is the lady who kindly invited you to come and eat here this morning.'

'I'm pleased to meet you again,' Colin said, wiping his mouth on his napkin and smiling up at Helen. 'You probably won't remember me. I met you when you were a little more than a baby.'

'Really?'

'Yes.' He pointed to his plate of food. 'My eggs and bacon were perfect, and as for the hash browns, well. . .' he grinned. 'I might have to come and stay here so I can eat like this every morning.'

'We'd love to have you here,' Helen said. 'I'm thrilled to meet you again but mostly I wanted to repay you for inviting my daughter to join you at the restaurant the other evening.'

Piper frowned as she finished wiping down the table. Maybe she had been wrong to be suspicious of her mother. It made sense that she was simply thanking Colin for inviting Piper to dinner.

'I'll leave you both to finish,' Helen said. 'Shall I fetch some more coffee?'

They thanked her but assured her they'd had enough to drink and Helen returned to the kitchen. Piper followed, carrying a tray of dirty plates and cutlery. She put the tray by the dishwasher ready for loading, startled when her mother's hand landed on her shoulder.

'Go next door quickly and ask Gran to come here.'

'Why?'

'Don't ask questions, just go,' she said, giving Piper a gentle push towards the door. 'Hurry up.'

Piper washed her hands and left the kitchen, shooting her mother a confused look over her shoulder. *What was she up to?* Was her mother trying to matchmake between Gran and Colin? she wondered. It wasn't like her to play games, but whatever she was doing, Piper knew the only way to find out was to do her mother's bidding and fetch Gran.

She knocked on her grandmother's front door

and walked in, as she always did. 'Hi, Gran, it's only me.'

Gran's cottage was smaller than the guest house. At some point in the past, the wall between the hall and living room had been removed so that anyone entering walked straight into the living area.

'Kitchen!'

Piper followed Gran's voice, not surprised to see her sitting at her round table, eating scrambled eggs on toast, as she did most days, while completing a crossword puzzle.

'Morning, lovey.' Gran indicated for Piper to take a seat at the small table. 'What brings you here so early? Shouldn't you be helping your mum with the breakfasts?'

'I was, but she sent me here to fetch you.'

Gran frowned and put down her Biro. 'Why? Is she all right? Nothing's happened, has it?'

'Not that I know of. I mean, she seems fine in herself if that's what you mean.' Piper shrugged. 'I have no idea what's going on with her. She's been acting a little oddly.'

'Interesting,' her gran answered, thoughtfully. 'I suppose there's nothing for it but to do as she asks.'

She ate the final two mouthfuls of her scrambled egg and finished her cup of tea. 'Let's go.'

Piper followed her grandmother back to the guest house.

'Helen?' Gran said, leading the way into the kitchen. 'You wanted to see me?'

Helen hugged her mother. 'Thanks for coming over so quickly.'

Piper sensed her mother hadn't been altogether confident Gran would appear, despite insisting she be brought over.

'I want to introduce you to someone,' she said, with a nervous smile. 'Let me just check they've finished their breakfast.'

'Why all the cloak and dagger stuff?' Gran asked.

'Yes, Mum,' Piper said, hoping her gran would be as happy to meet up with Colin after so many years as he had been to see Helen again.

Helen shot Piper a warning look. 'You won't have to wait long now.' She raised a hand, adding, 'Stay here for a moment,' leaving before they could reply.

'This is becoming annoying,' Gran said, folding her arms across her chest as she leaned against the worktop. 'I'd rather be doing my crossword instead of standing here, waiting.'

Seconds later, Helen returned. 'Right, if you want to come through, there's someone you should meet.'

Gran glanced at Piper. 'It had better be royalty at least keeping me hanging around like that,' she said, widening her eyes.

Piper followed them into the dining room, pausing as Gran gasped and put a hand to her mouth. 'Why have you done this, Helen?'

Colin rose and stepped forward, taking Gran's hands in his. 'Please don't be upset, Margery.'

'Did you arrange this with my daughter?'

He shook his head. 'I promise I'm as shocked as you,' he said. 'But after seeing you on the beach the other day, I was hoping to catch up and have a chat. There's a lot to discuss.'

'There is?' Gran looked stricken. 'I think it might be better to leave things as they have been for the past fifty-something years.'

Helen carried over a chair from one of the other tables. 'Mum, please sit down,' she said gently. 'I'm sorry you've had a shock, but when you came back from your swim the other day and mentioned meeting Alex's grandfather, I decided to get you together so you could clear the air.'

'*Why?*' Gran turned, colour in her cheeks. 'You don't know what happened between us. Why can't you leave things alone?'

Helen folded her arms and Piper could see her mother was now unsure about what she had done. 'I suspected he was Dad's friend from back in Harrogate, Mum.' Piper had no idea what friend of her grandfather's her mother might be referring to, but knew that if her grandmother had wanted to share the information with her she would have done so already. 'You need to speak to each other.'

Piper was aware of Alex and Colin watching their exchange and that Alex looked as uncomfortable as she felt.

'Why?' she repeated. Her gran was becoming angry, her hands clenched into fists. 'It's none of your business.'

'Because whatever it was that happened between you, it's not right to let it fester.' Helen sounded on firmer ground, never one to doubt her actions for long. 'You finally have a chance to resolve your differ-ences once and for all.'

Gran gave Helen a thunderous glare. 'If you felt this strongly, I would have preferred you to ask for my opinion before making arrangements behind my back.'

Colin shifted uncomfortably in his seat. 'I never wanted to corner you like this, Margery. I didn't know that this was going to happen.'

Piper saw her grandmother give him a suspicious look. 'He didn't know, Gran,' she confirmed, wishing her mother had taken the time to consider her plan a little better.

Helen sighed. 'I'm not doing this for Colin's sake.' She gave him an apologetic smile. 'Sorry, it's just that I know Mum has issues surrounding her past that I've always hoped would be settled. I had no idea what they were and when she reacted the way she did to seeing you, I decided this was the only way to engineer a meeting. I hope that once you've had time to talk things through, you'll un-derstand what I've done and my reasoning behind it.'

She motioned for Piper to follow her. 'Come

along. Let's leave them to chat in private. Alex, you're welcome to join us if you like.'

Gran shot her daughter a furious glare, but clearly recognised her tone. Helen was in no mood to argue and had made her mind up. At times like this, it was better to do what she wanted and get it over with.

'I'd much rather go for a walk to discuss this, Colin,' Piper heard Gran say. 'It'll be easier to talk about things outside rather than sitting here, facing each other.'

'That's an excellent idea, Margery. Let's go.'

As soon as they had left, Piper turned to her mother. 'Gran didn't look very happy with you, Mum.'

'Maybe not.' Her mother looked innocent. 'But, whatever their issue, it's not healthy for your gran to be bitter like this. They need to clear the air. How else were they going to do it?'

'They might not have wanted to,' Alex said quietly. 'Grandad isn't one for baring his soul, and by the looks of things, your mother didn't seem keen to speak to him. I'm not sure they're going to thank you for this.'

'I was thinking the same thing,' Piper admitted. 'I hope you're wrong, Alex.' She looked at her mother, who was filling the kettle under the running tap.

'That's a chance I'm willing to take,' Helen said, turning off the water and pressing the lid of the kettle back in place.

Piper and Alex stared at each other. She could see he was as anxious at the outcome as she was.

'I hope they're all right,' she said, loading the dishwasher. She glanced at her mother, who was staring silently out of the kitchen window. Piper suspected she wasn't as sure about what she had done as she was trying to make out. 'Mum, why don't you go and do something to keep your mind off Gran and Colin? I doubt they'll be back any time soon.'

Alex leaned against the kitchen table while Piper wiped the worktops. 'Do you want to go outside for a stroll? I need to do something to keep my mind busy until they return.'

'Yes, let's do that.' She rinsed out the dishcloth and draped it over the tap, then led the way outside. 'Let's walk along the pier. That way we can spot them coming back and see if they need us.' She was sorry not to have brought her sunglasses. It was already so bright. 'I wish Mum hadn't forced them together without any warning. I know she means well but Gran won't appreciate it and I hate to think of her being upset.'

* * *

Alex walked next to her, hands pushed into his jeans' pockets. 'Grandpa didn't seem very impressed either. Although I think he was more shocked than anything.'

'They obviously know each other from when Gran lived in England,' Piper said almost to herself. She had never known Gran to be anything other than friends with men. Gran loved telling her to be her own woman and never to rely on a man for anything. She'd reminded her mother of this when Piper's parents divorced, saying Helen should have taken her advice. 'Do you think they were in a relationship at some point?'

'I don't think so,' Alex replied. 'He's always said that my grandmother was the love of his life.' He shrugged. 'Then again, he might have said it because he thought it was what I wanted to hear? I just don't know.'

Piper thought back to when Gran had first seen Colin on Rozel Beach. She had seemed so shaken by the incident and, even now, her reaction had been more than someone meeting up with an old friend after many years. There had clearly been something between the two of them, but what? 'It's confusing, isn't it?'

'It is.' They reached the last house at the end of the pier. 'Can we go up here?' Alex asked, pointing to a flight of stairs between the last property and the sea wall.

'Yes, sure.'

'Where does it go?'

Piper looked up. 'To the back of the castle, and there's another few stairs taking us down to a small bit of beach. It's quite rocky, and not somewhere many people visit.'

He followed her up the steps to a small, paved area and looked up. 'Look, those stairs go right to the castle.'

'I don't think you'll be able to get through that way,' she said, realising that she had never bothered to go up the forty or so steps. She turned to her right. 'I'd much rather go down this way.'

Alex stopped to stare at the wide expanse of bay in front of them. 'It's so peaceful here. I'd have expected there to be lots of people making the most of the sunshine.'

'There probably will be a few later, but Grouville Beach is a nicer place to sunbathe.' Piper indicated the golden sand to their right. 'The beach here is small and rather pebbly,' she said. 'Shall we go down?'

'Yes, let's do that.'

Piper led the way down the worn, concrete steps to the small, pebbled beach with its rock pools. They sat on the wall separating the beach and sea and took off their shoes, dangling their feet in the cold water.

'I'm glad you're enjoying your stay,' she said eventually.

'It's been good to get away from everything for a while.'

She wondered what he meant by that. 'Do you have a significant other to bring with you next time?'

He shook his head. 'Not any more.'

'I'm sorry.'

He turned to face her. 'How about you?'

Piper took a deep breath to steady her emotions. 'No. Not any more.'

'I'm sorry.' He seemed to be searching her face for answers, but she wasn't ready to give them.

'Thank you,' she said. 'To be honest, it's been a while. And I'm fine.' She didn't add that since meeting Alex, she had felt more than fine. In fact, she felt more alive since his arrival than she had in a very long time. It was surprising, and a little exciting.

Alex looked out to sea and didn't say anything for a few minutes. She was glad of the chance to study his profile and her feelings for him without him realising. She had always preferred fair-haired men, but there was something about Alex's blue eyes and dark, wavy hair that stirred emotions in her she had presumed were dead. It was a little unnerving when she had almost forgotten how being attracted to another human being made her feel.

8

Piper arrived back at Gran's cottage and let herself in, catching a heated exchange between her grandmother and mother.

'Don't you ever again presume to take matters into your own hands where I'm concerned, Helen. Do you understand?'

'I was only trying to help.'

Piper walked through the living room to the kitchen.

Gran sighed heavily. 'I don't need your help. I'm a grown woman and have looked after myself since you were little more than a toddler. Why would you think I need you to make decisions for me now?'

'Hi, Gran,' Piper said when her grandmother took a breath. 'How did your chat go?'

'Obviously not that well,' Helen snapped.

Piper hated seeing the two people closest to her at loggerheads. 'Stop it, the pair of you.' They looked at her, aghast. She never interfered in their occasional arguments, but this one had the potential to escalate if she didn't step in quickly. 'Gran, you know full well that Mum only had your best interests at heart.' She gave her mother a cool stare. 'It's not her fault that she didn't realise you didn't want to have anything to do with Colin. And you, Mum, before you say anything, we all know that Gran is more than capable of fighting her own battles. I wouldn't like to be set up like that, and neither would you.'

As they opened their mouths to argue, Piper raised her hands. 'Stop it. No more arguing. Are you okay, Gran?'

Her grandmother rallied with a shrug. 'I'm fine.' She shot a fiery glance at Helen. 'Angry, but fine.'

'Gran, I said no more arguing. Please. The three of us have to stick together.'

'We do,' Helen said, looking rather sheepish. 'And I am sorry for getting involved, Mum.'

'Good.' Gran walked out of the kitchen and into the living room where she sat down on the two-seater sofa. Piper and Helen followed, each choosing a chair on either side. 'The fact is that your father wasn't the kindly man everyone took him to be. He hit me.' She stared at her hands as she spoke. 'I know I should have told you more about the early part of my marriage to your father, Helen, but for the first few years, it was too painful to go there. After that, there never seemed to be the right time to sit and talk to you about it. I wanted to move on and forget that part of my life.'

'I understand why you would want to move on from it all, Mum,' Helen said. 'But I'm horrified to think that Dad hit you.'

'It's an upsetting thing to have to think about. Thankfully, it was a very long time ago.'

Helen glanced at Piper and seemed unsure what to say next.

Piper couldn't believe what she was hearing. 'What did Colin do to upset you so much, Gran?' Piper asked.

Gran sat back in her chair and crossed her legs. 'Colin was your grandfather's best friend,' she said, staring at her hands. 'They were in business together and his wife, Iris, and I were best friends. We had grown up in the orphanage together.' Piper knew something of her grandmother's childhood, but very little detail. Her mother had mentioned a few times over the years how difficult Gran's childhood had been without parents or siblings, and Piper, aware that it wasn't something she liked to think about, never broached the subject. 'We spent all our free time in each other's company and even had our babies within a few months of each other,' Gran said wistfully. 'I thought we'd be best friends for ever.' She stopped talking and sighed.

'Carry on, Mum,' Helen urged.

Gran gave a shuddering sigh. 'She was as close to me as family, or at least, what I assumed having family felt like. We worked in the same hotel as waitresses.' She looked from Piper to Helen. 'We even started our jobs on the same day. We were more like sisters than friends, in some ways. We met our husbands when we both attended a local dance. The men ran a garage together.' She sighed. 'Our lives were simple, but I thought they were perfect.'

Piper watched her grandmother's expression

change as she reminisced. The pain in her voice was evident and Piper wanted to tell her to stop, but she had never heard her be so open about her past before. As difficult as it might be for Gran, Piper had the sense she needed to share it.

Helen reached out and took her mother's hand in hers before letting go. 'It'll do you good to get it all off your chest.'

'Yes,' Piper agreed. 'And we never have to refer to it again if you don't want us to.' She gave her mother a pointed look.

'At first, our marriage was perfect,' her gran said quietly. 'Then you came along, Helen, and I didn't think I'd ever want for anything else.'

Piper knew they were getting to the upsetting part. 'And then what happened?'

'Your grandfather, Peter, began to find fault in everything I did.' She lowered her gaze. 'Then he hit me for the second time.'

Piper gasped and covered her mouth, exchanging a shocked look with her mother.

'I know,' Gran said sadly. 'I was shocked when it happened. When I looked back, I could see the gradual control he had over me, but I was naive. I assumed this was what marriage was like. Until he hit me. Oh, he apologised, swore he'd never do it again.'

'But he did?' Helen whispered.

Gran nodded. 'Twice more. The second time, I decided I'd had enough. I tried to speak to Iris about it, but she refused to listen and told me to stop whining and be grateful to have such a handsome husband and adorable little girl.'

'I can't believe your best friend didn't believe you. You must have felt terribly let down by her.'

'I think it worried her that I might cause trouble and upset our happy foursome.'

'Oh, Gran, that's awful.'

Gran swallowed and took a deep breath. 'I was more upset that she didn't believe me than I was about Peter's behaviour, however unacceptable that was. I called at Iris's home to try and speak to her again, but Colin was there too. He walked in when we were speaking, told me that Iris had told him all about my accusations against Peter and that he couldn't imagine his friend being capable of hitting a woman.'

'You must have felt so alone, Mum,' Helen said. 'What did you do?'

'I put up with it for a few months and then it happened again, I knew I had to leave. Not having a family, I had no one to go to for support.' She closed her eyes briefly, pain crossing her face. 'I had always been frugal with my wages and put something by. I had savings.'

'Dad wasn't aware you had money?'

Margery shook her head. 'We were renting a flat and I was keeping my savings as a surprise, so we could buy furniture once he had enough for a deposit on a house. After I told them about Peter, Colin and Iris weren't as friendly with me, so I saved even more money, cutting corners with meals and being extra careful with my spending. Then, as soon as I had enough to leave your grandfather, I did.'

'And that's when you came to Jersey,' Piper said, relieved her grandmother had had the foresight to save money.

'Yes, lovey. I didn't want to stay in St Helier, or out west, because that's where we'd spent our honeymoon and I suspected if he ever did come looking for me on the island that would be where your grandad would expect to find me.'

They sat in silence for a few minutes, then Piper and Helen went to hug Margery.

'I'm so sorry you had to go through all that, Mum,' Helen said, sniffing. 'I hate to think he was so cruel to you.'

'You're incredibly brave, Gran. It must have been terrifying to come to the island with a small child not knowing what you would do when you arrived.'

Helen and Piper sat back down to give Margery a chance to continue speaking.

'It was, but I was lucky and applied for a job with Pearl Hayes.'

'The woman who sold you the guest house?' Helen asked.

'That's right.' Gran smiled for the first time since they'd arrived at her home. 'She took me on,' she said. 'She gave me a home and a job and was the first mother I had ever known. She had never been married and had always wanted children, but in those days one generally accompanied the other. I was surprised when I discovered after her death that she had left the guest house to me and a distant cousin of hers.'

'And you bought her half of the guest house from

her?' Piper's respect for her grandmother was increasing by the second.

Gran nodded. 'Yes.'

'And Colin?' Helen asked.

Gran shrugged. 'He wanted to apologise for not believing me back then.'

'I'm pleased,' Piper said.

'Oh, Mum, I'm so sorry I interfered.' Helen looked distraught. 'I wouldn't have pushed it if I'd realised how painful it would be.'

Gran raised a hand and shook her head. 'Don't fret, lovey. What's done, is done. Colin told me he and Iris had nothing to do with Peter after they fell out with him, which makes me feel a little better. He said he has no idea what happened to Peter and that he and Iris regretted the whole thing very much.'

'And now we understand what happened,' Piper said. She sensed there was more to it than just an apology, but her grandmother was clearly struggling with her emotions. 'Why don't we leave you in peace now, Gran?'

Margery nodded. 'I need a little time to mull it over. I'll pop over to find you both later.'

Piper watched as Helen bent to hug her mother

once more. She cleared her throat. 'Gran, I've always known you were a woman to admire, but you're even stronger than I imagined.'

'I don't know about that, lovey. I just did what I thought was best.'

'Can I get anything for you before we leave?' Helen asked.

Margery shook her head. 'No, thank you. And I don't want you both worrying. I might seem a little upset but I'm fine. I just need to... what is that word you use, Piper?'

'Process?'

'That's the one. I need some time to "process" my chat with Colin and everything I've just told you. I'll be fine.' She waved them away. 'Off you go.'

* * *

Piper followed her mother out of the cottage but instead of going home, Helen kept walking along the pier.

'You all right, Mum?'

'I will be.'

'It must have been frightening as a little girl to have violence and tension at home?'

'I don't really remember much, thankfully,' Helen said.

Piper reached out and stroked her mum's arm. '*Are you* all right? Would you rather I left you in peace to think? Or can I come with you?'

'Come with me.'

They walked slowly in silence for a few minutes. Piper felt sad that Gran had married an aggressive man. It must have been difficult and scary to leave without him knowing, and without anyone to help her. 'So brave,' she murmured.

'What was that?'

Piper realised she had spoken out loud. 'I was just saying how brave Gran was to do what she did.'

Helen nodded. 'She is amazing. I just didn't realise quite how much.' She stopped walking and shook her head. 'Why did I make her speak to Colin like that? I'm such an idiot.'

Piper rested a hand on her mother's arm. 'You didn't know what had happened between them, Mum. Gran said not to worry about it.'

'I'm just so annoyed with myself.'

'There's no point. Anyway,' Piper added, wanting to help her mother feel less guilty, 'she'll probably be happier now, knowing that Colin is sorry for what he did, and relieved to have told us about her past. Don't you think?'

Helen began walking again. 'Yes, I suppose you're right.' She slipped her arm around Piper's shoulders, and Piper was glad to feel her mother relax and to have put an end to their disagreement. How strange that she was the third generation of women who were single and self-reliant. Piper wasn't surprised she was happiest doing things on her own terms, especially when her mother and grandmother had done the same thing.

'Would you like an ice cream?' she asked, seeing two teens laughing as they walked away from the café along the pier and suddenly yearning for a cone of Jersey ice cream with raspberry sauce drizzled over the top of it.

Helen stopped. 'How did you guess that's exactly what I need right now? Come along,' she said. 'My treat.'

9

Later that evening, Alex arrived at the guest house and walked through to the backyard, stopping at the open kitchen door to knock on the doorframe. 'I hope you don't mind me turning up uninvited.'

'Of course not,' Piper said, closing her book and placing it on the small table next to her. Helen was out with friends and Piper welcomed Alex's presence. 'Come and sit. It's lovely and cool out here.'

'Thanks.' He sat and stared at her for a moment. 'Would you like to come for a stroll along the pier, or to the beach?' he asked. 'It's glorious out there.'

Piper gave him an apologetic smile. 'Sorry, but I

promised Mum I'd keep an eye on the place this evening while she's out.'

'No worries. How about when I come back to the island?'

'That would be lovely.' She watched him as he stared into space. 'I can sense there's something troubling you,' she said, presuming it had to do with Gran and Colin's earlier chat.

'Only that it's my last night here. I was going to ask you out for something to eat but spent longer with Grandad than I expected.'

She hid her disappointment, then reminded herself that she couldn't have gone anyway, not if she was stuck at the guest house. 'Is he all right, after this morning?'

Alex nodded slowly. 'He was thrown by the meeting with your grandmother earlier. I think their chat has reminded him of a few things he would rather have forgotten, but he was grateful for the opportunity to apologise after all these years.'

'I'm relieved. Mum will be too.'

'And your gran? How's she faring after all that's happened?'

Piper shrugged. 'She's a bit emotional about it all,

if I'm honest, but I think she appreciates his apology. Hopefully it'll help her settle the bad memories she's carried for decades. That can only be a good thing, can't it?'

'I think so.' Alex narrowed his eyes. 'When I return, I'd like to invite you, your mum and gran out for something to eat with me and Grandad. Clear the air properly and move on.'

Piper liked his suggestion and said so. 'So, this is your last night here for now.' She didn't know why she'd said it when they both knew it to be the case. 'Are you looking forward to getting home?'

'I am,' he said, but he sounded doubtful and she wondered why. 'I have a few things to sort out there with a business partner before I return to Jersey.' His voice trailed off a little. 'I'm hoping it won't be too difficult.'

She had no idea what he was referring to and sensed he didn't want to go into detail. 'I hope it won't prove as hard as you think to sort out,' she said.

'It's to do with money. I'm a bit of a nerd.' He laughed. 'I prefer dealing with technology rather than finances.'

'There's nothing wrong with being nerdy.' She was a bit nerdy herself.

He smiled. 'My sister, Fliss, has always teased me about being into technology.'

So that's who Fliss was, Piper mused.

'So, you're a computer buff and you develop apps?'

'That's right.'

Piper suspected he wasn't elaborating in case she found his job boring. 'I'm hopeless with computers,' she said, hoping to eke out more information. 'Obviously, I can do all the usual things, like sending emails and saving documents, but I'm not on any phone thingies.'

'You mean social media?'

'Yes, like Instagram. The ladies at Harbour Blooms are always taking pictures of their arrangements and window displays. They seem to be doing it every time I go in there, and posting stuff online, but it's not my thing at all.'

'I don't blame you.'

Aware that he wasn't going to tell her anything further, she decided to change the subject. 'Will you have enough time to see your Grandad again before you leave tomorrow?'

'Unfortunately not. I've got an early flight and he has a class first thing.'

'I can give you a lift to see him if that helps?' She didn't want a lack of transport to be the reason Alex didn't visit his grandfather before he left.

He shook his head. 'That's kind of you, but I'm sure he'd rather get on with his art class. He's not very good at goodbyes.'

'Did you tell him you were coming back soon?'

'I did, but he's probably had enough of an emotional assault course this week. Thanks for offering a lift, though. I appreciate it.'

She didn't want Alex to feel badly about what had happened between Gran and his grandfather, so offered to take him to the airport instead.

Alex's smile was full of warmth. 'You're very generous, Piper, but it's across the other side of the island and you have more than enough to get on with without spending an hour in traffic.'

He had a point. Not wanting to push it, she said, 'Well, if you change your mind let me know.'

'I will. Thanks.'

'Will you be going straight back to work?'

He sat deep in thought for a few seconds, as though the question demanded some deliberation. 'No, I've got the day off,' he said eventually.

There was something mysterious about Alex Cooper and Piper wished she could work out what it was. Maybe she would find out when he returned.

As the sun set and the temperature cooled, Piper shivered. She didn't want to bring their evening together to an end, but didn't fancy sitting in the living room where guests tended to congregate in the evenings.

'You're cold?'

'A little,' she admitted. 'But I'm not ready to go inside just yet.' She realised he was staring at her. 'What's the matter?' She brushed her fingers over her lips, hoping there weren't any crumbs from the toasted cheese and tomato sandwich she had eaten earlier.

'Nothing.' He gazed at her, before taking her hands in his and pulling her gently to her feet. 'I suppose I should go.'

'Er. All right,' Piper said, turning her back to him to hide her embarrassment. She had thought for a moment he was going to kiss her. 'I'll see you out.'

Mortified, she led him back through the guest house to the front door. Piper opened the front door and forced a smile. 'Goodnight.'

'Goodnight,' he said leaning forward and giving her a peck on the cheek before leaving.

10

'What's the matter with you?' Jax asked the following morning. He stopped in front of Piper, outside the coffee shop where she was headed to buy a cappuccino. 'Is this the treat you give yourself for finishing making up the bedrooms at the guest house?'

'Something like that. Why?' She bent to stroke Seamus's head.

'You look miserable, that's why.' He moved closer and stared at her. 'Has someone upset you? Because if they have, they'll have me to deal with.'

Piper stepped back and grinned. 'Jax, as much as I love you, we both know full well there's more chance of me dealing with someone than you. You might have the physique, but you're too laid-back to argue with anyone, let alone have a fight.'

He frowned at her before raising his eyebrows. 'Yes, you're right.' As she went to move past him, he added, 'Hey, you haven't told me why you've got such a miserable look on your face.'

'It's probably man trouble,' Nancy said, walking past them to her van with a bouquet. 'It usually is.'

'What?' Piper frowned. 'Not with me, it isn't!'

Nancy laughed. After placing the flowers inside her pink van she turned, ready to go back to her shop. 'Suit yourself, but I recognise that expression.'

Piper pulled a face at Jax when Nancy had gone. 'This place drives me nuts sometimes. There's so little privacy and everyone either knows, or thinks they know, everyone else's business.'

He slipped his arm around her shoulders. 'Aw, stop grumbling. You know as well as I do that you'd never want to live anywhere else.'

Was that still true? She supposed it was. She needed to stop feeling sorry for herself and cheer up and she would start by being nice to Jax. 'Can I buy you a coffee?'

He shook his head. 'I'm not letting you pay a

ridiculous amount for flavoured water.' He tapped the metal water bottle on the side of his belt. 'I have all the liquid I need in here. But thanks for the offer. I'd better get on, and if coffee is the thing that will cheer you up, I won't stand in your way.'

She nudged his shoulder. 'I was on my way before you interrupted me,' she teased. 'Have a good day.'

'You, too.'

* * *

Piper had an hour to spare and after buying a cappuccino, she walked to the end of the pier. Turning left at the end of the row of terraced houses, she made her way to where she had thought Alex was about to kiss her. The disappointment still tugged at her. As she walked down the uneven steps to the beach, she thought that coming to this place was probably the worst thing to do when she was missing him. But she was here now, and it seemed that for once she was the only person there. She sat on a rounded boulder and pushed her sunglasses onto the top of her head as she stared at the blue sea, the sun picking out silvery dashes of light as the waves peaked.

What was wrong with her? She was never this soppy over a man, but Alex was the first one to make her feel something since meeting Rick at university, when her heart had been full of expectation and plans to change the world.

Feeling miserable, she took a sip of her drink, careful not to scald her lips. It had been eighteen months since Rick had eloped with Stacy. Piper still found it hard to come to terms with the fact that she hadn't noticed any changes in her fiancé's behaviour before he and Stacy ran off together. She recalled only too well how stunned she had been returning home after attending a show at the Opera House to discover he had left a letter on her pillow. It had only occurred to her then why he had made an excuse not to go. Piper thought back to how oblivious she had been that night, as she enjoyed the musical with one of her friends, and how the embarrassment of her gullibility still stung.

She was still too sensitive about the whole incident – or so her mother insisted –but it was hard not to imagine people talking about you when something so devastating happened. Everyone knew Stacy. She had lived in a house on the hill, not far from the pier, all her life. Piper had worked for Stacy's husband, waitressing during summer holidays when she was younger, and had always seen her as elegant and beautiful. Stacy had seemed very happily married, or at least that's what Piper had assumed until she and Rick ran off together. Before Rick left the island with Stacy, Piper had believed the myth that men tended to leave their wives or girlfriends for younger women, but Stacy was at least twelve years older. No wonder she'd missed what was going on.

'I need to stop this,' she said to herself, determined to finally put the past behind her. She didn't need Alex's attention to do it either. She had always been strong, and although Rick's leaving had been awful, Piper didn't want it to define her any longer. She needed to stop being embarrassed by what had happened. After all, it wasn't as if she had done anything wrong. She wanted to start living again, and stop being the girl who had been dumped by Rick so that he could marry Stacy.

'You've got this,' she said, taking another drink

from the covered cup in her hand, burning her mouth and wincing in pain. 'Bugger.' She breathed in a gulp of air and, for a split second, felt like crying. 'Stop it,' she scolded herself, glancing round to check no one was listening. 'That's enough.'

She needed to change her life, but how? She wasn't going to let her mum down by leaving the guest house and finding another job, nor did she want to. She needed something more though. Something that would take her out of herself and bring more joy into her days.

'What's up with you?'

Piper turned to see Jax's mum, Sheila, still wearing the overall she wore at her salon when doing her clients' hair.

Piper forced a smile as Sheila sat beside her. 'I'm fine. I was just thinking, that's all.'

'Piffle.'

'Sorry?'

Sheila twisted to face Piper. 'I know you well enough to pick up when you're upset and when you're simply thinking. So, are you going to tell me what's wrong, or will I have to persuade my son to find out for me?'

Piper smiled. She knew Jax would never betray a confidence. She also didn't want Sheila to keep pestering her for the truth, which Piper knew from experience she would do.

'I was just trying to work out what to do next with my life.'

Sheila frowned as much as possible with her Botox-filled forehead. 'Aren't you happy working with your mum?'

'It's not that.' Piper didn't want her mum's friend to get the wrong impression. 'I do love living and working here, but I'm twenty-seven. I'd expected to be married and making a home and family of my own by now.' Her voice cracked with emotion.

'I could wring that bloody Rick's neck for what he did to you. Little sod.' She gave a growl and Piper couldn't help smiling. 'Never mind that snooty Stacy. Little tart.'

'She's not a tart,' Piper said. 'Not that I've forgiven what her and Rick did,' she added quickly when Sheila's face reddened angrily. 'Look, she obviously did me a favour.' For the first time, Piper believed it. 'If Rick didn't love me as much as I loved him then it's right that we're not married. Imagine having to go through a divorce.' She shuddered. 'No, I'd rather be single than with someone who prefers another woman.' She forced a smile. 'Honestly, I'm fine. But I do need to find some way to make my life busier and more interesting.'

'How are you going to do that?'

Piper stared at the water moving gently against the harbour wall. 'I'm not sure.'

11

The following week when the house was empty, and Piper had finished working at The Cabbage Patch, she drove her mother and Gran to Archirondel for an early supper. They chose an outside table at a small café. While Helen ordered food, Piper went with her gran for a swim to make the most of the warm evening and her new swimsuit.

Most of the beaches on the island were covered in fine, white-gold sand, but Archirondel was another pebbly beach. Piper dropped her towel next to her gran's and linked arms with her as they walked down to the seashore. The tide was on the way out and Piper was relieved to discover the sea was warm after a sunny day.

'This isn't nearly as cold as Rozel was the other day,' she said, carefully stepping over the pebbles as she walked deeper into the sea.

'It'll get a bit cooler as we go deeper.'

She was right. Piper grimaced as Gran suddenly lowered herself into the water up to her neck. 'Come along, Piper. What are you waiting for?'

Piper took a deep breath, wishing for once that her gran wasn't quite so hardy and was a little more patient. She stepped forward until the water lapped around her chest, the cooler temperature briefly snatching her breath.

'Just keep moving,' Gran said, beginning to swim away from her. 'You'll soon get used to it.'

Piper knew from experience that Gran was right, so did as she was told and within a minute was striking out to sea, loving the sensation of the water gliding over her skin. She let her mind wander and after a while lay on her back, closing her eyes against the evening sun.

'Liking it?'

'Loving it,' she answered dreamily. 'In fact, I think I'm going to start doing this more often.'

Gran laughed. 'I'll believe that when I see it.'

Piper let the gently rolling waves massage her body, and for the first time in ages, felt completely free. She might still live at home and not have the partner she had spent years imagining herself with, but she had this. Surely her independence and the close, supportive relationship she had with her mum and grandmother were worth more than anything else. And she had her own business, she reminded herself. It might not make her a fortune, but it provided her with enough income to live and save a little. Piper sighed. Yes, she was lucky, and she was grateful for all that she had.

* * *

'Food's ready,' Helen called eventually, snapping Piper out of her thoughts.

She opened her eyes and waved to let her mum know that she had heard. She would have loved to have spent longer wallowing in the gentle waves as they softly moved her back and forth.

'Come on, Gran,' she said, unsure if she had heard Helen's call. 'It's time we got out.'

They swam back to the beach, dried and pulled on their clothes before joining Helen at the café.

'Enjoy yourselves?' Helen asked.

'It was really relaxing.' Piper thanked the waitress as she placed the coconut prawns and chips she had ordered onto the table in front of her. 'This looks and smells delicious.'

After a few minutes sitting in silence while they savoured their food, Piper sensed her mother watching her.

'What's the matter, Mum?' she asked before eating another prawn and groaning in pleasure at the taste.

Her mother hesitated and glanced at Gran. 'I saw Sheila earlier.'

Piper knew instinctively where the conversation was going and wished now that she hadn't said anything to Sheila.

'Look, Mum,' she said unable to hold back a sigh. 'I'm fine.'

'That's not what Sheila told me.'

Piper groaned. 'I wish I'd never said anything now, but you know Sheila.'

'We all know Sheila,' Gran said.

'I don't want to talk about it,' Piper said firmly, not wanting to go over what had happened with Rick again.

After a moment, her mother and Gran began reminiscing instead about when Piper was a baby. She had heard the same stories all her life, but they loved remembering that time in their lives and were also completely biased when it came to her.

'It's true,' Helen said when she caught Piper's amusement. 'You had hair that was almost black, your blue eyes were so huge and your lips almost a cherry red. Gran thought you looked like Snow White.'

'So you're saying I looked like a cartoon character?' she teased.

'You know what I mean.' Her mother pulled a face. 'You were such a beautiful baby. So what if I'm proud and like to talk about you?'

'As long as it's only with Gran.' She leaned over to kiss her mother on the cheek. 'You're the best mum, do you know that?'

'What about me?' Gran asked before taking a sip of her drink.

'You're the best gran, Gran.' She blew her grandmother a kiss. Something grabbed her gran's attention and Piper turned to see what it was.

She raised her hand to shade her eyes from the sun and squinted across the beach. 'Is that Jax over there with a group of schoolchildren?'

'I thought it was him when I noticed Seamus playing with a couple of the children,' Gran said, smiling. 'He's such a good boy, that one. It's a shame you're related because he's the sort of chap I'd like to see you settling down with. Don't you agree, Helen?'

Helen nodded sagely. 'I just want you to find someone who loves you and supports you in everything you choose to do.'

Piper wouldn't mind the same thing. 'I'm sure I'll find him some day.'

She was glad when her mum and Gran changed the subject to chat about how well the season was going, giving Piper time to daydream. Her mind flicked to Alex for a few minutes as she ate more of her prawns relishing the delicious taste.

'Mind if I join you?'

Piper looked up. 'Jax.' She turned to look for the schoolchildren she'd seen with him minutes before. 'Where are your pupils?'

'Their school minibus arrived to collect them.'

Gran indicated the chair next to her and Jax pulled it out and sat. He waved at the waitress, who instantly hurried over to see what he wanted.

'May I have the same as her, please?' He pointed to Piper's plate and glass. 'And a bowl of water for my dog if that's all right?'

'No problem at all.'

Seamus sat under Jax's chair. 'Thank you.'

The waitress gave him a flirty smile before returning inside the café.

'What?' Jax asked when Piper shook her head, grinning at him.

'You. I don't know what it is about you.'

He flicked an imaginary speck of something from his shoulder and winked at her. 'I can't help it if I'm a handsome devil, can I?'

Gran nudged him. 'Stop showing off.'

Helen and Piper laughed at Jax's mock horror.

'We were just saying that it's a shame you and Piper are related.'

Jax groaned. 'You're not going on about how well-suited we are again, are you?'

'They are.' Piper rolled her eyes heavenward.

'We'll both find partners when we're good and ready. Won't we, Piper?'

'Yes.'

'Anyway, I'm happy being single.' He narrowed his eyes and looked from Helen to Margery. 'Just like you two. And Mum, come to think of it. We're a bunch of happy singletons. Let's embrace it and stop worrying.'

'Thanks,' Piper mouthed, relieved her cousin had taken some of the attention away from her.

The waitress brought Jax's food and drink out. After another flirty smile and brief hesitation, she went to clear the table next to them that had just been vacated.

He ate a few mouthfuls. 'Good choice, this is tasty.' After another mouthful he frowned thoughtfully. 'Did I see you and your gran swimming earlier?'

'You did.'

He looked stunned. 'Seriously?'

'Yes, I know,' she said, with a rueful smile. 'You've

tried for years to persuade me to join you for your daily swim.'

Jax turned his attention to Gran. 'How did *you* persuade her, Margery? I'd love to know because I've tried every trick in my not-inconsiderable-book and it's never worked.'

'Maybe you're not as persuasive as you like to think,' Gran teased.

'Obviously not.' He pointed at Piper. 'You have no excuse from now on. You're going to come swimming with me. It'll do you good to get outside more.'

'I'm out walking every day,' she argued, not wanting swimming to become a daily habit. It was one thing going into the sea at the end of summer when the water had heated up over the summer months, but another entirely once the weather cooled.

'Don't bother arguing. You've done it now and you can do it again. Tomorrow I'll come to yours and we'll go swimming.' He gave her a wide, satisfied smile. 'I'll make a fit person out of you yet, little cousin.'

'We'll see,' she said, pulling a face at him. 'Now,

stop badgering me and eat your food before I pinch those prawns.'

12

Piper made up the bedrooms, including the one that Alex would be staying in when he arrived later that day. Her stomach gave a little flip at the thought of seeing him again. She had kept herself busy since his departure two weeks before, but for some reason the atmosphere in the house seemed a little less exciting without him being there.

She spent a few hours in her room, sorting through some of her latest sea glass finds. Satisfied that they were all neatly contained in individual jars, she said goodbye to her mother and drove up to The Cabbage Patch. She was pleased to find Casey and

Tara already at their small concession next to hers in the barn.

'Hi, there,' she greeted them, placing her rucksack on her worktop. She sat on a wooden stool behind her counter and watched as Casey expertly wrapped one of her more elaborate homemade candles in coloured wax paper bought cheaply from one of the other sellers. Piper loved that Casey used beeswax from her father's beehives, left over after filling his jars of honey. 'Busy morning?'

'Not really,' Casey replied before deftly folding the paper and tying green gardening twine around it to hold it in place. 'You?'

'Nope. Just sorting more glass.'

'Oh, I meant to say, Tara and I have been collecting sea glass for you, and my mum has sent a tub full. She and her friends have been collecting it on their morning dog walks.'

Piper was touched that so many people supported her fledgling business. 'That's so kind of them. Please thank them for me, will you?'

'Sure.'

Casey, satisfied with her handiwork, pushed the

wrapped candle to one side of the counter with others in various sizes. 'You're looking pensive this morning,' she said, turning her attention to Piper.

'I'm just admiring your candles and mirrors and wondering whether I should diversify. But I'm not sure what else to do.'

Casey leaned her elbows on the wooden surface in front of her. 'You need to ask yourself what sort of things you like to do and take it from there.'

'I have.'

'And?'

Piper frowned. 'That's the problem. I still don't know.' *Why was am I being so indecisive? Because Alex was due to arrive, that's why.* She was on edge and spent the rest of the morning serving customers. Needing a break, she asked Casey and Tara to keep an eye on things while she took a stroll to the out-building where the artists congregated. Maybe she would see Colin and say a quick 'hello'. Her gran was still a bit down about seeing him again after so many years.

She opened the barn door and, hearing voices, realised a class was in progress. Not wishing to in-trude, Piper stepped inside, where natural light cascaded into the large space through the skylights in the roof high above them. She quietly pushed the door closed behind her and scanned the room, trying to spot Colin behind one of the easels. She looked at her watch. It was almost lunchtime. Hopefully the class would end soon.

'If you all want to take a fifteen-minute break,' the tutor said on cue. 'Then we can continue with the second half of our lesson.'

Most of the artists put down their paintbrushes. Piper noticed Colin, hands on his hips as he bent backwards in a stretch. Vivienne, one of the stall-holders who sold costume jewellery in the barn, walked in carrying a large plate with a chocolate cake on it. She seemed to make a beeline for Colin and Piper wasn't sure whether to wait for him, but he'd already spotted her.

'Piper? Piper!'

She smiled as he came to join her and then noticed Vivienne spot her and turn suddenly to head off in a different direction. How strange, Piper mused. She realised Colin was speaking.

'Nothing's wrong with Margery, is there?' He looked concerned.

Piper shook her head. 'Why would you ask that?'

He waved his hands. 'Ignore me. I'm a little pan-icky about things sometimes. I was worried she was still upset about seeing me and, well, we're not as young as we were. I would hate to think I'd given her a turn.'

Feeling guilty, Piper gave him a reassuring smile. 'There's nothing wrong with Gran. She's fine. I had a free couple of minutes and thought I'd come and see how you were getting along.'

'That's very kind of you.' He moved away from the door as others began to leave the barn.

'Shall we find somewhere to sit and chat?'

Piper pointed to one of the benches dotted around. 'How about over there?'

They sat in companionable silence for a moment.

'You're still enjoying it here?' Piper asked.

'Very much. It's a perfect setting. The other day a few of us went for a walk on the cliff paths. The views across the Channel were incredible. We're going back to paint them before the end of our visit.'

'They are pretty spectacular, aren't they?'

'You're very lucky living in such a pretty place.'

He looked a little wistful. 'I'm glad Margery came here and made such a pleasant life for herself.'

'Thank you. I'm happy she chose to come here too.'

'I've felt badly about how Iris and I treated your grandmother since discovering more about Peter's true character, you know.' He sighed heavily. 'I know that Iris missed your gran when she left suddenly.' He stared down at his hands and then looked at Piper. 'She must have felt very alone, especially with a small child to care for in a strange place.'

Piper didn't want Colin to dwell on the past. There was nothing he could do to change things now. She rested a hand on his forearm. 'Please don't give yourself a hard time about it, Colin. What's done is done and you didn't have all the information when you and Iris took my grandfather's side. It's good that you and Gran have resolved your differences.'

He seemed relieved. 'Thank you. That makes me feel much better. Although I still need to satisfy myself that Margery completely forgives me for what happened. I just hope she gives me another chance to do that.'

Piper wasn't sure Gran would be open to

speaking to him again, but decided to do her best to help make it happen when the chance arose.

Colin stood. 'I see the others are going back inside. I'd better get on, but it was very kind of you to come and speak to me today, Piper. I appreciate you taking the time.'

'It was good to chat to you, too.'

* * *

Feeling much better after her chat with Colin, Piper drove to town to collect some shopping for her mother. She arrived back at the pier and parked her car in the only available space.

She had almost reached her front door when the rumbling sound of a motorbike distracted her. She turned around to see who it was, but didn't recognise the rider in the black leather jacket and full-face helmet. It was quiet on the pier, and several people turned to stare, unimpressed at having their peace disrupted.

Piper was surprised when the bike pulled up next to her and stopped. The rider turned off the machine and pushed down the kickstand before dismounting. Embarrassed to be caught staring, Piper turned and opened the front door.

'Piper, it's me!'

Recognising Alex's voice, she spun round to see him lifting the helmet off his head. 'You brought your bike over?'

'I thought I might persuade you to come out on it with me,' he said hopefully. 'Grandad loves the bike. He had one for years and I take him out for the day at least once or twice a month when he's at home.'

'That's a lovely thing to do,' she said, trying to imagine them roaring around the countryside.

'It's always fun.' He put his keys in his jacket pocket. 'It's a little warm for wearing leather today. It was much cooler when I left home yesterday to catch the overnight ferry from Poole.'

'Poole? I thought you lived in London. Isn't Portsmouth closer?'

'It is, but I spent a night at my parents' home in Sandbanks. They're away and needed me to go and check up on my sister to see how she's getting on.' He frowned. 'She's younger than me and twenty now, but still acts like a spoilt teenager sometimes. She has a tendency to hold parties but not worry too much about people she doesn't know coming to the house, which my father would hate.'

Piper thought that sounded rather thoughtless of Fliss, but didn't like to say so.

'How did you find things?' she asked, stepping back to let him inside.

'Not too bad, thankfully. She had a few friends who had spent the night but they were old school-friends and they were making the most of the sunshine and lazing around. So nothing untoward.'

She was glad for his sake that his sister was behaving herself. 'Well, you're here now. Why don't you come inside, and we'll get you checked in. Then you can change into something a little cooler if you like.'

'Is it okay for me to park the bike here overnight?'

Piper nodded. 'There's not enough room for a car, so no one's going to mind.'

He took off a rucksack that Piper hadn't noticed him wearing and followed her inside. 'It's good to be back.'

His comment cheered her enormously. 'It's good to have you back here,' she said honestly.

'Really?'

She realised he was no longer following her and

turned to face him. His eyes sparkled and when he smiled, she couldn't help but mirror his expression. 'Yes,' she said. 'It is.' She continued into the living room to check him in and fetch his room key. 'I was up at The Cabbage Patch earlier and had a chat with your grandfather. He seems well and is still enjoying his time there very much.'

'That's good to know.'

She updated the computer and handed him the room key. 'Does he know you're here?'

'He does. I thought he could get together with some of the people on his course and come up with a few ideas of places we might visit together. He loves planning outings and since Granny died, he's had little opportunity to do much.' His voice took on a sad tone. 'I couldn't help thinking as soon as I saw my room upstairs that first time how much she would have loved it here.'

So that was why he had looked sad that day, Piper realised.

'They were always incredibly busy. He had a vintage car, a gorgeous pale-blue-and-cream 1953 Austin-Healey 100-6. It was his most treasured possession. They were always out and about, taking part in vintage car rallies. Boxing Day was a big rally I seem to recall, with them stopping off for lunch at a traditional pub along the way.'

Piper pictured the man who, until she discovered what had passed between him and her grand-mother, she had imagined to be kindly. Still, he had apologised, and she hated to think of anyone being lonely or miserable. 'He doesn't go on the rallies any more?'

Alex shook his head slowly. 'He sold the car soon after Granny died. He said he found it too difficult to even sit in it without her and couldn't bear the thought of his friends pitying him now that he was alone.' He tilted his head. 'Granny was a character. Lots of fun to be around.' He stared at Piper for a second before continuing. 'That's probably why she and your grandmother got along so well before they fell out.'

'They must have missed each other very much,' Piper said. 'Our two grandmothers.' She didn't want to offend him, so added. 'And your grandfather, of course.'

'I suppose they must have done. Such a shame that things happened as they did,' he said sadly. 'I would have loved for Granny and your gran to make up and become friends again before she died.'

'I'm sure Gran would have liked that too,' she agreed, realising for the first time that Gran's sadness after speaking with Colin hadn't only been about the way he had treated her, but the discovery that her childhood friend was no longer alive to make up with her. The thought upset her so much that she had to clear her throat before speaking. 'I'll leave you to freshen up.'

'Great, thanks. I'll see you down here in, say, twenty minutes?'

'Perfect.' He paused halfway up the stairs, and looked at her. 'I'd like to take you out if you're free tomorrow morning. We can go out on the bike and see where the day takes us. After you've finished work, of course.'

'That would be fun,' she said, equally wanting to go and unable to turn him down when he had such an expectant expression on his lovely face.

'I was even hoping you might come out for a ride with me this evening. Gramps is eating with his friends, but said he'd be free a bit later. So we could go out for an hour or two.'

Piper loved the idea. It had been hot today and a cool ride out on a motorbike seemed like a fun thing to do. 'Yes, that would be lovely.'

'Right. I'll catch up with you in a bit.' She smiled at him.

* * *

When Alex had gone upstairs, Piper took the opportunity to pop out and visit her gran.

'Hello, lovey.' Her grandmother frowned from her chair by the living room window. 'Is something the matter?'

Piper shook her head as she sat down opposite. 'I've just been speaking to Alex.'

'Oh, he's back then?'

Piper nodded. 'He arrived a few minutes ago and said something that made me think of you.'

Gran put down the tapestry she had been working on for weeks. 'Go on.'

Piper explained that she had realised that it wasn't just Colin who had upset her, but the fact that her old schoolfriend was no longer around to make friends with. 'Is that right?'

'It is. I don't know if Colin realised, and I was too emotional to be able to explain it to him. I needed some time alone to come to terms with it all.' She stared into space briefly. 'I always assumed that Iris and I would meet up again one day. That we'd be able to talk things through and that she would understand why I had made that difficult decision to leave. After speaking with Colin and learning that she had died a couple of years ago, I knew that it was too late. That I would never get the chance to speak to my old friend again.'

Piper got up and hugged her grandmother. 'Oh, Gran, I'm so sorry. That's heart-breaking for you.'

'It was.' Her voice was muffled by Piper's shoulder. Piper felt her grandmother's hands gently push her away.

Piper thought back to what Colin had said. 'Gran, I couldn't help wondering what Colin meant when he said that you had more to discuss. Do you know what he was referring to?'

Gran shook her head. 'I've no idea. I can't think that there is anything else. Maybe he realises that I needed time to come to terms with never being able to make things right with Iris, before I could talk more about our friendship, all those years ago.'

'Maybe,' Piper said thoughtfully. Wanting to make the most of them being alone together and give her grandmother the opportunity to speak about any hurt she might still be working through, Piper asked, 'So there isn't anything else you'd like to share from back then?'

Gran sighed. 'We all have memories that haunt us a little but any hurt I felt about Iris and Colin's reactions to me leaving your grandfather have been soothed slightly by Colin's admission that they didn't know Peter as well as they thought.'

'I'm glad,' Piper said, hugging Gran once again.

'You go off, lovey,' Gran said. 'Go and speak to that nice young man now that he's come back to spend time with you.'

'What?' Piper shook her head, not wishing her grandmother to get the wrong idea despite her secret feelings for Alex. 'He hasn't, Gran.' She gave a laugh that even to her own ears didn't sound convincing. 'He's come to spend more time with Colin. I think Alex needs a holiday.'

Gran gave her a knowing look, but it vanished

almost as soon as it appeared. She clearly didn't want to embarrass Piper by pushing the point about Alex. 'Has he been working hard?'

'I presume so.'

'What does he do?'

Piper shrugged. 'If I'm honest, I think he seems a little cagey about his life.'

She wasn't sure it mattered. She had been surprised by her own lack of curiosity about the details of Alex's life away from the island. She knew what he did for a living, although very little about what it entailed, and even though Piper sensed there was something he was keeping to himself, she didn't think it was anything untoward. At least she hoped not. Before Rick, she'd trusted her instincts about people, but since his betrayal hadn't trusted herself as much, until meeting Alex.

'What are you dreaming about?' Gran asked, interrupting Piper's thoughts.

'Nothing much,' she fibbed.

'Then you should get on. It would be rude to keep that lad waiting. He must be tired if he's travelled from the mainland.'

Gran was right. Piper kissed her soft cheek. 'I'll see you tomorrow then, Gran.'

'See you tomorrow, lovey.'

Piper left the cottage, excitement threatening to bubble over in her chest at the prospect of spending time with Alex once again.

13

For the first few seconds after Alex's bike took off along the pier and up the hill towards St Catherine's, Piper wasn't sure where to hold on. As if sensing her concern, Alex turned his head and shouted for her to hold on to him, taking her right hand and placing it around his waist.

Piper's hands rested against his tight abs and she had to concentrate on the pine trees as they sped past them along the coastline. She had seen this magical view of the sea beyond the line of trees many times before but today it seemed to give her a more intoxicating feeling of freedom. She felt happier than she had in a long time.

How had she reached the age of twenty-seven without riding on the back of a motorbike? Now she knew what she was missing, she wouldn't hesitate to repeat the experience, especially with Alex.

Feeling the warm air brushing her shoulders was much more fun than sitting in a car. It was exhilarating. Alex took a right turn, his muscles moving against her arms, and Piper wished they were going further than St Catherine's Breakwater so that the ride could go on for longer.

They slowed at the large mound that would take them to the parking area and café, and along the seven-hundred-metre pier. Parking up, Alex waited while Piper dismounted and then followed suit, unclipping his helmet before helping Piper remove hers.

'Well?' He grinned, ruffling his hair with his hand. 'Did you enjoy that?'

She handed him her helmet, aware her own hair was probably mussed up as she pushed her fingers through it. 'I loved it,' she said, honestly. 'It was incredible. Exhilarating. I can't wait to get back on and go somewhere else.'

Alex laughed. 'Good. I'm glad. I was worried I

might give you a fright if I went too fast and put you off ever joining me on a ride again.'

She liked hearing him talking about going out again. 'I think the opposite is more likely,' she said with a laugh. 'You'll be looking for excuses to not take me out with you.'

'So you're not frightened I'll go too fast?'

'Not on an island where the maximum speed limit is forty miles per hour,' she said. 'I can't see even me getting a fright at that speed.'

'Ah, I'd forgotten about that. We'll have to think of something else. Perhaps we can take the bike over to France for a day trip.'

'That sounds fun.' She nudged him gently in the ribs as they walked towards the breakwater. 'A little bit terrifying, but mostly fun.'

He studied her face momentarily, then smiled. 'I can see that would be moving things a little too fast.' When she didn't say anything, he added. 'Let's have a walk to stretch our legs before we get back on the bike.'

'Don't you want to spend time with your grandad?'

'Of course, but only when he's not busy with his

art lessons. I don't want to interfere with his schedule, especially as he's enjoying it and making new friends.'

Piper knew she would hate it if her gran didn't have enough people around her or things to keep her busy. 'You and your sister must be relieved he's having a good time.'

He nodded. 'Fliss was hoping to join me but had a conference to go to, unfortunately. She'd love to come to the island and see Gramps.'

'If you like, I could take some photos of you both to send to her.' Piper hoped Alex didn't think she was dreaming up new ways to spend more time with him. 'Or I could lend you an old selfie stick. I have one at home somewhere, if you'd rather.'

'I don't fancy carting one of those around. Although it could be fun, I guess.' Alex grinned at her. 'Anyway, I'd rather you came along. Much nicer.'

They walked on in a happy silence, the gentle breeze in their faces as they walked past other couples making the most of the granite walkway, the sea on either side. They reached the end of the breakwater and stopped to take in the view.

'Let's walk back along the top,' Piper suggested,

pointing to the steps leading up to the promenade where they could peer over the wall towards Les Minquiers and the French coast.

'Sounds like a good idea.'

* * *

As they returned to the parking area, Piper noticed a family of four sitting on a stone seat eating ice creams.

'Those look tasty,' Alex said. 'I wouldn't mind one to cool me down. How about you?'

'I am a little hot after that walk.' Piper glanced at the small ice cream parlour adjoining the café, relieved to see it was still open. 'Go on then. We'll need to be quick; I think they're about to close for the evening.'

Alex took her hand and pulled her into a run. Piper laughed as she tried to keep up with him. Running was not her best skill and by the time they reached the parlour she was slightly out of breath. 'Phew! I don't want to do that too often,' she giggled.

'Sorry, but the worry of missing out was too

dreadful.' Alex smiled at her, a mischievous glint in his navy eyes.

'You'd better choose what size you want.' Once the customer in front had paid for two cornets, she stepped forward. 'Two medium cones with flakes and chocolate sauce,' she said, turning to check that Alex wanted the same.

'Not a large one?' he asked a glint in his eyes.

'You haven't seen how much you get yet.' She smiled at the assistant. 'Make that two mediums please.'

'This is my treat,' Alex said.

'No, it isn't. You're a guest here.'

After a brief argument, Alex settled the bill. 'That's medium?' he said, looking aghast at the size of the ice cream he was handed.

Piper giggled at his reaction. 'Well, they are known for their huge, tasty ice creams here.'

They began walking back towards the sea. 'What do you think?' She wanted to watch him savour his first taste.

'Delicious. Is this your famous Jersey ice cream?'

'It is.'

'I'd give it a lick quickly,' he laughed. 'That

chocolate sauce you asked for is starting to run down the top of your hand. Let's go over there.' Alex indicated a boulder at the edge of the breakwater. 'I need to sit down to eat this.'

She sat awkwardly, trying to get comfortable while looking sideways at Alex enjoying his ice cream cone. He was a gentle man, thoughtful and kind. She hoped he didn't have a hidden agenda, or some personality flaw that would shatter her illusions.

'What are you thinking?' he asked before popping the end of his cone into his mouth. 'I hope it wasn't about me. You looked far too serious.'

She shook her head and hurriedly licked some of the melting ice cream. 'Just trying to fathom out how to finish this without ending up wearing it,' she fibbed. The bottom of her cone disintegrated, and a dollop of creamy liquid dropped onto her trainer. 'I was hoping that wouldn't happen.'

Alex shook his head. 'I've never seen anyone making such a meal out of anything.'

'I aim to please,' she said, matching his jokey tone, trying not to give away how much she was enjoying his company. She finished the rest of her cone as quickly as possible. 'I have to go to the ladies to clean up. You won't want me sitting pillion on your bike in this mess.' She raised her hands, palms outward and held her foot out. 'I'll be back in a few minutes.'

Moments later, refreshed and feeling much better, she walked back to join him. Noticing he was on his phone, she decided to give him some privacy and instead of going any closer strolled over to the white painted railings and looked out over the sea. She thought back to when she had first arrived at university and during a heatwave had commented about the lack of sea breeze, forgetting that she was no longer near the coast. Her friends had found her comment amusing, but it had been the first time she had realised that living inland meant the smell of the sea would no longer be part of her daily life.

Alex joined her. 'Everything all right?'

'I saw you were talking to someone, so gave you a little peace.'

He pushed his phone into his back pocket. 'Thanks.' He leaned against the railings next to her.

'When I was younger, I was desperate to get away

from here and go to uni in England,' she said. 'It was the thought of going on trains.'

'Trains?' He frowned.

Piper giggled. 'We don't have them here, so it was a new experience being able to travel on them.'

'Ah, I see.'

She recalled her excitement when planning to leave for Surrey. 'Knowing I could travel to London easily for a night out or just to meet friends without having to pay to catch a flight each time was liberating.'

'But the flight is only short. About thirty or forty minutes.'

'Yes, but it seemed enormously exciting to be on the other side of the Channel.'

He turned to face her. 'And how did you find living on the mainland?'

'I loved it. I had a brilliant time while I was there.' She had loved meeting new people from Europe and other islands. 'Most of the friends I made were Spanish or Italian, which was fun.'

'I suppose you could all find your way around together.' He smiled and she wondered if he was thinking back to his own time at university.

'Yes, and I've been lucky to be invited to their homes in Milan, Florence and Barcelona. How about you?'

'I didn't go to university,' he said, his smile slipping.

Piper could tell she had hit on something that he either wasn't ready or in the mood to talk about but was intrigued to understand more. 'You didn't?'

He shook his head. 'I had a place waiting for me but the summer before I was due to go, the app I had developed with a friend was picked up by an investor and I had to make the choice whether to go with that or start my degree.'

It sounded incredibly exciting. 'Surely that was what you were hoping to achieve, wasn't it?'

He shrugged. 'It was what we had both spent months dreaming about, but I never really imagined it would happen. Not so quickly, anyway. Don't get me wrong,' he said smiling. 'We were extraordinarily lucky and,' he hesitated. 'Well, we did rather well out of it. But then I was committed to keep working on the launch and having to help market it.'

'And you didn't enjoy doing that?'

Alex sighed. 'It's not my favourite part of the job

and I suppose I've always imagined what life at university would have been like, and I feel I missed out by not going and having that experience.'

So that was it, she realised. 'I should think those friends of yours who did go to uni were probably envious that you made a success of your career so young.'

'I suppose so.'

'It all comes down to choices, doesn't it?' she said thinking how different her life might have been if she had gone travelling when she and Rick had planned to. *Would she be happier than she was right now though?* She doubted it.

'Right, shall we make a move?' he said, straightening.

Back at the bike, she put on her helmet and climbed up behind him.

'Where shall we go next?'

'I don't mind,' she said, happy to be driven through the lanes. 'You go where you like and if you get lost I'll redirect us back home.'

'I'd love to watch the sunset, but you said we had to go to St Ouen to see it. Will we have time?'

'On this machine, yes. It's always quicker to travel

by motorbike here, you can overtake more easily if there's a hold up with a tractor or something. It's best if we follow the north coast. I'll give you a squeeze if you go the wrong way.'

'Sounds like a plan to me.' He laughed and lowered the visor on his helmet. 'Hang on.'

They had to go slowly for the first minute or so to keep to the fifteen mile per hour speed limit that was on some of the island roads. As soon as they reached the main road the limit increased to forty miles an hour and Alex sped up, turning onto a lane that gave them a breathtaking view of the coast. Piper took it all in. Usually, she was driving, paying attention to the traffic, but today she was happy to relax and enjoy the scenery.

14

They reached St Ouen's Bay just as the sky was morphing into an array of yellows and oranges. The sun wasn't far from dipping below the horizon and once Alex had parked, he took Piper's hand and they walked to the railings overlooking the wide expanse of beach to watch the sun sink lower, as if dropping into the sea; the sky gradually darkening. Piper had seen it many times but never tired of the sheer beauty of nature.

As the sun disappeared, she looked sideways at Alex and saw the unmistakable expression of someone transfixed by what they were experiencing.

'Wow. I'd like to come up with something a bit more expressive, but I can't think what else to say.'

'I think you've just said it,' she said, happy that they had managed to get to the bay in time.

Alex said nothing for a moment, then looked either side of them at the few people sitting and staring out to the horizon. 'I imagine this place is packed with people during the high season.'

'I suppose so, but I don't come down here that often. The roads are busier from June to the end of August and it takes longer to get here from Gorey when you're sitting in traffic.'

'I've travelled to many places,' Alex said, his voice quiet. 'I've queued for hours with hundreds of other people to watch the sun setting off Santorini, but nothing I've ever seen has been quite this perfect.'

Piper's heart swelled. 'It is rather amazing, isn't it?'

They stayed where they were for several more minutes until the sun had completely disappeared.

Alex took a deep breath and turned to face her. 'That was worth travelling all this way for.'

Piper smiled. 'I'm glad you think so. Now, if we don't hurry and get going you won't have time to drop me back home before going to fetch your grandad.'

He made a face. 'I'd almost forgotten,' he said. 'We had better get a move on.'

'It's a shame you're not here next week,' she said, pulling on her helmet. 'It's Jax's birthday and I always persuade him to do something fun.'

'I wish I'd known. I would have come back a week later.'

'Then you'd have missed the sunset.'

'True.' He mounted the bike and waited for her to follow. 'I suppose it's just as well. I wouldn't be able to stay then anyway.'

Piper was glad she was wearing a visor so he couldn't see her expression. She would have found it too difficult to hide her disappointment. Determined to make the most of him while he was on the island and free to spend time with her, she pushed away her thoughts and focused on enjoying the freedom of the motorcycle ride home.

* * *

Alex slowed as they reached the pier and pulled over, parking in a small space. He switched off the bike's engine and they dismounted, Piper waiting while he locked their helmets in the box on the back of the bike. It was quiet on the pier and Piper supposed most people were eating their evening meal.

Alex looked at her suddenly, his eyes widening when he spotted Piper staring at him. 'I like you, Piper.'

Unprepared for this unexpected declaration, she admitted, 'I like you too,' feeling brave for letting down her emotional barrier.

'Do you mind if I kiss you?'

Piper opened her mouth to speak but wasn't sure what to say.

'I don't want to make you feel uncomfortable,' Alex said gently.

Piper watched his lips as he spoke and an irresistible urge to kiss him came over her. She reached up and cradled his face in her palms, drawing his lips to hers.

When they broke apart, Alex took her hand and led her to the bus shelter nearby, where he pulled her close and kissed her again, a groan escaping as she pushed her hands into his hair.

His lips sent delicious sensations through her body and Piper didn't want the moment to end.

Someone coughed pointedly behind them. Alex instantly let go of her and Piper turned to see Jax's mum, Sheila.

'Sorry to intrude on your snog.' She looked amused by discovering them kissing. Piper cringed at her words. 'I think your mum wants you,' she said with a grin, raising her eyebrows at Piper before studying Alex and giving him an appreciative smile. 'You must be Alex. I believe your grandfather is over there on one of the benches.'

'He is?' Alex seemed confused as he peered around the side of the bus shelter along the pier. 'I was supposed to be picking him up.'

Sheila shrugged. 'He popped into the guest house looking for you a short while ago and asked that someone let you know he's waiting for you when you're ready.'

Mortified to have been caught kissing Alex by her mother's best friend, Piper forced a smile. 'Thanks, Sheila. I'll go and see what Mum wants.'

She thought of her grandmother and hoped she was busy working on her tapestry and not about to come out and spot Colin.

'I hope our grandparents haven't bumped into each other,' Alex said quietly as if reading Piper's mind. 'I don't want them getting upset again.'

'Me neither,' Piper said.

As Sheila walked ahead, Alex's hand brushed Piper's, shooting an electric current through her arm. 'I'll hopefully see you later, after I've dropped Grandad back at the retreat?'

'I'd like that,' she said, wishing more than anything that they could return to the bus shelter and kiss again.

15

Piper waited up, keeping herself busy by working on a few picture frames she had rescued from a house clearance. As midnight came and went, she accepted that Alex wasn't coming and put away her mosaics and got ready for bed. She had to be up early in the morning to help her mother before putting in a full day working at The Cabbage Patch.

She hoped Alex was having a good time and reminded herself he was on the island to spend time with his grandfather, not her.

She woke with the sunrise and seeing that it was only twenty-past five rolled over and closed her eyes. Fifteen minutes later, she knew there was no chance of going back to sleep. She sat up and stared out of the window at the blue, cloudless sky. Another perfect day. It was a shame she would be spending most of it in the barn, but she looked forward to having friendly banter with Casey and Tara. There was always news from her friends if she hadn't seen them for a couple of days, and hopefully she would sell some of her designs.

After finishing work on her picture frames, she packed them carefully, ready to take to her stall. Having showered and dressed in jeans and a T-shirt, Piper went downstairs to help her mother prepare breakfast for their guests. They didn't have a full house but that would change by the end of the week and Piper was happy to make the most of it being less busy.

As she reached the bottom of the stairs, she heard Alex's voice speaking to someone in the living room. Unable to catch what he was saying, and supposing he might be chatting to one of the guests, she went to say 'hello'.

'I'll be back soon, sweetheart, and we can talk then. I promise.'

Piper slowed to a stop and her stomach flipped over.

'I miss you, too,' Alex said.

Horrified that he might catch her listening, Piper quickly turned and made for the kitchen, her mind whirring and her heart aching. He had called someone sweetheart and the tone of his voice couldn't be mistaken for anything other than loving. Piper didn't know what to think. *Would he have kissed her if he was in love with someone else? Was there a partner waiting for him in England?* She cringed as it dawned on her that she didn't know whether he was married or in a relationship. *How could she have been so stupid, so free with her feelings?*

She bit her lip, wishing she had the chance to leave without him seeing her, but would have to go into the dining room and take his breakfast order.

Her mother came in from the backyard, carrying some parsley from one of her herb planters. 'What's the matter with you?' She frowned. 'You're not coming down with something, are you?' She reached out to touch Piper's forehead.

Piper stepped back. 'Mum, I'm not five. Anyway, I'm fine.'

'You don't look it.' She narrowed her eyes. 'What's happened?' Before Piper was able to insist once more that she was fine, Helen stepped closer, lowering her voice. 'Has that little bugger done something to upset you?'

Piper widened her eyes, mortified that her mother was being so overprotective. 'I presume you mean Alex and no, he's not done anything,' she fibbed.

'You don't sound very sure.'

Piper picked up an apron and tied it round her waist. 'Neither of us have time for this conversation. I'd better go and ask what our guests would like to eat this morning before they start complaining.'

It was an exaggeration. Their guests were mostly polite, but Piper had no intention of having this discussion with her mother and she didn't want to talk about Alex while he was staying at the guest house. And anyway, she hadn't decided what she thought about the conversation she had overheard.

'As long as you're sure you're all right.'

'Yes, Mum.' Piper kissed her mother on the cheek. 'I'm fine. Now, please stop worrying and concentrate on making breakfast.' She picked up her notepad and pen.

'Okay, but I'm going to make you some scrambled eggs and I want you to eat them before you leave.'

Piper gave a brief nod before leaving the kitchen. Cooking was her mother's way of showing she cared, and she knew that if Piper was upset the first thing to go was her appetite.

'Bugger,' she whispered as she stepped into the dining room. Now she would have to make herself eat when it was the last thing she wanted to do.

Alex gave her a smile as she entered the dining room and she forced herself to return it. 'Good morning,' she said, trying to keep her positivity from sounding unnatural. She pressed her pen against the notepad to hide the fact that her hands were shaking. 'Have you decided what you'd like to eat this morning?'

'I'll have two fried eggs with beans and bacon please.'

She wrote down his order. 'Tea and brown toast?'

'Perfect.' She went to turn away. 'Piper?'

'Yes?' She kept a smile on her face, not wanting to give away her feelings.

'I'm sorry I was back too late to catch up with you last night. I—'

She cut him off, not wishing to spend any more time speaking with him than was necessary. 'Did you and Colin have a lovely evening?'

'Yes, but—'

'That's good. Sorry, I can't hang around. I've got to go to work this morning. Loads to do, and all that. You know how it is.'

He seemed confused and a little hurt by her reaction, but she wasn't too interested in how he was feeling right now. She moved to the next table and gave the couple and their toddler son a beaming smile. 'And how are we all today?'

'We're going to the zoo.' The little boy grinned and held up a patched panda.

Piper hoped the boy wouldn't be too disappointed not to see a panda at Jersey Zoo. 'I'm not sure you'll find one of those there, but you will find some impressive brown bears. I saw one sleeping on a tree trunk the last time I was there. I spent ages watching him.'

The boy's eyes widened. 'Can I do that too, Mummy?'

'Of course you can.' The boy's mother smiled. 'But first you need to eat breakfast so that you've got the energy to walk around and see all the animals.'

'Have you decided what you'd like to eat?'

Piper took their order and, moments later, she was back in the kitchen. She gave her mother the orders and began making drinks.

'Take those through, then come and eat your breakfast,' Helen said, indicating the plate of scrambled eggs on white toast on the kitchen table.

Piper knew better than to argue. Anyway, the smell of the buttery eggs was making her mouth water despite her earlier reservations about eating. She would be grateful for the breakfast after a busy few hours at work. She ate her breakfast while her mother cooked, then took the plates of food through to the guests.

'I was wondering if you had any free time today?' Alex asked as she placed his food in front of him.

'Like I said, I'm working today.'

He went to say something further, but she didn't give him the chance before she hurried away. She had no idea who he had been talking to on the phone but could only think about the loving tone he'd used. Maybe it was perfectly innocent, but she wasn't going to ask.

She served the rest of the breakfasts and ignored his wave before leaving the dining room.

'Right, Mum, I'll be off now.' She gave her mother a quick hug, picked up her rucksack and the bag holding the well-wrapped mosaic mirrors and left before Alex had a chance to finish eating and follow her.

'Have a good day,' Helen called after her.

16

Piper parked her car and switched off the engine. The sight of the large, ancient barn always made her smile. She had never imagined being lucky enough to work somewhere so beautiful while she had been studying at university. She was grateful to Sheila who had asked Casey if there was a space for Piper at the barn to set up a stall. It was when she had been at her lowest ebb after Rick's shock announcement that he had fallen in love with Stacy and wanted to break off their engagement, and Piper's mother had asked her friends for ways to distract her.

'You've got no reason to put off setting up your business now,' Sheila had said. 'You and that prat

Rick might have been planning on travelling around the world, and I know how devastated you are that all your plans have been squashed, but that doesn't mean you can't find other ways to be fulfilled and happy. You've always talked about doing something with your designs and now's the perfect time. What are you waiting for?'

Piper had had to admit that she had little else to focus on and was desperate for a diversion from her humiliation and emotional pain. It served her right for investing so much of herself in Rick's life and going along so easily with all his wishes

In the end, it had only taken a brief lecture from Jax during a beach walk for Piper to make up her mind and go for it. That was eighteen months ago, now she couldn't be happier that she had done as Sheila had suggested.

'Morning, Casey, Tara,' she said. 'Hi, Irene.' She waved at the platinum-haired lady in her seventies who kept them all amused with her malapropisms from her stall. She sold handmade pictures of puffins painted on pieces of driftwood, and other beautifully decorated items.

Irene waved bejewelled fingers in Piper's direction. 'It's going to be a good day today,' she called. 'The cards said so.'

Piper gave Irene the thumbs up. Irene also gave Tarot card readings and occasionally gave advice to the stallholders if she had seen something in her cards that she felt might relate to them.

'You been working on more stuff, then Piper?' Paddy, a sixty-something farmer, who sold metal sculptures made from old pieces of farm machinery, stepped forward from his stall to take the larger bag from her.

'Phew, thanks, Paddy.' She gave him a grateful smile. 'Those were a little heavy.'

'Where do you want them? On the table?'

'That'll be perfect. Thanks.'

After arranging her stall, Piper carefully unwrapped her mosaic-framed mirrors and set them next to each other to inspect them one last time before attaching a price tag and hanging them up.

'They're beautiful,' Casey said, leaning over her counter to study the mirrors, one framed with pale-blue glass and the other with green. 'I'm not sure which I prefer, they're both gorgeous.'

'Thanks.' Piper stepped back and tilted her head.

'They've come out better than I'd hoped, which is always a relief.'

Tara returned from the communal kitchen at the back of the barn, carrying two mugs of tea. 'Sorry, Piper. I didn't expect you to be here yet or I'd have made you one. Here,' she said, holding out one of the mugs. 'You take this one and I'll pop back and make another.'

'No, please don't worry. I can make myself one later.'

'Let her go,' Casey said. 'She's dying for an excuse to go back and chat to Peregrine.'

'No, I'm not!'

Piper pulled a face at Casey. They both knew how much of a crush Tara had on the Cornish potter who had arrived on the island to live with his elderly uncle the year before. He had caused a bit of a stir when he had first taken on one of the stalls at The Cabbage Patch and Tara had been besotted with him ever since. 'Stop teasing her. Anyway, he said we should call him Perry. He doesn't like to be called by his full name.'

'Thank you, Piper,' Tara said. 'I'm glad you're here now. You can keep my friend in check. She never let up with the goading all day yesterday, just because she caught me studying him at work for five minutes.'

'Five! Twenty-five, more like. I had to look after all our customers while you gazed in adoration at him.'

'I did not,' Tara protested. 'Anyway, he's very talented. Don't you think?' She looked at Piper and waited for her to reply.

'He's certainly talented,' she agreed. 'His work is impressive, I have to admit.'

'Urgh. Just go back to the kitchen then,' Casey groaned. 'She really has got a crush on him and I'm not even sure he's noticed her. I hope she doesn't end up getting hurt.'

'Me, too,' Piper said, watching Tara hurry across the barn to the kitchen.

Seconds later, there was a shriek and Tara burst through the kitchen door. 'One of the artists has fallen,' she called. 'I think he's broken his leg.'

Piper gasped.

'I'll go,' Piper said, as Casey made to leave her stall. 'I've got first-aid experience. You keep an eye on our stalls.'

Casey nodded, not looking happy to be the one staying behind. Piper hesitated, feeling guilty. There wasn't time to waste she reminded herself as she ran off, closely followed by Paddy

Outside, she immediately spotted a small group of people and hurried over to them to see what she could do to help. One of them stepped back and Piper's heart gave a jolt when she saw who had been injured. 'Colin!' She stepped between two of the artists. 'We need to give him a bit of space,' Piper said, crouching next to Colin.

His face was pale with pain, his forehead creased, and his teeth clenched. Someone had placed a plaid blanket over him, and a bright-pink flamingo-patterned cushion lay under his head.

'It's all right, Colin,' she said, unsure but wanting to reassure him. 'Has anyone phoned for an ambulance?' she asked, looking up and scanning the worried faces above her. A few of them mumbled incoherently to each other. Frustrated and not wishing to waste any time, Piper pushed her hand into her back pocket to retrieve her mobile phone only to discover that she must have left it in the barn.

She swore under her breath. 'I'll only be a moment,' she soothed as Colin grimaced in pain. 'I'm going to call for an ambulance. We'll have you made more comfortable soon,' she promised, hoping she was right. She stood and ran back into the barn.

'What's happened?' Casey asked a duster in her hand.

'It's Alex's grandfather. I need to call an ambulance and let Alex know what's happened.'

She grabbed her rucksack and rummaged inside, relieved when her fingers closed around her mobile. She dialled 999 and gave the relevant details to the operator. She didn't want to keep Colin waiting any longer than necessary, but wanted to call Alex before going back outside. Realising she didn't have Alex's number, she called her mother.

'Mum? Do you know if Alex is still there?'

'Hold on, lovey, while I check.'

Piper held her breath, trying her best to remain calm while she waited.

'He was just about to leave, but I managed to stop him,' her mother said, seconds later. 'Here he is.'

'Piper?' Alex's voice was warm in her ear. 'I was hoping to speak to you before you left this morning.'

'You need you to come to the barn.'

'Now?'

'It's your grandad.' She swallowed. 'He's had a fall and we think he's broken his leg.'

'I'm on my way.'

Casey watched her. 'Who's Alex?' she asked as soon as Piper ended her call.

'Colin's grandson. He's staying at the guest house. He's on his way. Listen, I need to get back to Colin and let him know what's happening.'

As she rushed out of the barn she could hear Casey calling to Irene to keep an eye on their stalls, before following her. They found Colin still surrounded by worried artists, Tara and Paddy.

'The ambulance will be here any minute,' Piper reassured him, hearing the sound of a siren in the distance. 'There it is now.'

Colin grabbed her forearm. 'Alex?' he hissed through gritted teeth as pain gripped him more tightly.

'I've called him. He's on his way,' Piper said. 'If he doesn't get here by the time the ambulance leaves, I'll accompany you and one of the others will let Alex know where to find you. Try not to worry.'

'Thank you.'

She held his hand, hoping to comfort him and watched as the ambulance pulled up. Within what seemed like seconds, a paramedic was attending to him and Piper let go of his hand and moved out of the way so that his injury could be assessed.

Piper looked around her, willing Alex to get to the barn before the ambulance left. Fearing he wasn't going to make it, she turned to Casey. 'I'd better go with him. Please let Alex know how to find the hospital or ask someone to take him.'

With an oxygen mask over his face, the paramedics moved Colin into the back of the vehicle.

Casey pushed Piper gently towards the open back doors. 'Don't worry. We'll sort Alex out, you go and keep poor Colin company.'

Piper thanked her and stepped up into the vehicle. As one of the paramedics began closing the doors, she heard the unmistakable rumble of Alex's motorbike. Closing her eyes briefly in relief, she rested a hand on Colin's shoulder. 'That's your grandson arriving now.'

'He's a good boy, that one. I don't care what anyone says.'

Piper thought it an odd comment, but didn't say

anything. Now was not the time. She heard Alex calling for the paramedic to keep the doors open and a moment later, he was staring into the vehicle. 'Grandad? What happened? Are you all right?'

'They've given him something for the pain,' Piper reassured him. 'I'll get out so you can go with him. I'll see you soon, Colin.' She gave the old man a comforting smile before Alex took her hand to help her out.

'Thanks for calling me, Piper,' he said, taking her place in the ambulance.

As the paramedic closed the doors, she heard Alex's voice once more. 'Everything's going to be all right, Grandad.'

Close to tears, she stepped back and watched the ambulance race off.

'Poor Colin,' an elderly voice murmured beside her. Piper gave Vivienne a nod. She hadn't realised Vivienne had been taking part in some of the painting lessons. Most of the time she sold costume jewellery in the barn on a small stall. The woman's oversized shirt had paint spatters all over it and Piper assumed she had been spending time with Colin during their lessons. 'One minute, we were walking back from the meadow where we'd been painting for a few hours, talking about which course we're going to apply for next, the next, he'd tripped over a branch and fallen.' She gave a whimper. 'I'm so sorry. I don't know what's come over me.'

Relieved to have someone else to take care off, Piper put an arm around the older lady's thin shoulders. 'Why don't we go back inside, and I'll make you a nice cup of tea.'

The woman sniffed and wiped her nose on the back of her hand. 'I don't seem to have a tissue. I'm not usually one to cry.'

'You're probably in shock,' Casey said walking with them. 'Here, take this. It is clean.' She held out a tissue and Vivienne took it, dabbing her eyes and nose. 'Colin will be fine. Don't you worry.'

Piper hoped her friend was right. The poor man hadn't looked well at all and, depending on the damage he had sustained, might be in hospital for weeks.

It looked like he wouldn't be leaving the island for some time, and Piper couldn't help wondering whether that meant that Alex would be staying too. She wasn't sure what she thought about him being on the island for much longer, not if that call she had overheard was anything to go by. *What if the woman she had heard him talking to came over to join him?* Piper groaned inwardly. Discovering Alex might be involved with someone was upsetting enough, the last thing she needed was to have to see him with another woman.

17

'That poor man.' Helen sat on the beach next to Sheila and Jax where Piper had found them an hour and a half later. 'I hope he's going to be all right.'

'So do I,' Piper said, bending to pick up a small piece of glass and rubbing the damp sand from it before dropping it into her pocket.

Jax put his arm around Piper's shoulders. 'I'm sure he'll be fine.'

'I hope so.' She couldn't get the image of Colin's pain-etched face out of her mind, nor forget the fright in Alex's voice when she'd called him to break the news about his grandfather's accident.

She resolved to help Alex and Colin in any way

possible. Whether her grandmother still had issues with Colin was of little relevance now, as was her own sadness thinking Alex might have a girlfriend she hadn't known about.

'It's hot up here,' Jax said, taking her hand. 'Let's go for a paddle. I know Seamus will be happy to have another swim.'

'I'm not really in the mood.' She wished she hadn't come down to speak to her mother now, but had needed to talk about the upsetting news with someone. Piper knew Jax was trying to distract her, but she would rather go home and wait for Alex to return from the hospital.

'I won't take no for an answer,' Jax said lightly. 'So you may as well give in.'

'Fine,' Piper said, caving in. 'Come on then.'

She slid her trainers off. 'Will you keep an eye on them?' she asked her mum.

'Of course,' Helen said. 'Let Jax cheer you up.'

'I'll do my best.' Jax grinned. 'Hurry up, before the tide turns.'

Piper punched his arm playfully. 'Stop bossing me about.' Once they were out of earshot of Helen and Sheila, she added, 'What's so important you needed to speak to me alone?'

'Who said I need to speak to you alone?' He grabbed her round the waist and tickled her until she wriggled out of his reach.

'Stop it, you pain.'

He raised his hands in surrender, his expression suddenly serious. 'I'm concerned.'

'What about?'

He stopped walking and before she had a chance to ask what he was doing, bent to pick something up. He wiped whatever it was with his thumb and handed it to Piper.

She looked at the piece of worn glass. 'Thanks,' she said, slipping it into her pocket. 'So, tell me.'

'I spotted you coming back with Alex on his bike the other evening.'

Had he seen them kissing? 'And?'

'I can tell you like him.'

She didn't bother to deny her feelings. 'Go on.'

'Mum told me about your gran and Alex's grandad having history. And not a good one.'

Piper wished her mum had kept quiet. 'That's right, but what's that got to do with me?' she asked.

'Piper, we both know how loyal you are. I'm concerned that if you get too close to Alex that his
grandfather and your gran's differences, which, let's
be honest go back a hell of a long way, might cause
problems going forward.'

'I shouldn't think so,' she said. 'As far as I can tell,
Gran needs to come to terms with not ever making
up with her friend, but that's about it. I'm sure that
over time she and Colin will feel less awkward with
each other.'

He hesitated and stopped to turn to her. 'I'd hate
to see you being hurt though. You're the closest
person I have to a sibling, and I still can't stand to
think of that arse, Rick, without wanting to go and
have a strong word with him.'

Piper stepped forward and put her arms around
Jax, hugging him tightly. 'I love you too, Jax. You're
like the big brother I never had, and I know you always look out for me. But I'm not the fragile person I
once was.' When he looked doubtfully at her, she
added. 'I promise you. I do like Alex, you're right, and
I suspect he likes me.' She recalled Alex's phone call
that she had overheard. It wouldn't do to concern
Jax, especially as she didn't know yet what the call

was about. She made up her mind to ask Alex about it.

'I mean, how well do you know this guy?' Jax asked, his question invading her thoughts. 'He seems pleasant enough, but is he?'

Piper frowned. Colin had made that strange remark about Alex being a good boy and him not caring what anybody else thought. She wasn't sure what he could have meant by it. Maybe Alex had been in some sort of trouble when he was younger, but she had known several friends who had taken unwise detours in their lives before realising they were on the wrong path.

'I'm a little wary,' Jax said thoughtfully. 'That's all.'

Piper realised that he had taken her silence as her being upset and gave his arm a gentle squeeze. 'I know, and I appreciate your concern for me. But I don't have unrealistic expectations.' She smiled. 'I don't really have any expectations. I also know that the issue of him living on the mainland and me living here, and not knowing much about him, might add a layer of doubt against anything ever coming of a relationship between us.' She reminded herself of

Alex's fondness for the person he had been speaking to earlier on the phone. 'And anyway, he might even have a significant other back at home, so nothing will probably happen between us and you'll be worrying about me for no reason.'

'Have you asked him?'

'Not yet.'

'Make sure you do.'

She put her fingers over his mouth. 'I can look after myself, Jax.' She turned to walk back up the beach.

'Hey,' Jax called. 'Where are you going?'

Piper stopped. 'I thought we'd cleared everything up?'

'You agreed to come for a swim.'

'Er, no, I didn't. I agreed to paddle. There's a difference.'

'Then come and paddle.' He grinned at her. 'You know you want to, really.'

Piper sighed heavily. She wasn't quite as cross as she was making out. She watched Seamus bound into the water and start swimming in front of them. Now that they were down near the sea, she found that she was happy to go in. She began running into the water, amused to give Jax a surprise by doing something he didn't expect. 'Last one in buys the drinks.'

'What?' He guffawed. 'When?'

She didn't stop running and was wading deeper, slowed by the weight of her jeans.

'You little cheat.' He soon caught up with her and grabbed hold of her, lifting her high as she screamed in excitement before throwing her back into the sea.

Piper regained her footing and splashed him over and over again, laughing as he retaliated. Her foot slipped on a pebble and she slid under the water, taking in a mouthful of sea.

Within a couple of seconds, Jax had hold of her arms and lifted her up. 'You OK?'

She coughed, spluttering until she cleared her airways. 'Yes. No need to panic. But thanks anyway.'

He put his arm around her waist as she tried to splash him again and carried her back to the shore. 'I think you've had enough.'

She laughed, pushing him away gently. 'I said you were like my big brother, but that doesn't mean you'll get away with being bossy.'

He stepped back and ran his hands over his hair,

pushing it back from his face. 'No harm in trying once in a while,' he said before calling for Seamus to join them.

The two of them wrung out their clothes for a few minutes. Piper knew from experience that her mother and Sheila would have a fit if they dared to go home dripping wet. She looked up towards the sea wall; both women had gone. Neither of them worried when she and Jax were together and clearly weren't worried about their shoes! She thought back to some of the times when they were younger and had been in terrible trouble with their mothers.

'Hey, do you remember Midnight Mass that time when we were about seventeen?'

'I do. My mum still hasn't forgiven me. In fact, that was the last time she allowed me to attend church with her. She said I disgraced myself.'

'You did.' Piper elbowed him in his side. 'You had been drinking and began singing all the Christmas carols out of tune.'

He pulled a face at her. 'I wasn't trying to be annoying, that's my actual singing voice. I can't help it if I'm tone deaf.'

Piper giggled. 'No, but it didn't stop you from annoying everyone else by ruining the carols.'

'Anyway, I'd only had a little of my mate's bottle of cider.' He shook his head. 'I was such a lightweight.'

'You still are.'

'True.' They reached the granite slipway and wiped the sand off their feet as well as they could manage. 'Anyway, you encouraged me.'

Piper rubbed her hands together to try and rid them of some of the sand. 'Only in so far as I was laughing. You didn't have to play the fool and keep singing.'

'I guess not.'

'Sheila might have forgiven you enough to allow you to go with her this Christmas.'

Jax looked horrified. 'Can we please not start discussing Christmas yet? It's only April and we've still to enjoy summer before thinking that far ahead.'

He had a point. She loved Christmas but wanted to make the most of the good weather they were enjoying. The thought of celebrating Christmas brought Alex into her mind. *What would he be doing this year?* She pushed the thought away, deciding that it was safest to keep to the present and not get ahead of herself.

They picked up their shoes and followed Seamus to the top of the slipway where Piper and Jax would part ways.

'Thanks for persuading me to do that, Jax,' she said gratefully, bending to give Seamus a light pat. 'I had fun in the end.'

He laughed. 'Good, I'm pleased.' Something caught his eye. 'Hey, isn't that Alex getting off the bus?'

She turned. It was. He didn't look happy.

'Where's his bike?'

'He rode it to the barn and left it there.' She realised how she might be able to help him. 'I'd better go and offer him a lift to collect it.'

Jax inclined his head towards her. 'You'd better change first.'

'Good idea.'

18

She waited for Alex to reach her and walked with him to the guest house. 'How's Colin?'

'He's going to be all right. They've given him an X-ray and pain relief. He has a hairline fracture. Thankfully, the damage isn't as bad as they suspected, which is a relief.'

'I'm glad. I presume they've kept him in hospital?'

He nodded. 'They want to keep an eye on him. He won't need a cast but will need some sort of leg brace for a while and will have to take things easy.'

They reached the door and Piper opened it, indicating for Alex to go inside first. Her mother walked out of the front room just as Piper closed the front door.

'You can go out the back and take off those wet, sandy things straight away, my girl. I don't want them in here.'

'But, Mum.' Piper tilted her head towards Alex. 'We have guests.'

Alex smiled for the first time. 'Don't worry about me. I'll go upstairs and leave you in peace.'

'How's your grandfather, Alex?' Helen asked, noticing him standing there. 'Is there anything I can do for him?'

Piper waited while Alex repeated what he had said to her moments before. 'Thanks though, Helen. It's kind of you to ask.'

'If you'll wait for me to change, I can give you a lift to collect your bike. Or you could wait until the morning, if you prefer,' she added, realising he might be too tired and stressed to want to do anything further.

'I'd rather collect it today, if that's all right with you?'

'No problem at all.'

'Thank you. Don't rush though. I could do with a shower to freshen up first.'

Helen rubbed her hands together. 'I'll make you both a quick bite to eat before you go. By the look of you it's been a difficult day and I can't let you go back out without something in your stomachs.'

'Thanks, Helen.' Alex looked emotional. 'That's very kind of you.'

'Cheese and tomato omelette with salad all right?'

He nodded. 'Perfect.'

Piper whispered her thanks to her mum as Alex took the stairs two at a time. 'Can you grab me a towel, Mum, so I don't have to go to the flat naked?'

'Ah, yes,' Helen said, frowning. 'I hadn't thought of that. I'll fetch you one now.'

As Piper stood in the warm shower in the bathroom she and her mother shared, she couldn't help thinking about Alex and how difficult it must be without the usual support system he probably had around him in London.

She poured a dollop of shampoo onto her hand and massaged it into her curly hair before rinsing it off and applying conditioner. She decided that as soon as she returned from dropping Alex off to collect his bike, she would pop round to speak to Gran and tell her what had happened. Alex needed the support of everyone around him and she was going to make sure he got whatever he and his grandfather needed. Now wasn't the time to focus on old arguments, or even her own concerns that he had a girlfriend at home. There would hopefully be plenty of time later for Gran and Colin to confront each other when Colin was fully recovered, and Alex wasn't needed to support him in the same way.

She dried herself off, combing through her damp hair and not bothering to dry it, then dressed in a pair of shorts and a clean T-shirt and went down-stairs to the kitchen to find her mother and tell her that she thought the two of them and Gran should help Colin and Alex in any way they could. Even if it meant Gran putting aside her dislike of Colin, and letting him use her spare room when he was dis-charged from hospital. Gran wouldn't like it, but she had had enough years of experience running the guest house to cope with someone she wasn't used to, staying in her home.

'So, what do you think then?' Piper asked,

taking out plates and cutlery and putting them on the side, ready for her mother to finish cooking the omelettes. 'Do you think Gran will go along with it?'

Helen flipped the omelettes over and rested one hand on her hip. 'Hmm, I'm not sure. You know how bloody-minded your grandmother can be at times.' She pointed to the fridge. 'Take the salad out. These are nearly ready.'

Piper did as she asked, unsure what to do. She felt that despite Colin's apology, her gran still seemed rattled, as though now that old memories had been brought back to the surface, she needed time to come to terms with them. 'Maybe I should try talking to her about it again?'

'Tell you what,' Helen said, serving both omelettes. 'I'll have a word with her tonight, so she's primed. I'll pretend I haven't told you I'll be speaking to her. You leave seeing her till the morning. It'll give her time to mull over what I say to her tonight. If she thinks we're both on the same wavelength then she might be more inclined to agree with you and do as you suggest.'

'I'll cross my fingers that you're right.' Piper

hoped her mother sounded more positive than she felt about her gran's reaction.

'Me too.'

They heard footsteps and Alex appeared in the kitchen doorway. 'I haven't kept you waiting, have I?'

'Not at all,' Helen said, picking up both plates. 'Your timing is spot on.'

Piper picked up the cutlery and what condiments she supposed he might want and followed Helen outside.

'It's still warm enough to eat out here this evening,' Helen said, putting the plates onto the small two-person metal table she and Piper used whenever the weather was warm enough. 'Right, tuck in.'

* * *

'It's very kind of you to give me a lift,' Alex said as Piper manoeuvred past streams of cyclists making the most of the warm evening to enjoy the lanes. 'I hope all your guests don't put you to as much trouble as Grandad and I have done?'

'No, they don't.' She gave him a quick smile to

show she was teasing. 'Mum and I are happy to help in whatever way we can. I suppose you'll want to stay for a bit longer now your grandad is in hospital?'

'I would like to but I must leave tomorrow and return home, but will be back again. Not until next week though. Would you be able to reserve a room for me?'

'I know we're fully booked at the moment, but I can let you know if we have any cancellations.' Concerned that they wouldn't have any, Piper tried to think how else she might help him.

'That's kind, thanks.' His phone buzzed and he withdrew it from his jeans' pocket. Piper, now driving slower and unable to overtake the bikes in front of them, glanced at his face when he didn't say anything. He scowled. 'Is everything all right,' she asked. 'It's not the hospital, is it?'

'No.' He turned his phone over and rested it upside down on his knee. 'Just a little issue I'm trying to rectify.'

'Sounds ominous. I hope it's not too difficult.'

He smiled at her, but it didn't reach his eyes. 'A friend has asked me for some help, but it is not my biggest concern right now.'

She remembered that they had been discussing him staying for longer before he'd been distracted. 'I know this is probably a question you won't be able to answer, but do you have any idea how much longer you'll want to stay when you do return next week?'

'I'm not sure yet, sorry. I don't want to put you out. I know you're already very busy with your work and the guest house and I'm sure I can find somewhere else to stay if I look hard enough.'

'I'd like to think I can find you something.'

'Really? Where?'

'Leave it with me.' She wondered if Gran might consider letting Alex stay with her for a bit, but decided to think about it more later on.

His smile was genuine this time. 'That's generous of you, but you can hardly turf out people who've booked to stay at the guest house, especially when they have little hope of finding anywhere else.'

'We wouldn't get away with that,' she said, returning his smile. 'But we could think of something else.'

'Like what?' He raised his eyebrows expectantly.

'I don't know yet, but I'll tell you as soon as I do.

It will help though to know how long you'll be able to stay.'

She sighed with relief when the fifteen or so cyclists turned left down another lane and she was able to accelerate slightly.

'Probably only a couple of days initially. When I'm certain Gramps is settled and know what's happening, I'll return to the mainland for a short time. I can do a lot of my work remotely, but some things, like the thing I can't tell you about, need to be dealt with face to face. I'll be back here again as soon as I can. I can let you know my plans as soon as they're confirmed?'

Piper was cheered up to think he would be coming back and forth to the island. She reminded herself he wasn't doing it for fun, or to see her, but to be with his grandfather. The reminder that Alex took such care of his grandfather made her heart ache with affection for him. If only he lived on the island too, they might be able to spend time getting to know each other better. If he was, in fact, single. They might even decide they liked each other a lot. She shook her head to rid it of the silly daydream and focused on where she was going.

'Everything all right?'

Piper's face reddened. He must be wondering what was going through her mind. 'Yes, thanks. I was thinking about something I mustn't forget to do,' she fibbed. 'Right, we're here now.' She indicated and turned down the lane that led to the barn.

'This really is kind of you, Piper. I'm going to have to stop taking you away from your busy life with all these favours.'

'It's no problem at all, I'm happy to be able to help in any way I can.'

'That's generous of you.'

She parked the car and switched off the ignition. 'Not at all. You're our guest,' she said, not wanting him to know quite how much she enjoyed these extra unexpected times she was able to spend with him.

A shadow crossed his face. 'That's good to know.'

She had said something wrong, but wasn't sure what, and then realised he wasn't happy to be considered nothing more than one of their guests. Wanting to change the subject, she asked, 'I hope you haven't forgotten the keys for your bike.'

His eyes widened for a second as he pushed his

hand deep into his jeans' pocket. Then he withdrew them and held the keys in the air. 'Nope. All present and correct.' He studied her face for a moment, and she realised he was trying to decide something. Then he leaned forward and kissed her on the cheek. 'I'll leave you to get on now. Thanks very much for the lift.'

'No problem at all.' She didn't want to be left with her scrambled thoughts on the drive home just yet, so got out of the car.

'You're staying?' He seemed surprised.

She hoped he didn't think she was vying for another ride on his bike, or worse, another kiss. 'I can check up on a few bits on my stall while I'm here. May as well make the most of the place while it's quiet.'

'Right.' He walked over to his bike and hesitated. She hurried towards the huge double barn doors, eager to get inside and away from the awkwardness of their conversation.

'Piper?'

She stopped and turned to face him, surprised to hear him calling her name. 'Yes?'

'Do you fancy going for a ride?'

There was nothing she'd rather do. 'I'd love to,' she admitted. Then, thinking it might seem a little odd to be too eager, added, 'I'll just be a few minutes, if that's all right?'

'Of course. Take your time. I'm not in any hurry. I'll wait here for you.'

As she unlocked the smaller barn door, it occurred to her that he might want to have a look at her stall. 'Would you like to come in while it's closed?'

His mouth widened into a grin. 'I'd love that. Thanks.'

* * *

Alex ran over to join Piper and together they went inside.

'This is some place,' he said. There was no need to put on any lights as, although the doors were closed, there were high windows and it was still light outside. The sunlight cast shadows onto the corner stalls and Piper realised she had never been in the emporium when all the business owners had left for the day. She liked it.

'Where's yours then?'

'Over here.' She pointed and led the way, slowing when she realised Alex was trying to take in the different stalls: In locked, glass-fronted stands behind each stall they could see Vivienne's costume jewellery, some vintage homeware, French enamelled items, a stall selling beautiful silk flowers in exquisite vases, and another displaying the Sanderson Sisters' Speciality Knits – a vast array of brightly coloured, knitted toys, tea cosies, intricate baby blankets, and even keyrings.

She reached her stall and stopped to let him catch up.

He didn't say anything immediately but looked around at her mirrors, picture frames, plates, pictures and the smaller placemat sets. 'This is magical, Piper,' he said.

'Do you really think so?'

'I do.'

She was ridiculously pleased to hear him say so. She wasn't sure why it mattered so much that he appreciated the things that she made and sold, but it did, very much.

'It's completely different to your clever tech business.' Her confidence dipped when she considered how far from each other their passions lay. They were complete opposites. She upcycled discarded items using glass and pottery she picked up for nothing on the beach, while Alex invented apps that she would probably never have a need for.

He studied her for a few seconds. 'What you do is clever too,' he said.

She smiled, then something struck her.

'What is it?' His voice was gentle, encouraging her to open up.

Piper took a deep breath. She wanted to know what his grandfather had meant when he said how wonderful Alex was regardless of what others thought, but didn't want to get Colin in trouble. After a brief struggle her curiosity got the better of her. 'Your grandfather was saying what a great chap you are.'

Alex gave her a knowing smile. 'Did he follow that up with "despite what they might say about him", or something like that?'

Piper laughed, surprised. 'Yes. I was wondering what he might be referring to. I understand if you'd rather not tell me.'

'It's fine,' he said. 'He and my father have always

disagreed about where their thoughts on education lie. Grandad, being the artistic type, thinks children should be allowed to follow their heart with their careers.'

'And your father doesn't agree?'

'No. He believes you should do your best to become as highly qualified as possible, follow a sensible career, like he did with law, and then when you retire follow any dreams you still have.'

Colin's sentiment made sense now. 'I imagine your father wasn't happy about you letting your place go at university then?'

'Exactly that.' He shrugged. 'It's probably why I still feel torn about my decision not to follow my friends and study for my degree.'

'But you've been successful with your apps.'

'Not all of them.' He smiled.

'Yes, but my work must seem so basic compared to what you do,' she said instead. 'Your apps must help thousands of people.'

He gave her a puzzled look. 'The first and most recent ones were my biggest successes,' he said. 'The most recent app is for elderly people who live alone. It helps them connect with others who live nearby in similar circumstances to them. I'm told it has helped hundreds of thousands.'

She supposed his grandfather might have been his inspiration for the app since he had become widowed and now understood how proud of him Colin must be. She could tell Alex wasn't boasting, but what was he trying to get at by saying something that only proved she was right to think of his work as so much more valuable than hers? 'That's great,' she said.

'Piper,' his voice was gentle. 'We both create things for people. Mine just happens to be for a bigger market but isn't any more special than yours, even if it is helpful. What you create gives people a lot of pleasure. You can't put a value on that.'

She felt a little silly now, wishing she could simply take a compliment. 'But your creations are massively successful.'

He laughed. 'Not all of them, I can assure you. I just got lucky with a couple.'

He stepped closer to the silvery-grey, chalk-painted sideboard she had found in a skip on which she now displayed her stock. 'What you do makes someone's day.'

'As do you, I'm sure.'

He gave her comment some thought, and shrugged. 'I suppose so, but you get what I mean.'

She relented, happy that he considered what she did of value. 'I do. And I'm glad you appreciate my bits.'

His eyebrows lowered in confusion for a second and then he smiled. 'Oh right. Yes, I do.'

She realised what she had said and held back a grimace. This wasn't going as well as she had hoped. 'Right, enough of that. Let me show you around some more and then we'd better leave.'

'Didn't you want to do something first?'

She had no idea what he meant. Piper stared at him, trying to read his face. *Was he imagining she might have lured him in here to kiss him?*

'You wanted to check up on pieces of stock, or something.'

So she had. 'Thanks for the reminder.' She walked over to the sideboard and pulled open one of the cupboards under the row of drawers. Then, reaching inside, she took out a large punchbowl that her grandmother had discovered at a car boot sale the year before. It was badly scratched and wasn't of any value, so she had bought it and given it to Piper to upcycle.

'Would you move those candlesticks and that plate to the side, please?' she asked.

Alex lifted the items, holding them out of her way while she lowered the heavy mosaic bowl. 'That looks really impressive. It must have taken you days to do that.'

'Thanks.' She took the candlesticks and arranged them on each side of the colourful bowl, checking each were perfectly centred on the dresser. 'What do you think?'

'Eye-catching.'

'Kind of you to say so.' She closed the dresser drawer. 'Right, come and see what else is in here. You might even find a birthday or Christmas present for family and friends.'

'Good idea.' He followed her to check out the elaborate display of acid-etched mirrors and array of coloured candles in different shapes and heights that Casey and Tara made. He stopped to study them. 'These are amazing. My sister would love these mirrors and some of these candles. I can just picture them in her flat.'

'Well, I'm sure the girls would give you a discount if you bought a couple of things.' She pictured him travelling on his motorbike. 'They'd arrange to post them if you can't carry them.'

He smiled. 'Thank you, I'll bear that in mind.'

'Sorry, I'm being pushy. Let's go and have a look at Paddy's stall. That's probably more your thing.' She led the way to the middle of the emporium to where Paddy's metal sculptures and metal art had stood since the barn had opened up to traders. 'He was one of the first to have a stall here,' she explained. 'It's why he has the best spot.'

Alex studied the strange metal shapes, some painted with primary colours, others left rusted, which Piper thought added to their appeal. 'He's very talented.'

'He is. I like most of the things in here,' Piper said. 'I feel honoured to be one of the stallholders. I've learned so much from the others.'

Alex clasped his hands behind his back as he leaned forward to study a metal horse rearing from a dark-wooden base. 'By the sounds of things, you all get along very well.'

'We do,' she said with pride. 'We look out for

each other and watch over each other's stalls if one of us is called away or unable to work that day.'

Alex stood up straight once more. 'That sounds really friendly. I like working from home and enjoy my own company, but it must be fun to interact with colleagues.'

He sounded sad. 'But you like working from home.'

He gave her a reassuring smile. 'I do, most of the time. I like the quiet when I'm concentrating, and I've always been a lone bird when it comes to work. I like to do things my way and am a bit of a workaholic if I'm honest. I'm the sort of person who doesn't know when to step away from his job.'

'I'm a bit like that too,' Piper said. Her mum often told her off for working into the night on a project. 'My mother worries that I don't get enough sleep.'

'Grandad is always asking whether I'm sleeping properly.' He laughed. 'We might do different jobs, but it sounds as if we work in a similar way.'

'We do.' She liked the idea of this parallel in their lives. It felt good to have a connection.

She realised it was close to dusk and glanced up through the windows to the sky. 'We should get going soon, or it'll be too dark to see anything and I don't want to turn on the lights.'

'Why not?'

'The old sisters who run this place live in the big house. If they see lights on they might worry. I wouldn't want to frighten them.'

'No, of course not.'

They moved to Vivienne's stall, where she sold her costume jewellery.

'This is much smaller than the others,' Alex noticed.

'I don't think Vivienne could afford one of the larger pitches and the sisters, Meg and Amy Ecobichon, offered her this one. Don't you think her jewellery is clever?'

'It's lovely, but I'm not that knowledgeable about jewellery.'

'She makes it with her daughter. Vivienne says the money adds to her pension, and gives her daughter a second income. I think she likes the companionship here, too, now she's retired.'

'Vivienne?' Alex thought for a moment. 'I think Grandad has mentioned her once or twice.'

Piper grinned, recalling Vivienne's concern about

Colin and when he would be back. 'I think they probably quite like each other.'

Alex raised his eyebrows. 'Really?'

'Maybe.' She didn't want to say the wrong thing. His grandfather might not like them speculating about his friendships.

'Come on, let's go before we can't see where we're going and end up bumping into something. I can't bear the thought of breaking someone's work of art and upsetting them.'

'Good point.'

Piper showed Alex out and locked the door behind them.

'I liked the paintings hung around the walls,' he commented.

'They're mostly by people who took the art course here,' Piper said. 'Their work was good enough to be put on sale.'

'I wonder if Grandad will be able to have one of his paintings displayed. He would be delighted if that happened.'

'I hope so,' Piper said, wondering if he would be able to finish his painting course after his recovery.

'Shall we go for that ride?' Alex asked. 'You could show me a few of the places I haven't discovered yet.'

'OK, but I think we've missed the sunset.' She looked into the dusky sky. 'I was going to say it'll soon be too dark to see much, but look at that moon.'

He glanced up to where she was pointing. 'Is that a super moon?'

'No idea, but I do know it's bright enough to light up most things tonight.' She locked her car then walked with him to his bike. 'I'm looking forward to this.'

'So am I,' he said, taking hold of her hand.

19

Piper directed Alex to the bay at La Saie Harbour. They left the bike and helmets in the tiny parking area and walked through a tree-lined archway and down a narrow slope to the beach. There was a grassy bank on one side, and wooden railings and a wild hedgerow on the other.

'This is a bit like going back in time,' Alex said warmly.

'Watch your footing.' Piper was being careful with every step. 'It's fairly even going down here be-cause the pathway is worn, but you need to be take care not to slip on a bit of seaweed or trip on one of the smaller rocks. I don't want to have to carry you back up to your bike.'

Alex laughed. 'I'd like to see you try.'

'You'll have a long wait,' she giggled.

As she stopped to stare at the pearlescent moon lighting up the gentle waves lapping the shore, Alex bumped into her. 'I thought I told you to look where you were going,' she said with a laugh as he grabbed hold of her to stop her from tripping.

'You said to watch my footing and that's what I was doing,' he joked, letting go of her. 'I didn't expect you to suddenly stop.'

She pointed upwards. 'Look at the moon. Isn't it magnificent?'

'Wow. It certainly is. It seems bigger here some-how, but that must be some sort of illusion.'

'Shall we go on?'

His hand reached for hers again. 'I think I'm going to hold on to you this time. I don't want to risk falling over you again.'

Piper enjoyed the sensation of his hand wrapped around hers. His touch was cool and firm. She would happily walk like this more often. They reached the beach and stopped once more.

'Let's go to the water's edge,' Alex suggested. 'I fancy a paddle.'

'I like that idea.' The tide was high, leaving only a strip of sand. Piper knew from her many visits to the bay that the flat sandy area was in stark contrast to the rocks hidden below the surface of the water. 'We'll have to be careful,' she cautioned. 'It won't be sandy in the sea.'

'That's fine. I only want to stand with my feet in the water.'

'Shall we leave our shoes here?'

He let go of her hand and they both removed their footwear. 'I like feeling sand between my toes.'

'It's one of my favourite things,' she agreed. 'I love warm, fine sand but also cooler damp sand on hotter days.'

'I can tell you grew up spending time on the beach.' He smiled at her. 'Most people would only think of sand as being dry and warm.' He bent to pick up a handful of sand and let it run through his fingers. 'It's so pale and fine,' he said. 'Do you ever come here searching for glass and bits of pottery?'

'Not so much. I go to other beaches, but usually

the larger ones. Having Grouville Bay on my doorstep is more than a big enough area.'

They walked on to the water's edge and stepped in ankle-deep and stood in silence. Piper gazed at the moonlight shimmering on the water. It was a still, warm evening as if it was high season rather than April. She closed her eyes and listened. The gentle ripple of the waves as they danced slowly over the pebbles in the sand and Alex's breathing were the only sounds she heard. She wished she could stay there for ever.

She gave him a discreet look before facing forward again. Even if nothing came of her liking this man, spending quiet time like this on this serene evening with him was helping to heal her soul. She realised she felt calmer than she had in years.

His fingers grazed hers before taking hold of them lightly. 'Isn't this a perfect evening?' he whispered.

'I was thinking the same thing,' she said, her voice breaking. Piper cleared her throat. 'I want to thank you.' She kept her voice low, not wishing to disturb the peaceful atmosphere in the bay.

'Whatever for?'

'For this. For reminding me that life does move on and does get much, much better.'

He tugged gently at her hand, pulling her closer to him until their chests were touching. 'I should be thanking you, Piper. Not the other way around.'

Confused, she went to ask what he meant, but before she managed to do so, his lips found hers and he kissed her.

Piper was thrown for a second but then he let go of her hand and his arms slid around her waist, pulling her tightly against him. Her arms slipped up to his neck, and she gave in to the bliss of Alex's kiss.

Eventually they relaxed their hold on each other. 'I've been wanting to do that again ever since the last time,' he murmured.

'Me, too,' she admitted. 'I wish you didn't have to leave.'

He kissed her again. 'I would much rather stay here and spend more time with you, but I must go back.'

'I wish you didn't have to go,' she said, unable to hide her disappointment.

'So do I, but I don't have a choice. I'll be back next week though, don't forget.'

She recalled the person on the other end of Alex's phone call.

'You don't have a girlfriend, or anyone waiting for you at home, do you?'

He frowned, looking surprised by her question. 'I wouldn't be here with you like this if I did, Piper.'

'Sorry.' She could tell she had tainted the atmosphere between them. 'But I overheard you on the phone to someone you're obviously fond of.'

'That was probably my sister. Although I mostly feel irritation towards her rather than affection,' he joked.

'Good.'

He laughed and Piper realised what she had said. 'Not that your sister irritates you, but that I'm not here kissing someone's boyfriend. I'm not that sort of girl.'

'And I'm not that sort of man,' he assured her, kissing the tip of her nose.

Piper sighed. This really was the most perfect, romantic evening. She was so relieved that he didn't have a girlfriend. *Would he ever consider staying on the island permanently?* 'I'm glad you'll be back next week,' she said softly. 'And that you won't be gone for too long.'

He took her hand in his and they turned to face the sea again. 'It's such a perfect night. I'm glad I got to come here before returning to the madness back home.'

Madness? She realised this was her cue to ask him more about his personal life. 'What's going on there?'

He shrugged and kissed her again. 'It's fine. I'm being overly dramatic. I resent having to leave here, and you, and Grandad, of course.'

A thrill coursed through her. *His words, the way he kissed her, how he made her feel – could it mean he liked her as much as she was beginning to like him? Was life ever actually that perfect? Not if he had secrets,* she reminded herself. She had thought she knew everything about Rick and look how badly that had turned out. She pushed her doubts to the back of her mind, determined not to ruin the moment again.

'At least you can escape again soon,' she said, desperate to summon up the courage to ask him more about himself, and wanting to make him feel better. She wished he didn't have to leave at all. 'If you've got a lot to deal with at home then the time will fly by.'

'I hope you're right.'

It occurred to Piper, as they stood hand in hand and she wriggled her toes in the cool sea water, how little she actually knew about him apart from his name, that he was close to his grandfather, had a sister, and his parents were away on a cruise. It was little more than she learned about most of the guests who came to stay at the Blue Haven. Then again, Alex knew where she worked and her daily routine, but not much about her past, she reminded herself.

'Are you all right, Piper?'

'Yes,' she fibbed, aware that she had probably stiffened while she was thinking and had tipped him off that something was wrong. 'Why?'

'I just wondered.' He stared at the sea silently for a moment. 'You can talk to me about anything you like.'

'That's kind of you to say so. Thanks.'

He turned to face her. 'So, what's on your mind?'

She realised she had no choice but to be honest with him. After all, how was she to get to know him if she acted as if she didn't want to? 'It just dawned on me how little I know about you, that's all.'

It was his turn to appear awkward. 'Ah. I can understand why.' He cupped her chin lightly and bent his head to kiss her. 'I don't mean to be secretive, but — ' He thought before continuing to speak. 'There are some things I need to deal with that I can't speak about yet. I know that probably sounds a little sinister, but I promise you, it isn't.'

'It's fine, I understand,' she said, not really understanding at all but not wishing to ruin the short time they had together. She decided to go with her instincts about Alex and pushed aside the thought that she had also trusted her instincts with Rick. Piper squeezed her eyes shut to force her concerns away.

Anyway, she reasoned, she had sort of got to know Colin and he thought that Alex was the best thing walking the earth. The thought soothed her for a few seconds before she recalled how badly her grandmother had reacted to seeing Colin again on Rozel Beach the day they went swimming. Piper sighed. They might have come to some sort of resolution, but her gran was holding onto a lot of hurt from all those years ago.

'Are you OK?' Alex was watching her intently. 'Do you want to leave?'

She shook her head. 'I was just thinking about Gran.'

'And her issues with my grandparents?' he asked, his voice solemn. 'It's sad how they fell out and wasted so many years, isn't it?' Piper agreed with him. 'Do you think we can help?' Alex added.

'I wouldn't bet on it,' Piper replied, honestly. 'Maybe when you come back to the island we can work on it. There's no time to do anything about that now and, anyway, your grandfather has more than enough to deal with. Maybe if I can persuade Gran to let him stay with her they might find a way past their differences.'

'Good plan.' She heard the smile in Alex's voice. 'Now, would you mind if I kissed you again?'

'I don't mind at all.' She would worry about any concerns she had when he came back. Right now, all she wanted to do was enjoy kissing him. 'In fact, I was wondering when you were going to get round to doing it again.'

He laughed and then took her in his arms once more.

* * *

Piper lay in bed that night, going over her time with Alex on the beach. She knew she was opening herself up to potential heartache but found that she liked him too much to do anything about it. After all, she thought as she stared out at the marine-blue sky, he was leaving in the morning, and she would have more than enough time to consider what was between them before he returned to the island. She closed her eyes and willed sleep to take over, but her mind whirred busily.

What was so important that his friend couldn't wait a few weeks? She tried to conjure scenarios that would be more important than being with his grandfather and couldn't come up with anything.

She wondered whether Alex was lying awake, too, thinking about her.

When her mind wouldn't relax she threw back the duvet and as quietly as she could, so as not to disturb the guests in the room below, crossed the room and took out her tubs of glass and sorted them into different colours and categories to distract herself.

When she noticed the sky lightening, she glanced at her bedside clock. It was five-fifteen and she hadn't slept a wink. She rubbed her neck, which was stiff, and rotated her shoulders to loosen them. Placing the tubs on her dressing table, she lay back down in bed and closed her eyes.

* * *

When she woke, Piper was shocked to discover it was after nine. 'Damn!'

She kicked back the duvet and hurried to the bathroom she shared with her mother for a quick shower. After drying herself and dragging a brush through her wet hair, she dressed in record time, slipped her feet into her trainers and hurried downstairs, willing Alex to still be there.

Everything was quiet. She had a quick glance in the dining room but apart from an elderly couple eating silently, the place was empty. Running through to the kitchen, she spotted her mother.

'Why didn't you wake me?'

Helen finished wiping the worktop and looked up. 'Good morning to you, too, Piper.'

'Sorry. Good morning, Mum.' She forced a smile. 'Why did you let me sleep so late?'

'Because I heard you tiptoeing around your room

at silly o'clock and thought you might need a bit of a
lie-in. I could have done with your help this morning, too.'

Feeling guilty that her mother had set the tables,
taken orders, served breakfast and cleared up, as well
as cooking and making drinks, Piper walked over
and gave her a gentle hug.

'Sorry, Mum.'

'It's fine,' Helen said, always quick to forgive after
an apology. 'What's got into you this morning? You'll
make it up to the barn in time for opening, won't
you?'

'It's not that.'

Understanding registered on her mother's face.
'Ah,' she said. 'You wanted to see Alex before he left.'

'He's gone, then?'

'He left...' Helen glanced up at the wall clock.
'About three-quarters of an hour ago. I think he was
hoping to see his grandfather at the hospital before
catching the ferry to Poole.'

Piper struggled to hide her disappointment, unsure why she was bothering when her mother knew
her so well. She turned to leave the room.

'He left you this.'

Piper spun round to see her mother's smiling face as she withdrew a letter from between two cookery books on one of the kitchen shelves.

'Now, please calm down,' her mum said. 'I don't want you leaving here in a state and ending up crashing your car on your way to work.'

Suitably chastised, Piper grinned. 'I promise I'm fine.'

'Good.' Helen handed over the letter.

'Thanks, Mum. I'll catch up with you later. Have a good day.' She gave her mother a brief wave and left the kitchen feeling happier than when she had arrived. After grabbing her rucksack and car keys, she left the house, wanting to be alone to read the letter. Sitting on a bench outside, she opened the envelope and took out the single sheet of paper.

Hi Piper,

I was hoping to say my goodbyes to you face to face, but you weren't around, and I have to leave now. Don't worry about finding me somewhere to stay, Fliss is going to speak to her friend, Phoebe, about me staying at her home on my next visit.

*What I really want to say is how much I en-
joyed being with you last night on the beach. It
was special and I hope we can do it again
when I return.*

Take care and I'll see you very soon,
  Alex X

'Why are you looking so miserable?'

The voice made her jump. 'Bloody hell, Jax,' she snapped, quickly folding the sheet of paper before slipping it back into the envelope. 'Don't creep up on people like that.' She bent down and unzipped the front pocket of her rucksack, folding the envelope and shoving it inside.

'Who's upset you? Not Alex, surely?' He raised his eyebrows and pulled a silly face.

Piper stood up and pushed his shoulder. 'Shut up,' she said, embarrassed. 'No one's upset me,' she fibbed, not wanting to sound like a jealous teenager if she told him about Alex's hopes to stay at Phoebe's home.

'Yeah, right. Some people might believe that, but I know you too well to be fobbed off.' He narrowed his eyes and bent closer to stare at her face. 'Yup, it's

Alex. What's he gone and done? Let me know so I can go and defend your honour.' He clenched his fists and raised them theatrically.

'Shut up, Jax,' she said with a giggle. 'Don't you have anyone else to annoy?'

'Not right now. My next client is due to arrive in a few minutes. Actually, it's a group of nine-year-old boys. One of them has a birthday and is looking forward to setting up camp and searching for rock oysters.'

'You would have loved a birthday treat like that when you were a kid.'

'True.'

She looked around for Seamus but couldn't see him. 'Seamus not with you today?' she asked, forgetting her woes.

He looked glum and shook his head. 'As you know I always check when people make their bookings that they're happy for Seamus to come along with us.'

'That's right.'

'The kid whose birthday it is today is frightened of dogs, so they asked me if I could leave Seamus at home.'

Piper knew how much both Jax and Seamus would have hated that. 'So where is he now?' she asked, wondering if she should offer to take the little dog for a walk.

'He's fine,' Jax grinned. 'I've left him with Mum.'

'In the salon?'

'No. She's taken the day off. She's taken him for a walk in St Catherine's Wood.'

Piper thought of all the shaded paths and streams the little dog would enjoy. 'He'll love that.'

'He will.' Jax laughed. 'I'm not so sure how much Mum will though.'

She spotted a people carrier driving slowly towards them along the pier. 'I have a feeling this might be your group of youngsters now.'

'Looks like you're right.' He playfully dug her in the ribs. 'Off you go, and don't give that bloke another thought. Enjoy your day.'

'I will.'

She walked to her car, smiling. Jax would make someone a great boyfriend, one day. Although the woman in question would need to enjoy being barefoot a lot of the time, and knee-deep in sea water or rock pools, if she was to be attractive to him.

20

Alex had been gone three days and still Piper hadn't heard from him. She was beginning to wonder if absence wasn't making his heart grow fonder and decided to focus on work.

She also visited Colin in hospital. He seemed better, but miserable at missing out on the rest of his retreat.

The second time she visited, she was told he had a visitor already and as Piper wasn't a relative, she wouldn't be allowed to see him. She was trying to imagine who his visitor was when Vivienne came out of the ward to ask a nurse if Colin could have some more water.

She was glad his art class colleagues were coming to see him. At least he had made friends here and if she heard from Alex she would have some good news to share with him, though she supposed he was already keeping in touch with the hospital.

She was walking away down the hospital corridor when she overheard a woman talking.

'Is that her?'

Vivienne confirmed that it was.

Footsteps approached and Piper turned to see a beautiful woman around her own age with long, sleek, fair hair, perfectly curled.

'Excuse me,' the woman said. 'I'd like a word with you.'

Surprised, Piper stopped walking. 'Sorry, I don't think we've met.'

'I'm Fliss. Alex's sister. I was wondering if you're free to give me a lift to this barn place, and then on to a friend's house?'

Piper was taken aback at the woman's self-confidence. She had barely introduced herself before asking for a favour, or even two. Interested to know more, Piper nodded. 'I'd be happy to. The car isn't too far away.'

Fliss gave her a thoughtful look and seemed surprised Piper had agreed so readily. 'OK. Great.'

As they made their way along the lengthy corridor, Piper, desperate to ask about Alex and how he was, reminded herself that Fliss had just been to visit her grandfather. 'How's Colin?'

'He's great. His leg is healing well. They remarked on how fit he is for his age, and that he should be well enough to return home in a couple of weeks. Not that he's in any rush to go home.'

'No?'

'He'd rather stay here with his new friends, but I was telling him he'd need somewhere to stay and shouldn't be on his own. Not until he's properly recovered.'

She thought of Vivienne and wondered whether she would take the opportunity to offer him a place in her home but didn't say anything in case Fliss didn't know that Vivienne had a soft spot for her grandfather.

'Ma and Pa are away on a cruise right now which is why I had to come here. I was hoping Alex might do it, but he's tied up with *all* his personal stuff.' She rolled her eyes heavenwards. 'Typical Alex.'

Piper wasn't sure if Fliss expected her to know what this 'personal stuff' entailed, and she had no intention of asking.

'Where are you staying?' she asked, wondering if it was the same place Alex had mentioned. 'There isn't much available at this time of year.'

'So my brother tells me. Thankfully an old uni friend lives here. She's always trying to persuade me to come to the island and stay with her and the sweetie was very excited to hear from me and offered me one of her spare rooms for as long as I needed. She invited Alex to stay there, too, since he tells me your guest house is fully booked.' Fliss grinned at Piper. 'She was even more determined he should stay at her place when she spotted a photo of him on my Instagram account.'

Piper's heart dipped. *Why would Alex ever choose to stay at the guest house when he'd been offered somewhere private and, by the sound of things, more upmarket?*

'No idea how the damn photo slipped on there,' Fliss said. 'He hates it when I share anything about him on social media. Not that I often do, you understand. But sometimes I do it accidentally.' She stopped talking and looked sideways at Piper, presumably expecting her to say something.

'It was kind of your friend to offer to put you both up.'

Fliss beamed at her. 'That's what I told Alex.'

Piper returned her smile, unsure how to respond. They reached the car park, and she unlocked her Mini. 'Here we are.'

The drive to the barn didn't take long and Piper was relieved that Fliss didn't stop talking, seeming to require no input from her. She was obviously excited to see her uni friend again.

'What's your friend's address?' Piper asked, after she'd popped into the barn to collect the takings from her stall and Fliss had packed up and collected her grandfather's belongings.

Fliss took her mobile phone out of her pocket, scrolled through and then read out an address Piper didn't recognise. 'Why is everything in French?'

'The island was ruled by Normandy for about three hundred years, until the beginning of the thirteenth century when we swore allegiance to the king of England,' she explained, then noticed Fliss's bored expression. Aware that she was wasting her breath, Piper focused on where they were going instead.

'Can I look at your phone? I don't know the address.' Fliss gave it to her. 'OK, we need to drive along La Rue De La Bachauderie,' she said, picturing the route. She handed back the phone. 'I think I know where I'm going now.'

After a couple of wrong turns, Piper finally saw the house name on one of two imposing granite gate posts.

'I thought you said you knew the way,' Fliss grumbled.

Piper gritted her teeth, not wishing to get into an argument with Alex's annoying sister.

'Sorry, that was rude of me,' Fliss said eventually. 'I practically kidnapped you and forced you to bring me here today and you probably have other things to be getting on with.'

Piper forced a smile. 'It's fine,' she said. After all, she had agreed to bring her.

She drove up the gravel driveway and slowed as she reached the circular parking area in front of the impressive Georgian house. 'Here you are,' she said, stopping the car. *This was the place Alex would be coming to?*

'Thank you.' Fliss opened the door and stepped out while Piper stared through her open window at the huge building that had at least twenty windows facing to the front.

Piper noticed that Fliss was only carrying a tiny cross-body bag and a large weekend holdall. 'Don't forget your grandfather's things,' she said, trying to be as helpful as possible.

Fliss turned, a confused expression on her perfect face. 'What things?'

'The stuff you just collected?'

Fliss groaned and stopped. She stared thoughtfully at Piper, hesitated for a moment, and then looked over her shoulder. 'You can take it back to your place, can't you?'

Annoyed at her presumption, Piper said stiffly, 'I'm not sure what you expect *me* to do with it?'

Fliss sighed heavily, clearly keen to get away. 'I obviously don't have anywhere to keep his things. I'm staying here for the first time. I don't like to impose on my friend's hospitality.'

'But we've only just met and you don't mind imposing on mine.' Piper heard the irritation in her voice. *Was Fliss always this rude?* Alex's manners were impeccable and she couldn't imagine him acting in this way. The least his sister could have done was ask if she didn't mind finding somewhere to store her grandfather's things rather than just assuming she would be able to do it. It was difficult to imagine she and Alex were siblings.

Before Fliss could respond, the front door opened and a glossy, dark-haired woman gave a delighted scream. 'Flissy! You're here!'

Fliss waved and blew her a kiss. 'I won't be a sec, Phoebe.' She bent down to Piper's car window and gave her a pleading look as she whispered, 'Please can you keep Grandad's things with you? Put them in Alex's old room until he gets back or something.'

'You know we're fully booked and that he doesn't have a room. Other guests are in there now.'

'Alex didn't tell me you were so difficult,' Fliss said huffily. 'The way he spoke about you, I assumed you were kind and helpful.' She turned to blow another kiss at her waiting friend. 'Look, I don't care what you do with Grandad's stuff. If you don't have somewhere to store it, which I'm sure you must do, then take it all back to the barn. As you can see, I am not in a position to take it.'

Without waiting for Piper to say anything further, she marched off, breaking into a run, dropping her bag as she reached the front door and flinging her arms around her friend. 'Phoebe, it's so kind of you to invite me here.'

'I hope you've got a costume because I thought we'd go and have a swim. Daddy and Mummy are away so it might be fun to invite a few friends over and introduce them to you, have a few cocktails. What do you think?'

Having been dismissed, Piper put her car in gear and began to drive off.

'Thank you for dropping Flissy off,' the girl – Phoebe – shouted after her. Piper raised her hand out of the window. Tempted to make a rude gesture, she gave a polite wave instead.

Annoyed, she wondered what to do with Colin's things. Maybe Gran would agree to store them, at least until he was discharged from hospital. Then, remembering that she still needed to broach the subject of Colin staying in Gran's spare room, decided to take them home. They had little space for their own things in their tiny attic flat, and Colin had accumulated quite a few canvases, as well as books, paints, and the clothes he had brought with him to the island, but they shouldn't take up too much space.

* * *

Piper parked the car further away from the house than she would have liked, knowing she was lucky to find a space at all with so many holidaymakers visiting the island. She lifted everything out of her Mini and placed it on the tarmac while she tried to work out how to carry it all.

'What on earth have you got there, lovey?' Nancy asked, standing in the doorway of the florist's. 'You look like you could do with some help.'

Piper smiled and hoped Nancy might send Vicki out to help her. When she didn't, Piper said, 'That would be great, thanks. I'm looking after it for someone who's had to go into hospital.'

Just at that moment her grandmother walked out of the nearby sweetshop. Spotting Piper, she hurried over, putting a half-unwrapped sherbet lemon back into its white paper bag. 'Where's all that junk come from?' she said with a frown.

Relieved Alex wasn't there to hear Gran speak so disparagingly about his grandad's possessions, Piper shook her head. 'It's not junk, Gran. I've brought it home to ask Mum if we can store it for a bit.'

Gran narrowed her eyes. 'They're Colin's things, I suppose.'

'How did you guess?' Piper asked, realising she hadn't managed to get round to asking Gran yet about the possibility of Colin sleeping in her spare room.

'I heard he was in hospital.'

Hearing the disapproving note in her voice – as though Colin had hurt himself deliberately to annoy her – Piper said firmly, 'I can't not help him, Gran. Alex has had to return to England.'

'I know,' she said, sounding hurt. 'I'd never be uncharitable enough to suggest you shouldn't help.'

'Oh,' Piper said, thrown. 'Sorry. I'm a bit out of sorts this afternoon.'

'Why?' Her grandmother picked up Colin's bag and a couple of the canvases, leaving Piper to carry the rest. 'What's the matter?'

'I've just met Alex's sister, Fliss.'

'And why is that so bad?'

Piper told her grandmother about being commandeered by Alex's snooty sister at the hospital, and how rude she had been when Piper dropped her off at her friend's home. Not wanting her gran to feel sorry for her, Piper decided not to mention how pretty Phoebe was or that she had offered for Alex to stay with her when he was next back on the island. 'I suppose she's come to the island with little notice, and is concerned about her grandfather,' she said, trying to make allowances for the girl's behaviour. 'I suppose I could have been a little friendlier.'

'It's possible that you felt awkward because she was Alex's sister?'

Piper hoisted her rucksack onto her shoulder, struggling with Colin's things. She needed time to think before replying. Gran would see through any attempt to fob her off with a vague answer.

'They're just so different,' she said. It was as far as she intended going on the topic. She wasn't ready to share her feelings about Alex with anyone.

'Piper?'

She realised that while she had been lost in

thought they had reached her gran's house. 'Why have we stopped here?'

Gran put down the holdall she had been carrying and unlocked her front door. 'Bring it all in then,' she instructed. 'No need to stand on the pavement where everyone and his mother can see what you're doing.'

Piper couldn't help laughing. For someone who was interested in everyone else's business, her grandmother was intensely private about her own. She did as she was asked, relieved to put down all the items she was carrying onto the living room floor.

'You don't mind keeping them at yours?'

Gran frowned. 'How uncharitable do you think I am, young lady?'

Piper was at a loss for words. She was unable to think of a reply that wouldn't insult her grandmother, so kept quiet.

'You can stop for a cup of tea and then carry that lot up to the spare room. We both know how little space you and Helen have, and while I have my issues with Colin the least I can do for a fellow human is store his belongings until he's well enough to come and fetch them.'

'Thanks, Gran.' Piper felt a rush of relief. She sat

on one of the chairs, glad to be doing nothing for a
minute. 'Don't worry, I'll make the tea,' she said,
seeing her grandmother's expression. 'I'm just gath-
ering myself for a few minutes. That lot was heavier
than it looked.'

'You're telling me.' Gran moved her tapestry to
give herself room to sit. She looked over at the bags
and other bits Colin had amassed in his short time
on the island. 'I wonder how he was expecting to get
this lot back to the mainland? It's too much to take
on a plane.'

'Post it?'

'It would cost a fortune.' Gran shrugged. 'Why
are we bothering ourselves about this?'

Piper shook her head. 'I've no idea.'

'You've had your rest,' Gran said, smiling. 'Now
get up and fetch your tired old Gran a cuppa.'

Piper knew her grandmother had more energy
than most people half her age, but she didn't argue.
She was rather thirsty herself. 'One delicious cuppa
coming up.'

21

Piper waited impatiently for Alex to arrive. She had been keeping an eye out for the Jersey Harbour arrivals all day. The boat had docked over an hour ago and she presumed he would have gone from the harbour straight to the General Hospital to visit his grandfather.

Her stomach did a little flip when she heard the deep roar of his motorbike as it slowed in front of the guest house mid-afternoon. She hadn't been able to secure a room for him and hoped he would agree to a suggestion her mother had come up with.

Not wishing to seem too eager, Piper held back from going outside to greet him. She waited for him in the front room, busying herself by tidying the already immaculate reception desk.

She heard the front door close and his footsteps coming into the room.

'Hello there,' he said, beaming at her. He looked around the room and then walked over to her and kissed her lightly on the lips. 'I'm glad you're in here by yourself. I couldn't wait to do that.'

Piper's heart raced from the touch of his lips on hers. 'It's good to have you back,' she admitted.

'It's a relief to be back.' He put his rucksack down on the wooden floor and leaned on the reception counter. 'I gather from my little sister that you two didn't hit it off all that well. I must apologise for her. She can be a bit of a princess at times.'

Piper shook her head. 'It's fine.'

'Fliss has always been a little spoilt as the youngest. She expects to get her own way.'

'It was just one of those things. Nothing for you to worry about anyway.'

'That's a relief.' He seemed to relax slightly. 'She said something about you storing Grandad's stuff?'

'Actually, Gran saw me unloading my car and offered to keep it in her spare room.'

Alex's eyes widened. 'She did?'

Piper grinned. 'I was as surprised as you. She said it was the kind thing to do. I have a sneaky suspicion she wants him to have something to thank her for.' *Was she being uncharitable?*

'If it gets them talking and being friendly then I don't mind what she does.' He walked round the small counter and took her in his arms. 'I just want them to make up properly, then we can all relax.'

Piper slipped her arms around his neck and kissed him. 'So do I.'

Alex kissing her neck, making her body tingle, asked: 'What are you thinking?'

'That Fliss and I are going to be friends too.'

He laughed. 'Whether she likes it or not?'

She kissed him. 'I can be very persuasive when I want to be.'

He tickled her sides, making her squeal and then cover her mouth when footsteps crossed the wooden floor in the bedroom above them. 'Stop that.'

His gaze was full of laughter. 'You were telling me how persuasive you can be.'

'So I was.' She pulled him close and kissed him

again, happily forgetting everything when he kissed her back.

When they came up for air, she said, 'I'm afraid we haven't had any cancellations, so we don't have a guest room for you.'

'That's fine. I'm only popping in to say "hello",' he said, taking a strand of her hair and letting it run through his fingers.

'I do have another plan,' she continued, a flush travelling to her cheeks.

'Really?' His eyes were alive with desire.

'You can move into my room.'

His eyes widened. 'I could? I love the sound of that.' His breath was warm against her lips.

She let a moment pass. 'Just so you know, I won't be in there.'

'What?' His eyes twinkled with amusement. 'Where will you be?'

'I'll stay in Gran's spare room.'

'No, I can't let you do that.'

'It's fine. She won't mind at all.'

He shook his head. 'It doesn't seem right. I just can't let you do that.'

Disappointed he wasn't going to be persuaded,

she said, 'I can ask Gran if you can take the spare room in her cottage then?'

'Another kind offer, but no. We both know that wouldn't be fair on her. Not with how she and Grandad are right now. Fliss has already suggested I stay with her at Phoebe's house. Apparently, there's more than enough room.'

'Fair enough,' Piper said quietly only just managing to hide her dismay. When Alex saw the house, he would no doubt be relieved he'd gone with his sister's offer. A thought struck her.

Was Fliss trying to set Phoebe up with her brother? She hoped not, but Fliss obviously had no idea that Alex and Piper had become close.

Alex rested a hand on her cheek. 'Hey, don't be sad. We can still spend time together, but I will have to see my sister while I'm here. We have quite a few things to discuss and being away from her friends at home is a good opportunity for me to get her to listen to what I have to say.'

'Of course.'

As if sensing her dip in mood, he added gently, 'I'd rather stay here, but I can't push you out of your bedroom.'

'It's fine, I get it.'

'I'm taking Fliss and Phoebe out for something to eat this evening, to thank Phoebe for inviting us to stay. You're more than welcome to join us.' He took her hand in his. 'In fact, I wish you would.'

'I don't think I'll be welcome,' Piper said with a sinking heart. 'It's not as if either of them knows me and your sister didn't exactly warm to me this morning.'

'She's fine once you get to know her.'

Piper shook her head. 'Thanks for the invitation though.'

He leaned forward and kissed her. 'I'll come back and see you at the barn tomorrow morning. If you're free, we can nip out for a bite to eat before the lunch rush. It'll be quicker on the bike, it's easier to park.'

Cheered by his offer, Piper smiled. 'I'd like that very much.' She would rather spend time with him when Fliss and Phoebe weren't there. She'd certainly be more relaxed.

'I'll leave it up to you to decide where we go.'

'I've already thought of the perfect place.'

'Good,' he said, drawing her to him and kissing her once more. 'I'll look forward to it.'

She walked with him to the door and watched him drive off on his bike, staring out at the bay for a moment, wishing she was with him, before turning back inside to continue her chores.

* * *

By seven o'clock, Piper decided that while she hadn't wanted to spend time with Alex's sister and friend, she wasn't in the mood to while away a perfect evening alone in her room. Her mum was out with her 'man friend', Dave, and Piper was left with nothing to do but think.

Deciding to go for a walk and get some fresh air, she grabbed her bag and went out.

The pub down the road was busy with people drinking and chatting outside. On impulse she made her way over. She was bound to see someone she knew, and even if she didn't, she could have a drink on her own.

She stopped to chat with a couple of people she recognised, then walked inside to the bar where she spotted Jax, laughing at something the two women he was with were saying.

'What can I get you?' the barman asked.

'A white wine spritzer, thanks,' Piper ordered.

'Put that on my tab, will you?' Jax said, putting his arm around her shoulders.

Piper couldn't miss the irritation on the women's faces. They'd been enjoying Jax's full attention, but he seemed oblivious to their annoyance.

'Why the long face?'

'I'd rather not talk about it, if you don't mind.'

'Suit yourself.' He took the spritzer from the barman and handed it to her. 'Let's drink these outside. We'll regret it if we don't make the most of this perfect weather.'

'Would you like to settle your tab first, sir?'

Jax pulled a face at Piper. 'We almost got away with that,' he joked in a loud whisper.

The barman waited for Jax to produce payment.

'Bye, ladies.' Jax gave both women a brief hug. 'It was great meeting you.'

'We might see you back in here later?' the blonde one asked hopefully.

'Yeah, maybe. Have a great evening.'

They went outside, squinting against the early

evening brightness. 'No spare tables,' Jax said. 'Let's go onto the beach.'

'We're not supposed to do that,' Piper argued, sounding, even to her own ears, like a little goody-two-shoes.

Jax put his arm around her waist. 'I'm going to pretend I didn't hear that. No one will mind as long as we return the glasses later.' He nudged her, causing her to spill some of her drink and led her across the parking area and down the slipway onto the beach.

They kicked off their shoes and found a spot against the wall, settling down to enjoy their drinks.

Jax drank some of his lager before saying, 'OK, talk to me.'

'I can't be bothered. It's all too ridiculous.'

He nudged her again, making her spill more of her drink and causing her to almost topple sideways.

'Will you stop doing that? If I lose any more of this you're going to owe me another drink.'

'I bought that one.'

Piper laughed. 'I don't care. Stop being so rough, we're not children any more.'

'Don't pretend you can't stand up for yourself, missy.'

'Shut up.' She leaned back against the wall and closed her eyes for a couple of seconds. 'I'm glad I bumped into you. You always take me out of myself when I get in my own way.' She smiled at him and saw him frown down at her. 'What?'

'I'll pretend I understood what you just said, but I really have no idea. I'll take it as a compliment though.'

She laughed and looked at him. 'It was.'

'If you've got nothing you want to talk about, I do.'

Piper was intrigued. 'Go on.'

'I was wondering if your mate, Alex, would like to come out on a sea safari this week to see the dolphins?'

'I'm sure he'd love that.' Piper had been out with Jax and his friend a few times over the years and the excitement of watching the enchanting creatures never waned. 'Although his sister is over here now and they're staying with her friend up in Trinity. He'll probably want them to come too.'

'That shouldn't be a problem. I love watching

people enjoying new experiences.' Jax raised his glass. 'The more the merrier. Just clear it with him, work out what day suits you best and then let me know and I'll set it up with my mate.'

'I'm invited too?'

'Of course, if you want to come.' He gave a knowing smile. 'I can't think why.'

Ignoring his raised eyebrows, Piper took a sip of her drink before saying casually, 'Like you, I like helping people enjoy their stay.' And whatever happened, she wanted Alex and his sister to leave with good memories of the island.

22

The following morning was busy at the barn. Piper sold three of her best pieces to a newly divorced woman, who was delighted with them.

'I've been looking forward to having my own place for two years now,' she said as Piper wrapped a large bowl and two candlesticks in white paper. 'Now I have my own house, I'm going to fill it with everything I like. I've spent years living with my ex's dull taste in everything.' She helped Piper carry the items out to her gleaming Audi. 'I've already chosen brightly coloured wallpaper for each room.'

Piper was cheered by the woman's happiness

with her new life. 'Good for you. And thank you for choosing some of my pieces for your new home.'

'You must spend hours making them. I couldn't do something this intricate if you gave me a year.'

Piper thanked her again and returned to her stall in the barn to tidy up before Alex arrived to take her to lunch. She had just reached the barn door when she heard the roar of his bike engine coming up the driveway.

She watched him dismount and returned his smile as he strode over. 'You ready to go?'

'I'll be a couple of minutes,' she said. 'I'll just let Casey and Tara know I'll be out for an hour or so.'

'I hope you've chosen somewhere nice.'

'I have, and I have a proposition for you.'

He gave her a quizzical smile. 'That sounds intriguing.'

Without saying anything further, she hurried in to speak to her friends and grab her bag before running back out to join Alex.

He handed her a helmet. 'Where are we going then?'

'St John's way. Along the north coast.' She finished

fastening her helmet and swung her leg over the back of the bike, nestling in behind Alex. 'If you go left out of here and then left again and keep going, I'll let you know when we're there. It's a small place, on the cliffs.'

'Sounds great.'

She wrapped her arms around his firm waist and breathed in the leather scent of his jacket. It felt good to be sitting behind him once again, just the two of them. Even if it was just for one hour, Piper intended to make the most of every second.

As they neared their destination, she tapped his shoulder and pointed to the turn off. Alex slowed his bike and swerved into the small parking area.

'What do you think?' Piper asked as she removed her helmet, hoping he would be as impressed as she had been the first time Jax brought her here, a couple of years ago.

Alex looked around him. 'You couldn't find a more spectacular view, that's for sure.' They walked over to the edge, passing several picnic tables where people were eating and drinking from the varied menu of full English breakfasts, burgers, ice creams and hot drinks.

'It is pretty good, isn't it?'

'Good choice, Piper. I like it. Very much.'

As two cars pulled in and parked, Piper said, 'We need to get a move on and order before it gets too packed. Lunchtime is their busiest time.'

'It's a horsebox,' Alex whispered as they walked up to the tiny mobile café.

'Yes, I know.'

'My mother used to have one, but she used it to transport hers and my sister's horses to horse shows.'

They stood in the queue and discussed what to order. Piper usually ended up eating the same thing, despite intending to try something different.

They settled on bacon and egg baguettes and coffee and stood aside to take in the view over the Channel, where the calm sea glistened in the bright spring sunshine. A few minutes later, they were facing each other across one of the picnic tables.

'Did you ever ride?' she asked, picturing him on horseback like a modern-day Mr Darcy.

'No, not my thing. I prefer motorbikes.' He took a bite of his lunch and, after swallowing, added, 'Don't get me wrong. I love horses. We had several over the years and I was usually roped into helping muck out the stables. I did learn to ride but never competed like my mum and Fliss did.'

'That's a shame.'

'Not as far as my father was concerned. Horses are an expensive luxury, especially when you're taking it to a competing level. He was delighted that one of us gave up. My mother wasn't though. She hates my bike and has tried all sorts to get me to give it up.'

Piper blew on her coffee to cool it. 'Like what?'

'Sorry?'

'What sort of thing did she try?'

He gave his answer some thought. 'The usual lectures about the dangers of riding motorbikes, which was to be expected, I guess. When that didn't make any difference, she tried bribery.'

'What kind of bribery?'

'She offered to buy me a dog, something I'd longed for as a child. I told her she was at least fifteen years too late.'

Piper laughed and, breathing in too quickly, almost choked on a piece of bread. 'Oh, sorry,' she coughed.

Alex held up her drink. 'Here, take a sip.'

'Thanks,' she said, swallowing the hot liquid. 'So embarrassing when that happens.'

'It was my fault,' he said with a grimace. 'Sorry.'

'I would have given up a motorbike for a dog.'

'I must admit, I was tempted.'

She finished the rest of her delicious baguette and wiped her mouth and hands with the napkin. 'What's your verdict on this place? Would you come again?'

'Certainly. Although probably not in a howling gale or driving rain.'

The place was getting busier. 'Shall we take our drinks and leave the table for others to use?'

'Good idea.'

They threw away their rubbish and took their coffees closer to the edge of the cliff. 'There are brilliant walks around here.' She pointed to a pathway disappearing down to their left. 'Once a year there's a walk around the entire island for charity. Lots of people take part.'

'Sounds interesting.' Alex drank his coffee as he gazed out to sea.

'What, the cliff paths, or the charity walk?'

He turned his head and smiled down at her. 'Both.'

'Look.' She pointed out three pony-riders coming along the path. 'I wouldn't be brave enough to do that up here, I'd worry about falling off.'

'I definitely feel safer on my motorbike.'

Recalling Jax's offer the previous evening, Piper said, 'I have something to ask you.'

Alex raised an eyebrow. 'I'm all ears.'

'How do you fancy going on a RIB to the Minquiers with Jax and his mate, Dan. It's his boat and he does sea tours when he's not skippering some wealthy local's yacht. He's offered to take Jax and a few friends out and Jax wondered whether you'd like to join them.'

Alex was nodding. 'I'd love to.' He frowned thoughtfully for a moment. 'Are they the islands to the south here somewhere? I think I read about them on the boat coming over.'

'That's right. The Minquiers and Écréhous form part of the Bailiwick of Jersey.' She presumed Dan or Jax would point out the different islands when they were on the boat, so didn't elaborate.

'Right.' He gave her a cheeky smile. 'I would ask

what you mean by Bailiwick, but I'm not sure there's much left of your lunchbreak.'

She was reluctant to have to leave so soon. 'It's Jersey, some small islands and the small islets that make up the jurisdiction,' she explained. 'Guernsey has its own bailiwick.' She was used to holiday-makers asking questions and hoped she wasn't getting anything wrong.

'I see.'

Piper realised she hadn't mentioned Fliss and Phoebe to him. 'Jax said your sister and her friend are very welcome to join us. It will be for most of the day, but should be great fun.'

'You're coming too?'

'I wouldn't miss it,' Piper said, a smile curving her lips. Remembering how Casey and Tara were taking care of her stall, she checked to see how long they had been. 'Hell, it's quarter to one.' She drank the remainder of her coffee. 'I'm afraid we're going to have to go.' She stood as he did and took his cup from him. 'We'll come for longer next time.'

'I'm glad there's going to be a next time, Piper.' He bent down and gave her a quick kiss. 'Please thank Jax for his generous offer. I'm sure Fliss will want to come, and I'll let you know if Phoebe is up for it.'

'No problem. I've got your number from when I registered you at the guest house but I don't think I've given you mine yet.' He handed her his phone and she keyed in her mobile number. 'I'll wait to hear from you before letting Jax know.' She pictured the two immaculate women. 'If they come, they should wear their hair up, so it doesn't whip them in their faces when the boat goes fast.' She touched her own curls. 'It's what I do with mine.'

'I'll let them know.' Alex smiled. 'I'm going to visit Grandad after I've dropped you off and collected Fliss. We're trying to get organised for when he's allowed out of hospital.'

'Fliss said he didn't want to return to his home on the mainland.'

'He doesn't.'

'Where will he stay?'

'Not sure, but I'll work something out.' Alex kissed her again and handed her a helmet. 'Put this on and let's get you back to work.'

* * *

The afternoon flew by at the barn. Piper was looking forward to seeing Alex again and buoyed by the thought of their expedition to the Minquiers with Jax.

She noticed Vivienne had been watching her on and off all afternoon and it was becoming a little disconcerting. When there was a lull in visitors, she walked over to Vivienne's costume jewellery stall.

'Hi, Vivienne.'

'Good afternoon, Piper,' Vivienne replied, rather formally. 'You've had a good afternoon today. How many sales have you had so far? Five?'

'Six,' Piper said automatically. She wasn't interested in small talk. 'Vivienne, is everything OK?' She kept her voice low. 'Have I done something to offend you?'

Vivienne's face reddened. Her mouth opened, forming a perfect 'O'. 'No, not at all,' she said finally, shaking her head.

Piper decided to change tactic. 'Did you want me for something?'

Vivienne looked around. Thankfully, the other sellers were busy and not taking any notice. 'This is rather embarrassing,' she began, twisting the large moonstone ring on her finger. 'I'm not sure you're the right person to speak to about this, but I noticed you being picked up earlier by Colin's grandson.'

'That's right.' Piper was confused. 'Is something wrong?'

Vivienne cleared her throat and took a deep breath, as if to steady herself. 'I've been to see Colin a couple of times. However, the last time, his grand-daughter arrived and told me and his other friends that we were tiring him out too much and that she wanted to spend time with him alone.' She clasped her hands together. 'She told us to leave. It was rather humiliating to be honest with you. I've never been asked to leave anywhere before. I have to admit I was a little upset by the way she spoke to me.'

Piper felt sorry for Vivienne, who had been so kind to Colin. 'I'm sorry that happened,' she said, patting the older woman's arm. 'I'm sure she's grateful for your support and probably just worried about her grandfather.' Piper wasn't sure at all, having been on the receiving end of Fliss' sharp tongue. 'Would you like me to speak to Alex? I'm sure he won't mind you visiting Colin again and I'm sure Colin would like to see you.'

'If you wouldn't mind, I'd appreciate that.' Vivienne rested a hand on the short necklace around her throat and fiddled with one of the pearls. 'I don't wish to cause Colin any angst or upset his family in any way.'

'I'll be sensitive,' Piper reassured her. 'I'm sure he'll understand you wanting to resume your visits. He's probably desperate to find out how the rest of you are getting on at the retreat. It's horrible that he had to cut short his time there with you all.'

Vivienne let go of her necklace and smiled. 'Thank you, Piper. I feel much better now I've spoken to you.' She pushed her small glasses up on the bridge of her nose. 'You're very kind.'

'I don't mind at all,' Piper said honestly, noticing that a small queue of customers had built up while they were talking. 'Looks like you've got a few sales coming up,' she added with a smile.

As she returned to her own pitch, Piper decided to try to get to know Fliss a little better on the boat trip to see the dolphins, and find out what made her tick. It would be nice to get along with her if she and Alex were going to be seeing more of each other.

23

That evening, Piper and Alex sat near Le Pinacle, watching a small shoal of dolphins swimming in the sea below.

'This is breathtaking.' Alex put his arm around her shoulder. 'I never imagined I would get to see this.'

'I've seen seals further along, near Stinky Bay,' Piper said, using the local nickname for the small rocky bay they had passed on the motorbike on their way over.

'And you say this huge piece of granite, and the grassy bit behind it, is special?'

'I've never dared climb down there,' Piper said, shuffling closer to him. 'But yes, it's special. It's an important prehistoric site where pieces of axes and pottery have been excavated. According to Gran, it's believed to have once been a ceremonial site back in Roman times, or even possibly before.'

'Impressive.'

'I thought so, too.'

Piper gazed at the magnificence of the scene around them. 'If you had come here in late July, you would have seen the headland covered with purple heather with splashes of bright-yellow gorse. It's terribly pretty. People come up here to walk their dogs and over that way' – she pointed – 'on the other side of that huge tower, built during the Occupation, is Grosnez Castle. It's a ruin now. All that's left is a heart-shaped archway. Coaches come up every so often with visitors wanting to take photos of the area.'

'I don't blame them,' Alex said. 'I must bring Grandad here when he's well enough to go on my bike. He'd love to visit all the bunkers and gun emplacements across the headland. They've been well preserved. It must have taken an enormous amount of work renovating them. The amount of fortifications along here is staggering.'

'I've never given it much thought before. We're used to it, I guess.'

'It must have been so different here when the German army was on the island.'

Piper shuddered. 'I am thankful that Gran was only a baby then so didn't come here until after the war.'

'I'll bet you are.'

They sat in silence. They were so lucky to live now and not nearly eighty years ago when things were so different. Piper watched a sparrow hawk hover over a grassy patch to the right of them and then looked at the waves crashing against the bottom of the cliffs.

Was it the right time to bring up Vivienne's wish to visit Colin?

'Alex?'

He smiled. 'Yes?'

'Why are you looking at me like that?'

'You had a certain tone in your voice that reminded me of the one Fliss uses when she's asking for something that's all.'

She wasn't pleased to be compared to his sister.

'Sorry,' he said, grinning at her. 'Please, you were about to say something.'

She took a deep breath and explained about Fliss asking Vivienne to leave the hospital, saying that Colin was too tired to see his friends. 'I'm sure your grandad would like to see Vivienne again,' she said. 'I saw them chatting a couple of times at the retreat and they seemed to get along well. I thought the whole reason you persuaded your grandfather to come to the retreat was to take him out of himself and cheer him up. Help him make new friends and a new life.'

'Of course.' Alex didn't look very pleased.

'I'm not trying to be mean about Fliss, but I promised Vivienne I would ask you if she could visit Colin again.'

He narrowed his eyes. 'My sister can be abrupt with people, but I don't think she realises how she comes across sometimes.' He groaned slightly. 'Poor Vivienne. I don't want anyone to be put off visiting Grandad. He wouldn't be happy if he knew.'

'He probably does. I think Fliss asked Vivienne and the others to leave while they were at his bedside.'

'I see.' Alex closed his eyes briefly. 'He probably doesn't want to upset Fliss by saying anything. I do wish my sister wouldn't boss people around. In her defence, she was probably only looking out for Grandad.'

'That's what I thought,' Piper said, though that wasn't the impression she'd got.

'Don't worry,' he said, hugging her to him. 'I'll have a word with her.'

Relieved, Piper asked, 'Can I tell Vivienne that it's all right for Colin to have visitors?'

He leaned forward and kissed the tip of her nose. 'Of course you can. And if my sister says anything, say that I gave them permission and she's to speak to me if she has any objection.' He sighed. 'I'm hoping he'll be discharged soon anyway, so Fliss won't have any say in who sees him then.'

'Fingers crossed.'

His face brightened. 'By the way, this Thursday will suit everyone to go out on the boat, if the offer still stands.'

'Great,' Piper said, realising it would also be Jax's birthday. 'I'll let my cousin know.'

24

Piper was relieved when Jax told her later that night that he was more than happy to spend his birthday at sea.

'What else would I be doing?' he asked in his laid-back way. 'I'd much rather be out showing tourists the delights of our island than sitting at home.'

Me too, thought Piper, deciding she needed to find a way to sneak a small birthday cake out with them on their trip.

The following morning, Alex called her mobile to speak to her.

'Is everything all right?' She hoped nothing had

happened to Colin since they had last spoken.

'Fine thanks. It's just that Grandad is being discharged from the hospital this morning. I hadn't expected him to be let out so soon and I need to find him somewhere to stay. I know everywhere is full due, and was wondering—' He hesitated.

'Go on,' Piper encouraged. 'I'll do anything to help if I can.'

'This might be a bit tricky.'

'What is it?'

Another hesitation. 'I'll just spit it out,' he said. 'Do you think your gran would let him stay in her spare room? You said before that she might agree to me staying with her, so I thought—'

'Ah, right.' Piper couldn't imagine anything less likely.

'I'm not sure who else I could ask and she was kind enough to take care of his belongings while he was in hospital. I was hoping that she might consider putting him up until you have a vacancy there. What do you think?'

'It's a good idea, Gran might not agree though, Alex. I'll pop round and speak to her for you. You never know, she might be more open to the idea than we expect.'

'I do hope so,' he said. 'Otherwise, I'm not sure what I'll do with him.'

'There would be room at Fliss's friend's house.'

'Probably, but I would rather not ask if I don't have to.'

She was about to end the call then remembered her conversation with Jax and explained that their proposed trip was the same day as his birthday.

'That sounds fine to me,' Alex said, sounding a little happier. 'Please thank Jax from us and say we'll all be looking forward to it.'

Piper couldn't help wishing just her and Alex were going on the trip. 'I'll call you as soon as I've spoken to Gran.'

Without giving herself time to dwell, she headed next door, knocking once and walking in before she lost her nerve. 'Hi, Gran,' she called, noticing a steaming cup of tea on the table next to her grandmother's seat, her tapestry lying on the arm of the chair. 'Where are you?'

'Out the back, lovey.'

Piper took a deep breath and forced a smile onto

her face. She hoped that if she looked confident when she approached Gran, she might be more inclined to react positively. It was worth a try. She stepped outside into the small yard where her grandmother was dead-heading the scarlet geraniums she grew each year, positioned between lavender bushes in the border.

'Need any help?'

Instead of Gran answering, she straightened up and narrowed her eyes. 'What's the matter?'

'Who said anything is wrong?' Sometimes, Piper wished her gran didn't know her so well.

'Something's up.' Gran dropped the handful of dried-up flowers and stems into a bucket at her feet and rested her hands on her hips. 'Don't try to fob me off with piffle about work because I won't be fooled.'

Maybe her grandmother was psychic. 'It's nothing, really.'

'Well spit it out quickly. I want to finish this before my tea goes cold.'

Piper braced herself. 'Colin is being discharged from hospital this morning. We're fully booked, and Alex wondered whether you would let his grandfather stay in your spare room for a few days.' She picked up a stem that her grandmother had dropped so that she didn't have to keep eye contact. 'As soon as we have a vacancy, he can move into the guest house until he's fully recovered. What do you think?'

'Fine.'

'It's just that he doesn't know anyone over here. Well, not anyone he can ask to stay with.'

'I said, it's fine.'

'I'm happy to bring food around for him at mealtimes so that you don't have to—' Her gran's words sank in. 'Did you say it was fine for him to come and stay here, or did I imagine it?'

Gran turned her back on Piper and resumed her dead-heading. 'You heard correctly.'

She couldn't believe how easy it had been. 'Are you certain you don't mind?'

Gran stopped what she was doing and turned. 'Do you want me to change my mind?'

'No! Absolutely not.'

'Right. Then, if you'd like to leave me in peace for now and pop back in an hour to help me make up the bed in the spare room, that would be perfect.'

'Yes, of course.' Piper stepped over to her gran

and kissed her on the cheek. 'Thank you. Alex will be incredibly grateful.'

'Yes, OK. No need to make a fuss.'

Piper left before she annoyed her grandmother any further. She walked a little way along the pier, replaying their conversation, wanting to be certain she hadn't misconstrued Gran's answer in any way. Remembering she had promised to let Alex know, she returned home and called his mobile.

'She said yes.'

'Who did?'

'Gran. She's happy for Colin to stay with her.'

She listened to the silence at the other end of the call. 'Really?'

'I know,' Piper said, unable to help laughing. 'I was as stunned as you are. But I only had to ask her once and she agreed straight away. In fact, I have to go back to her place and help make up his room.'

'I'm amazed, but relieved,' Alex said, sounding both.

'What time will you be dropping him off?'

'He has to see the doctor first and I don't think he starts his rounds for another hour or two. There's no panic. As long as your grandmother doesn't change her mind when she's thought about what she's agreed to.'

'I'm sure she won't.' Gran wouldn't go back on her word once given.

'Thanks very much, Piper. We really appreciate this.' He laughed. 'Well, I'm hoping Grandad will. He'll probably be terrified when he knows where he'll be staying. I'll pop round to see you a bit later once I've settled him in. It would be nice to go out for something to eat, or a walk?'

'That would be lovely,' she said, already looking forward to seeing him again. 'You can let me know how it went once Colin is next door.'

* * *

She went to find her mother and found her sitting quietly, reading outside in the shade for once. Not wishing to disturb her rare opportunity for some alone time, Piper hesitated at the back door and turned to retrace her steps.

'What's the matter?' Helen asked without looking up from her book.

'I don't want to disturb you while you're relaxing,'

Piper said, wishing she had gone straight to her room to do some mosaic work.

Helen placed a slip of paper in between the pages and closed her book, resting it on her lap. 'I'm not reading now, so why don't you come and tell me what's bothering you?'

Piper pulled out the chair opposite her mother's and sat, before explaining what had happened that morning.

'If you'd have asked me to place a bet on your grandmother agreeing to let Colin stay with her, I wouldn't have wasted even fifty pence,' Helen said, clearly astonished. 'But it's good news, right?' Piper nodded. 'Is that what you wanted to talk to me about?' She raised her eyebrows questioningly. 'Or is there something else?'

'I wondered whether I could take over meals for Colin to save Gran from having to buy extra food in and cook it for him.'

'And you'd like *me* to cater for him, I suppose.'

'If you don't mind. We all know how useless I am at cooking anything.'

Helen laughed. 'I'm still trying to recover from

the burned offerings you served to me on Mother's Day.'

Piper thought of the roast she had invited her mother and Gran over to eat that day and what a disaster it had been when she had mistimed how long it would take to roast the chicken and vegetables. 'Exactly.' She gave her mother her most appealing smile. 'Can I take that as a yes?'

Helen gave an affectionate shake of her head. 'You know I will.'

Piper stood and, leaning across the small metal table, kissed her mother on the cheek. 'I'm doing a lot of kissing and thanking people today.'

'I'm probably still in shock about your grandmother being so obliging.' Helen pressed her lips together. 'I hope she's intending on being nice to him.'

'Gran wouldn't be mean to anyone.' Piper was indignant on Gran's behalf.

'Usually I'd agree with you, but we both know that Colin's not her favourite person after turning his back on her when she needed help, all those years ago. He'll be a captive audience, staying in her cottage.'

Piper thought her mother was overreacting. 'I'm

sure he'll be fine,' she said, less convinced than she sounded. 'Hopefully this way they'll have the privacy to find a way to resolve their issues once and for all.'

'Let's hope so,' Helen said. 'Now, if that's all I'll get back to my book. It's really interesting and now that I've got an extra mouth to feed I want to make the most of not cooking while I can.'

Piper knew her mother was teasing. 'I'll leave you in peace then. And thanks again, Mum.'

Her mother blew her a kiss and then waved her away.

* * *

An hour later, Piper shook the top pillow on Gran's spare bed before placing it neatly on the one below. She stepped back and folded her arms, studying the room to be certain she hadn't forgotten anything. She straightened the small carafe and glass sitting on a floral square tray on the bedside table. 'I think that's everything, Gran.'

Her grandmother draped a couple of towels over the vintage towel rail beneath the window. 'I'll be glad when he arrives, and we can get any awkward-ness over with.'

Piper was pleased Gran was being open about her feelings as she often kept them to herself. 'You are all right about this, Gran? I don't want you to feel pressured.'

'It's a bit late for that.' Gran folded her arms across her chest. 'And what would Alex do with the old devil if I did change my mind about having him here?'

Piper thought again of the house where Fliss was staying. There would be plenty of room there. 'He would think of something.'

'Well, as I've already said, it's fine.'

There was a knock at the front door and her grandmother stiffened momentarily before raising her chin, looking more determined than worried.

'I'll run down and let them in,' Piper said.

She reached the door, her heart pounding and a smile fixed on her face. 'Hello, Colin,' she said, opening the door. He looked pale and didn't seem happy to be there. 'Your room is ready for you. We hope you'll be happy here.'

'Hello, Colin,' Gran said, coming to the door behind Piper. 'Welcome to my home.'

A look of discomfort flashed across Colin's face. She shot a glance at Alex, who stepped forward and helped his grandfather inside, placing a leather holdall at the foot of the stairs. Colin was resting heavily on a pair of crutches and looked frail.

'Would you like to see your room first?' Piper asked. 'Or if you'd rather, we could have a cup of tea?' She turned to Gran. 'What would you prefer?'

'I say we sit and have a cup of tea.'

Piper could tell she was enjoying being the one in control. She wasn't sure why Colin seemed so unnerved and wondered whether Alex had only just broken the news about his grandfather's accommodation.

'I'll go and make us all a drink,' she said, eager to have something to do away from the tension in the room.

'I'll come and help you.' Alex followed her into the galley kitchen.

As soon as they were out of earshot, Piper turned to him. 'You didn't warn him where he was going, did you?'

'No.'

'Why ever not?'

'He might have refused to come.'

Piper sympathised. 'But he must feel like he's been ambushed.' She filled the kettle and set it to boil.

Alex had the grace to look troubled. 'I was worried that if he refused to come here then I would have nowhere else to take him.'

Taking a tray, Piper placed four cups and saucers on it. 'Does Colin take milk and sugar?'

Alex nodded. 'A dash of milk and two sugars, please.'

'Pass me the tin in there, will you?' She pointed to a cupboard. 'I'm sure we could all do with a chocolate digestive right now.'

'At least we can't hear yelling,' Alex said dryly.

She gave a reluctant smile. 'Not yet.'

Alex took the tray from her hands and set it back down on the worktop.

'What are you doing?'

He smiled at her. 'I was hoping to make the most of a few seconds alone with you.'

'Oh?'

Placing his arms around her, he lowered his mouth to hers. Piper slid her arms around his neck, and gave herself up to his kiss – he really was the best kisser she had ever met – until Alex suddenly moved back from her, his arms dropping to his sides.

'What's the matter?' she asked, as Gran shouted through from the living room.

'What on earth are you two doing in there?'

Piper heard the amusement in her grandmother's voice, as though she knew exactly what they were doing. 'I do wish she wouldn't do that,' she grumbled, reaching for the tea tray.

'I'll carry that,' Alex said, sighing heavily. 'You take the biscuit tin.' He picked up the tray and gave Piper a smile. 'I was enjoying that, too.'

'So was I,' Piper said, grinning

In the living room, the atmosphere was chilly. Piper was disappointed but reminded herself that Gran had spent many years resenting Colin. Even though he had apologised, it was probably going to take longer than five minutes in her house to forgive him.

She handed a cup to Gran. 'Sorry about the wait.

We were deciding whether or not to put the biscuits onto a plate.'

Gran's look suggested she didn't believe a word. 'I see you decided to bring the tin.'

Piper handed a cup of tea to Colin, who was sitting in the armchair by the window, and held out the biscuit tin. He peered inside and took one. 'These are my favourites,' he said, clearly making an effort to be friendly.

'I remember,' Gran replied without looking at him. 'I'll have one too, please, Piper.'

Piper glanced at Alex and the pair of them sat on the sofa and sipped their drinks. Unable to bear the silence, Piper cleared her throat. 'It's good to have you staying here, Colin.'

Colin looked from Alex to Gran. 'It was kind of you to offer, Margery.'

'My mum will be making your evening meals,' Piper explained. 'She loves cooking and wanted to do her bit to make you welcome.'

Piper sensed her grandmother glaring at her and made a point of not catching her eye. She knew that Gran was a capable cook, but hoped she would accept the help.

'That's very kind of her,' Colin said, dropping biscuit crumbs down his shirt front.

Seeing Alex's tense expression, Piper guessed he was as nervous as she was to leave his grandfather in her grandmother's care.

'So, Colin,' Piper said, trying her best to appear relaxed. 'Did the hospital give you all the medication you need?'

Alex shot her a grateful look. 'Do you need anything, Grandad?'

'It's kind of you both to ask,' Colin said. 'I have everything I need right now. I have your number if I need to call you, Alex.' He looked at Gran and Piper saw something pass between them. She was a little surprised to note that her grandmother didn't seem as put out to have Colin in her house as Piper had expected. *Was she secretly pleased that he wasn't yet fully fit and would have little choice but to listen to anything she said?* Piper shuddered. She hoped that Colin was mentally strong enough to deal with Gran. Her grandmother was tough – she'd had to be, especially after Colin and his wife had turned their backs on her.

'Why don't you two pop off now?' Gran said, interrupting Piper's thoughts. 'Colin and I are perfectly fine left to our own devices. I have all the shopping I need. And if I do need anything I'm more than capable of going out to the shops and getting it for us.'

'If you're sure?' Piper replied, finishing her tea and putting her cup down on the tray.

Alex did the same before turning to his grandfather. 'Is it OK if I leave now, Grandad?' He looked a little unsure.

'Yes, of course. You go off now, my lad.'

Alex rose and rested a hand on his grandfather's shoulder. 'Sure?'

'I'll call you if I need you.'

Alex nodded. 'Thanks, Mrs...?'

'Call me Margery, please.'

'Thanks, Margery.' Alex looked at Piper. 'You ready to go?' Piper nodded and Alex turned his attention back to her grandmother. 'Can I pop in to visit Grandad a bit later?'

'You come here anytime you like,' Gran said, adding as Piper bent to pick up the tray of cups, 'Leave those. I'll do them when we've finished our drinks.'

'OK.' Piper gave her Gran a kiss. 'I'll come around later with supper.'

Piper led the way outside. Alex closed the front door behind them and, without speaking, they began walking down the pier.

'That was a little odd, don't you think?' Piper asked.

'Were you expecting it to be more tense between them?'

'Exactly that.' She frowned and crossed the road to look down at the harbour.

Alex put his arm around her shoulders. 'They'll be fine. They've still got quite a bit of talking to do, I suspect. Let's hope they find a way to put everything behind them and become friends again.'

'I'm sure they'd both feel better if they can do that,' Piper said.

'Either they'll do that, or fall out in a big way,' Alex said grimacing. 'We'll just have to hope it's the former.'

'I'd better get my things from home and then get to the barn.' Piper wished she had a bit more time with Alex. She wasn't sure how much longer he would be staying on the island now that Colin had been discharged from the hospital. 'See you later?'

'That would be great,' he said, bending to kiss her. 'At least we can worry about our grandparents together.'

Piper puffed out her cheeks. 'Honestly, we're supposed to be the difficult ones, not the older generation.'

He laughed. 'Wouldn't that be nice?'

25

Piper walked into the barn and was greeted by Vivienne, who seemed a little overwrought.

'Hi, Vivienne. Is everything all right?'

The older woman followed Piper over to her stall. She seemed to be struggling for words. Piper unlocked her cupboard and took out a stand for the mosaic frame she had brought from home. After locking her rucksack away, she hung up her cotton jacket and waited for Vivienne to speak.

'Colin isn't at the hospital any more.' It was a statement rather than a question. 'Is he staying at your mother's place? I would have expected you to be full this week.'

'He's staying with Gran until Mum has availability to take him in,' she said. 'Alex told me to tell you that you were welcome to visit him in hospital, but he was discharged unexpectedly. I'm sorry I didn't get a chance...' Her words trailed off. Vivienne looked as though she'd been slapped.

'With Margery?'

Piper hadn't realised the two women were acquainted and was taken aback at the way Vivienne almost spat out her grandmother's name. 'That's right. Gran kindly gave him her spare room.'

'I didn't think she liked sharing her home with anyone. Not after so many years running the guest house and having little peace.'

Piper didn't like the tone Vivienne was using. She seemed to be insinuating that there was something underhand in what Gran had done. 'That's probably true, Vivienne,' she said, trying hard to remain polite. 'In this instance, though, she has kindly put herself out to give him a place to stay. After all, it was a little unexpected, and he was rather desperate. Or rather, Alex was desperate to find him somewhere to stay.'

'Desperate, eh?'

Piper could see Casey and Tara were trying not to listen to her conversation. She didn't want to disturb the other stallholders while they were working, and was also beginning to lose patience. 'I'm sorry, Vivienne but I really need to get on.'

'Yes, of course.' Vivienne smoothed down her finely knitted sweater. 'I should be doing the same.'

Piper pretended to tidy her display table. 'No problem at all, Vivienne,' she said politely, relieved to see the woman leave and return to her own pitch.

A coach must have arrived because seconds later the doors opened and thirty to forty people flooded in. One of the first stalls they reached was Vivienne's and while she chatted, Casey and Tara walked over to Piper.

'What the hell was that all about?' Casey whispered.

'We were getting ready to plough in and rescue you,' Tara teased. 'She really was on one, wasn't she?'

Casey pulled a shocked face. 'I've always thought she was a quiet, gentle lady. I've never seen her so animated and furious.'

'Nor have I.' Piper glanced over at Vivienne, now the picture of grace and charm as she smiled and showed off her jewellery to the tourists. 'Talk about having a darker side.'

The cousins giggled. 'Never mind,' Casey said. 'At least you survived.'

Piper sighed. 'Just about.'

Customers made their way over and for the next twenty minutes the three of them were busy making sales. Piper was relieved to have her mind taken off her concerns about Gran and Colin and, glancing at Vivienne, couldn't help thinking that Colin had had a lucky break in more ways than one.

* * *

That afternoon, after all the customers had left and she had locked up her stock, Piper gathered her things and said goodbye to Casey and Tara as she left the barn. Vivienne had already gone, and it occurred to Piper that she hadn't seen her for at least half an hour.

She pushed her thoughts away and focused on seeing Alex again and taking supper round to Gran and Colin. Hopefully, they had spent a pleasant afternoon together.

It was only as she neared Gran's cottage that she realised there was someone else there and decided to go straight in.

'What the—' She stopped dead when she saw who was in the living room. 'Vivienne? What are you doing here?'

Vivienne, standing in the middle of the living room, spun round, seeming surprised to see Piper. 'I've come to collect Colin. He's going to stay at my bungalow.'

'He's what?' Piper gave her grandmother a questioning look, realising that Colin wasn't in the room. 'Where is he?'

'Upstairs,' Gran said through gritted teeth. 'Packing his things.'

'He can barely have unpacked yet, surely,' Piper said. 'Why would he stay with Vivienne? He's perfectly fine here.' Colin entered the living room carrying his small bag a little awkwardly with his crutches. 'Colin? Why are you going? Is something wrong?'

He gave her a sheepish look. 'Vivienne thinks it's probably for the best.'

Piper shook her head. She had no idea what was

going on and wished Alex was there to reason with him. 'Does Alex know where you're going?' She stepped forward and took Colin's bag from him.

'I've left my address on the coffee table,' Vivienne said, taking the bag from Piper.

Piper raised her hands. 'Can we just take a moment? Colin, I don't understand why you're going to stay with someone you barely know. And especially not when it was arranged for you to stay here.'

'But he knows me better than he does Margery,' Vivienne said. 'I might not have known him for years, but we've become close friends during Colin's time at the retreat.'

'Even so, we've arranged for him to stay here.'

Vivienne sighed. 'Piper, I understand this seems odd to you, but Colin has told me all about the... situation with Margery.' She gave Gran a look of distaste that made Piper's hackles rise. 'He should be somewhere he can relax properly while he's recuperating.'

'Now you wait one minute,' Gran said, speaking for the first time. She placed her hands on her hips and jutted her chin in Colin's direction. 'I can deal with her barging into my home because I expect that sort of behaviour.' She didn't bother to address Vivienne. 'But I am surprised that you've confided in someone you barely know about what happened fifty-odd years ago. I thought that was between the two of us.'

'Are you calling me a gossipmonger?' Vivienne asked, her face turning puce.

Gran still didn't address her. 'Colin, obviously you must go if that's what you want, but I won't be coming to find you. I've lived with what happened for all these years, but I'd hoped that after our chat on the beach we could at least talk to each other. Am I wrong?'

Colin looked utterly miserable, and Piper felt sorry that he was being put in such a difficult situation. He turned to Vivienne. 'Margery is right,' he said. 'It is very kind of you to offer me a place to stay, and I do appreciate it.'

'Colin, what are you saying?' Vivienne's eyes widened in surprise.

'I'm afraid I'm going to have to decline your kind invitation. Margery is right. I want to make amends with her. We were friends many years ago and it was my fault that she had no one to turn to when she really needed someone. I need to put things right and staying here will give me the opportunity to speak to her at length,' he said, glancing at Gran. 'We have a lot to talk about.'

Gran seemed to glow with satisfaction at Colin's reply. 'Piper, will you be kind enough to return Colin's case to his room please.'

'Of course.' She took the case gently from Vivienne's grip. 'I'll see you at the barn tomorrow, Vivienne.' She watched as Vivienne's eyes filled with tears and, despite everything, felt sorry for the elderly woman. 'We can talk then if you'd like to.'

Vivienne gave Colin a disappointed glare and then looked at Piper. 'Thank you.'

Piper waited for her to leave before carrying Colin's bag back upstairs, relieved he had spoken up for himself and made a decision that couldn't have been easy.

She returned to the living room to see Gran and Colin seemingly more relaxed with each other than they had been earlier. Piper didn't want to impose on them for one second longer than was necessary.

'I'll leave you be now,' she said, not waiting for

either of them to answer. 'I'll be back with your supper a bit later.'

She arrived home and met her mother coming out of the front room. Helen studied her face. 'You're looking a little troubled. Is anything the matter?'

Piper waved for her mother to follow her and once they were in the kitchen, filled her in on all that had happened next door.

Helen leaned against the worktop and crossed her arms. 'I'm glad he decided to stay with your gran.'

'So am I,' Piper admitted, opening the fridge and taking out a cherry tomato which she popped it into her mouth, letting the sweet flavour fill her senses. 'It got a bit tense in there for a time, but I think they'll be fine.'

'Jax came here earlier, looking for you,' Helen said. 'I gather he's taking a few of you to the Minquiers on Thursday.'

'That's right. I'm looking forward to it.' She was, Piper told herself – even if she couldn't be alone with Alex.

'He asked me to make up a picnic for you all.' Helen indicated the notepad by the toaster.

'That reminds me,' Piper said. 'I need to buy a cake for Jax. It's his birthday that day.'

'Is it?' Helen frowned. 'I must buy him a present, though heaven only knows what. He's impossible to buy for.'

'He is,' Piper agreed. 'Which is why I always make a point of arranging something fun for us both on that day as a treat. At least this year we'll be out for the day, so a cake will have to do.'

'It'll be fun.'

'I hope so.' Piper read the shopping list, written in her mother's neat, rounded handwriting. 'I'm not sure if Fliss and her friend, Phoebe, are vegetarians or vegans,' she said. 'Maybe we should take that into account.'

'Why don't you phone Alex and ask him,' Helen said. 'Then you'll know for certain either way.' Her mother tore off the sheet of notepaper and handed it to Piper. 'I'll let you do the shopping.'

'I'll do it in the morning before I go to the barn.' It would keep her mind from fretting about Vivienne and how she would react when Piper next saw her. She hated to think that there might be an atmosphere between them at work. There were rarely issues among the stallholders and if there were, one of the Ecobichon sisters would intervene and the matter would be resolved.

* * *

Piper was about to call Alex when he arrived at the house. 'I was just about to phone you,' she said, closing the cover on her mobile phone.

'I've just visited Grandad,' he said. 'Do you have time for a walk on the beach?'

'Sure. Come on.'

They walked there in silence. Alex's face was pensive as they reached the bottom of the slipway and took off their shoes.

'Grandad told me what happened with Vivienne,' he said. 'I'm glad you were there.'

'I'm just pleased he changed his mind about going to stay with her.'

'So am I.' He picked up a shell, turning it over in his fingers. 'I found him and your gran in deep conversation when I got there.'

Piper's interest was piqued. 'How did they seem to you?'

He cocked an eyebrow at her. 'Tense. But I believe they were being honest with each other about their feelings and that can only be a good thing, can't it?'

'If they hope to move on from the past, then, yes.' She imagined her grandmother would have found it hard to not talk over Colin and let him say his piece. 'I think Gran has needed this closure for a very long time.'

'Grandad too.' Alex's hand reached for hers. 'It's a shame he didn't reach out sooner.'

'Maybe he was ashamed and put it out of his mind.' Piper tightened her grip, enjoying the warmth of his fingers clasped around hers.

Alex stopped and turned to face her. 'I hope that whatever happens between them, we can still be friends.'

Friends? She would like to be more than that to him but kept quiet and nodded. 'I'd like that.'

'Good.' He moved forward and gave her a light kiss before they walked on again. 'I'm looking forward to our trip with Jax. I've read up online about Les Minquiers or "The Minkies" as they're sometimes known.' He grinned at her. 'They look like something out of a movie.'

'The islands aren't very big, but there's a lot to see over there,' Piper said, pleased he was taking an interest in the place she loved.

'The weather forecast is good, which is just as well,' Alex continued. 'My sister's a bit of a lightweight when it comes to boats.'

At the mention of their outing with Jax, Piper recalled why she had been going to phone him. 'Mum is making us a picnic to take with us on Thursday,' she explained. 'We were wondering whether Fliss or Phoebe are vegetarians or vegans.'

'Fliss is a vegetarian *when* it suits her.'

Piper laughed. 'What does that mean?'

'She eats chicken when there's a roast going at home and also fish. But she's not one for red meat.' He bent to pick up a shard of dark-green glass, dusted off the sand and passed it to Piper. 'I've seen Phoebe eating a ham sandwich, so I'm sure you don't need to worry about her.'

'Great. Thanks.'

'Is there anything I can bring?'

'Maybe a few large bottles of water. Jax probably

won't think to bring basics. He can be a little switched off at times.'

They laughed and Alex raised her hand to his lips and kissed the back of it. 'He's a good bloke, your cousin. I liked him straightaway.'

'Most people do, apart from his father, who never understood why he didn't choose a more sensible occupation.'

Alex pulled a face. 'Like what exactly?'

'Jax is excellent with figures and his father always boasted that he would make a first-rate accountant. Unfortunately for him, Jax had other ideas.'

'I can't imagine him being satisfied sitting at a desk for seven or eight hours a day, can you?'

'Not at all.' Piper thought of her shorts-wearing cousin with his messy hair and relaxed attitude to life. 'I've never seen him in a suit, and I think the last time he wore long trousers was at school.'

'Not even in the middle of winter?'

Piper shrugged. 'Possibly, but only jeans. I don't think Jax has anything formal in his wardrobe.' She shook her head. 'I doubt he even has a wardrobe.'

'The most important thing is that he's a decent chap and he seems to be that.'

Piper was happy that Alex liked Jax. Her cousin was one of the closest people to her and she recalled only too well how much Rick had disliked him. Probably, she thought, because Jax hadn't held back from letting him know that he didn't think Rick was the right person for her. And he had been proved right.

'Now that Colin's out of hospital, I suppose he'll want to go home soon,' she said, anxious to hear the answer.

Alex shrugged. 'I'm not so sure about that. He said to me yesterday that he's hoping to finish the painting course, or at least, sign up for the next one.'

Hope surged through her. 'Then you'll be staying too?' She tried not to show how excited she was at the prospect. 'Or do you have to get back to England for work?'

He stopped walking and looked around as if to check that no one was near enough to hear what he was about to say. 'I'm not supposed to tell anyone but I'm doing a little urgent work as a location manager for a friend of mine.'

'What's that?'

'I'm looking for locations for him. Doing a bit of planning for something.'

Intrigued, Piper tried to imagine what he might be involved with. Nothing came to mind. 'Can you tell me what it's for?'

He smiled, clearly amused by her interest. He cocked an eyebrow and tapped the side of his nose. 'I'd love to tell you, but I'm sworn to secrecy.'

Piper frowned. 'What if I promise not to tell anyone?' She didn't imagine he would tell her, not if he wasn't supposed to, but it was worth a try.

Alex sucked air in through his teeth and clamped his lips together. 'You'd like me to betray my friend just to quell your interest?'

'Why not?' She hadn't grown up with Jax and not learned how to take charge of the situation when someone was teasing her. She grinned and grabbed his waist. He immediately laughed and twisted away. 'I knew it,' she squealed. 'You're ticklish.'

He grimaced and moved away, grasping her by both wrists. 'I am, so you can stop that, young lady.' He laughed loudly and leaped back, holding her at arms' length. 'Stop it. Or I'll—'

'You'll what?' she asked, amused.

'I'm trying to think of something you won't like.'

'Like?' she giggled, confident that he wouldn't do anything nasty to her.

'I'll kiss you.'

Piper stopped trying to grab him. 'That's no threat.'

He shrugged and pulled her towards him, still holding on to her and keeping her from touching his waist. He moved her hands behind her back and held them there. 'Ha! Now, I've got you exactly where I want you.'

'You're not going to fob me off that easily,' she giggled. 'And I'll tickle you again as soon as you let me go if you don't tell me why you're looking at locations. And why it couldn't wait until your grandad was well again?'

Alex kissed her nose. 'I never took you for being nosey,' he teased. 'I guess I was mistaken.'

'Please tell me. By being mysterious, you're making me want to find out more.'

'Right, but if I let you go, you have to promise to sit quietly and listen. And then not repeat a word. Deal?'

She could hardly refuse, not after all the fuss she'd made. 'Deal.'

He let go of her wrists and sat on the sand.

Piper sat opposite him; legs crossed. She leaned her elbows on her knees and cupped her chin in her palms. 'Go on then. I'm listening.'

Alex took a deep breath. 'One of my closest friends, Matteo, is a singer.'

'Don't tell me. It's Matteo Stanford, isn't it?' she joked.

Instead of Alex laughing and giving her a different name, he nodded. 'That's him.'

Piper's mouth dropped open in surprise. 'Are you messing with me?' She grabbed hold of his knee. '*The* Matteo Stanford?'

Alex gave a knowing nod. 'I forget he's pretty famous after that album of his did so well.'

'Did well! Are you kidding me?' She leaned forward and lowered her voice. 'You do know his album was number one in thousands of countries, don't you?'

'Thousands? That many?'

'OK, I can see you're not madly impressed, but I am.' She stared at him. Alex was friends with Matteo Stanford. She couldn't take it in. Close friends. 'This is massive.' She remembered she had promised not to tell anyone. 'And I can't tell Casey or Tara? Or Jax?'

'No one.'

She wished she hadn't been so quick to make promises she was desperate not to keep. 'You're enjoying this, aren't you?'

He grinned at her. 'I am. Very much.' He laughed. 'Matteo is just a regular guy once you get to know him.'

'That's easy to say when you're his buddy.' She should stop acting like a hormonal teenager. It hadn't been a good look when she was younger and certainly wasn't the image she wanted to portray.

'Tell you what, I'll introduce you to him when he comes over.'

Piper gasped in shock, her hand flying to her chest. 'Seriously? You'd do that for me?'

He laughed. 'Of course, I will.' He leaned forward and kissed her. 'Then you can see for yourself what a nice bloke he is. I never think of him as famous. Although,' – he held up a hand as she started to argue with him – 'I am aware that he is. He always wanted to be a singer-songwriter so now he's making something of himself we're happy for him, but it's hard to be starstruck by someone you've known since you were four.'

It struck Piper afresh that she was in the company of a man she liked very much. More than liked. 'I'm sorry,' she said. 'I don't know what's come over me.'

He shrugged. 'It's fine. My sister was the same and she's known Matteo forever, like I have. I don't think she took much notice of him until her friends began to make a fuss after his first single hit the top of the charts so quickly.'

Alex was making Matteo sound very down to earth. Piper liked to think that the handsome singer was the same in real life as he appeared to be in television interviews. 'Has he changed at all since he became successful?'

He gave her question some thought. 'A little, but not as a friend. He's just more wary of people than he used to be, but that's something he's had to learn to do to protect himself.'

'Poor guy. He'll probably be fine here. The locals are used to seeing well-known people around the island. They don't tend to get all silly over them.'

Alex looked at her, amusement dancing in his eyes.

She punched his shoulder lightly. 'I might have just acted like a fool, but I wouldn't if I saw him out in public. I'd be calm and dignified.'

'You're sure about that?'

'Shut up!' She remembered that he still hadn't told her exactly what he was doing for Matteo. 'So, why are you looking for locations and why the rush?'

'He's coming over to record his next album at a recording studio on the west of the island. While he's here he wants to shoot his next music video.'

'When?' She didn't want to sound too enthusiastic but reasoned she may as well get all the information he was willing to give her in case he decided to change the subject.

'In a few weeks' time. He has to fit it in between a massive tour he's doing. It was supposed to be a little later in the year but it was such a sell-out that his management team have asked him to agree to a few extra dates, which he has. Now he's in a bit of a panic to get the recording sorted. He wants me to find somewhere suited to the song where they can film it.'

Piper's mind raced. 'If you let me hear it, I might

be able to help you. I know lots of people. I'm sure I can come up with the perfect place.' She wasn't sure at all, but she had no intention of letting an opportunity like this pass her by. Anyway, she reasoned, she did know lots of amazing places on the island and was fairly certain she would be able to find somewhere suitable.

'Maybe. I'll have to clear it with Matteo first.' He grinned at her. 'It won't be for a while yet though, so I wouldn't get too impatient.'

Piper brushed sand from her hands. 'That's fine,' she fibbed. 'I can be very patient when I want to be.'

Alex stood and, taking her hands in his, pulled her to her feet. 'For now, though, we should concentrate on our outing with your cousin. I'm looking forward to it.'

'So am I.'

'The weather forecast has changed,' he said. 'I checked online and it looks like there's a stormy front coming from France tonight.'

Piper knew Jax and Dan didn't take people out for trips in stormy weather and said so. 'I'd hate for you all to miss the experience,' she said, aware that he and Fliss probably wouldn't be on the island for much longer, but relieved that his scouting meant he would be coming back more often.

Piper felt anxious at the prospect. 'Is it supposed to be better tomorrow?'

'Yes, a bit. I suppose we'll just have to cross fingers that it is.'

She crossed fingers on both her hands. 'We certainly will.'

26

'Fliss, why are you standing over there?' Alex grumbled, raising his hands before letting them drop to his sides in annoyance. 'You look as if you're waiting for someone.'

Piper heard the irritation in his voice and was glad he had asked the question that had been going round in her head. Fliss did seem intent on delaying their departure, for some reason.

Alex walked away from his sister, shaking his head, and went to help Jax load the rest of the cool bags onto the craft.

Piper wondered if there was something wrong that

Fliss was too embarrassed to share with her brother. She decided to go and check. Jax was a patient man, but liked to be punctual where work was involved.

She walked over to where Fliss and Phoebe were talking in voices so low she couldn't hear what they were saying. Phoebe noticed her and nudged her friend. Fliss stopped talking, raising her chin. 'Yes?' she said, looking at Piper as if she'd just belched in her face rather than smile at her.

Piper didn't understand why Fliss seemed so intent on disliking her. As far as she was aware, she hadn't done anything to offend her. 'I was wondering if there was anything I could do to help?'

Fliss frowned and then glanced at Phoebe and they shared an amused giggle. Phoebe walked away towards the slipway, leaving them together.

'I heard Alex asking whether you were waiting for someone.'

'Why would I confide in you if I was?'

Stung by the nasty comment, Piper felt her hackles rise. 'Listen, Fliss, today has been kindly arranged by my cousin, but if you don't want to come just say so. I'm sure you can catch the bus back to

Phoebe's place. If you do want to join us, then let's get a move on.'

'Fine,' Fliss snapped. She glanced once more in the direction of the oncoming traffic as it rounded the bend towards them. 'Come on then,' she said, marching towards the slipway and down to the boat where the rest of their group was waiting. Piper followed, trying hard not to lose her patience. So much for them getting along.

'Nice of you to join us finally, Fliss,' Alex said, helping her onto the boat.

A few minutes later, they were all in their seats and settled. Alex sat next to Piper and murmured his thanks, cocking his head to his sister sitting in front of them next to Phoebe. 'Sorry about my badly behaved sister. She's not normally this annoying, but she does have her moments and they're usually when you'd least like them to be.'

'It's all right. We're here now.' Piper smiled over at Jax, who gave her a thumbs up.

'Now we're all strapped in securely, let's go and enjoy our adventure together.' Jax then waved from his seat and gave Fliss a shy smile as his friend Dan started the engine of the ribbed inflatable boat.

Several groups of visitors strolling above them along St Catherine's Breakwater stopped to watch as the RIB slowly moved forward. As soon as the craft reached deeper waters, the boat took off at a speed that made Piper's heart sing, and Fliss and Phoebe shriek noisily.

The weather was perfect. The threatened storm hadn't materialised and the sun was shining, the water almost mirror-like in its stillness. It couldn't be much better.

It was eleven forty-five, but Piper had been up since six o'clock, setting up the dining room for her mother and helping clear away the breakfast dishes after taking a cooked breakfast to her gran and Colin who, she was relieved to note, appeared to be fairly relaxed in each other's company.

She had collected Jax's blue-and-white iced birthday cake from the bakery in the village where she and her mother always bought their cakes. She glanced at the square cool box her mother had lent her for the cake. So far, Jax hadn't noticed it or wondered what was inside.

'I'm sorry we kept everyone waiting,' Alex said, reaching out to take her hand and apologising for the third time. 'Fliss is usually quite good with timing, but she and Phoebe are a bad influence on each other.'

'It's fine, really.' Piper gave his hand a squeeze. 'They're here now and it's not as if we had to take any other visitors into account.' Jax had started to look annoyed that his friend was being made to wait, but relaxed as soon as he spotted Fliss. 'And my cousin seemed to get over it quite quickly.'

'My sister does tend to have that effect on men, for some reason.'

Piper looked at the women sitting in front of her and Alex. She hadn't missed the surprise on Jax's face on being introduced to Fliss. She was so different to the types of girls her cousin had been attracted to in the past that Piper hadn't thought, for one second, he might have chemistry with Alex's fashion-perfect sister. The women he usually dated were mostly beach-loving, dog-loving, make-up free, shorts and T-shirt wearing women. Fliss, on the other hand, had a line-free forehead, long lashes that Piper suspected came from a clinician, and lips that were a lot fuller than her brother's, suggesting they didn't run in the family.

Fliss and Phoebe giggled happily in front of them. Piper had heard the nervousness in Phoebe's voice when she got on the boat and hoped she would be all right. She didn't fancy them having to cut their outing short, especially when it was Jax's birthday, and her mother had spent so much time making the lunches.

Piper had been out a couple of times before with Jax but the weather had never been this idyllic. She closed her eyes and gave herself over to a sense of freedom as the wind whipped through her hair.

The boat slowed and Jax waved his hand up and down to indicate they should be silent. He pointed ahead and Piper peered in the direction of his finger and gasped as she saw a pod of dolphins playing in the sea.

'Alex,' she whispered, tugging on his arm. 'Look, over there.'

He did as she instructed, and his mouth opened in surprise. 'Oh, Piper. Aren't they magnificent creatures?'

'They are.' She had seen dolphins swimming close to the island's shores many times over the years, but the novelty never wore off. Piper felt enormously lucky to be able to enjoy a spectacle like this so near to her home.

Even Fliss and Phoebe seemed impressed, snapping photos on their phones, the sun shining on their glossy hair, while Jax watched their reaction with a smile on his face.

After a while the boat moved slowly forward, picking up speed when they were far enough away from the dolphins. She spotted the tiny islands coming closer and looked forward to Alex and the girls enjoying the unique experience for the first time.

* * *

As Dan docked, Jax held out a hand to help everyone disembark from the rubber vessel. She noticed him hold his smile for Fliss a little longer than he did for everyone else, and when they were all on land he signalled for Piper to join him.

'Help me get these off, will you?'

Piper took the first load of brown bags containing the picnic lunches her mother had prepared.

'Here, let me carry those for you.' Alex stepped

forward to take the cool boxes of drinks from Jax.

'Cheers, mate. Put all that over there, will you? We'll get everyone settled and then figure out who has what.'

Finally, having chosen where they wanted to sit and who with, Piper helped Jax hand out the picnic bags and serve the drinks. She was enjoying herself, despite the earlier frosty confrontation with Fliss.

'Come and sit here with me,' Alex said, patting a smooth boulder next to him and taking their bags of food from her. She fetched them each a bottle of beer and made herself comfortable.

'What do you think of the trip so far?' she asked, indicating the tiny islands surrounding the one they were on. 'This one is the largest island and is called Maîtresse Île.' She pointed to the little cottages built many years before.

'It's incredible,' Alex said, looking around them. 'Who are these cottages for?'

'I gather some are used by the fishermen and others are owned by locals who come out here for brief visits. I wouldn't mind having something like this to escape to occasionally.'

'Neither would I.' He frowned thoughtfully. 'Although you wouldn't want to be here during a bad storm.'

Piper laughed. 'Why would you even think of something like that when it is so beautiful today?' Then again, he had a point. These little stone cottages might look strong, and had survived many storms over the years, but it wouldn't be remotely fun to have to sit through one.

'So, how far from Jersey are we now?' Alex asked.

'Nine miles, give or take,' Jax said, overhearing. He cocked his head in Piper's direction. 'I hope my cousin has been filling you in on the interesting background about this place?'

'I have, actually.' She pulled a face at him. 'I'm trying to imagine anything I might have forgotten.'

Jax rested his hands on his hips. 'Have you told him the name of this island?'

'She has,' Alex said. 'And about who owns and uses the cottages.'

Jax thought for a moment. 'I bet she didn't mention that these buildings are Britain's most southerly properties, did she?' He gave her a knowing wink before walking away to speak to Dan about something.

'Bugger,' Piper groaned. 'I always forget something.' Secretly she was glad Jax had come over to help share the information about Les Minquiers. He was so much better at these things than she could ever be.

* * *

'Magical.' Alex pulled his T-shirt over his head and unbuttoned his jeans, letting them drop and kicking them off. Folding them roughly, he placed his clothes on the rock next to them.

Unable to resist staring at him, Piper then squeezed her eyes shut and shook her head. She was behaving like a teenager. Deciding to make the most of the sun, too, she took off her T-shirt and shorts, folding them neatly next to Alex's. She was glad she had thought to put her bikini on under her clothes. She knew from experience that they would have enough time to let their swimming costumes dry if they didn't leave swimming until too late.

Alex picked up the towel he'd brought and spread it on the ground. 'I see we've both had the same idea.' He indicated his red swimming shorts. 'Shall we eat first?'

'Good idea.' She handed him one of the bags and took the bottle of water he was holding out.

'I know we were going to have beers, but I'm rather dehydrated after being on the boat,' he said.

Piper took out the Portuguese roll with lettuce, tomato, edam cheese and mayonnaise that her mother had made. It was her favourite. She was so hungry after missing breakfast that morning and she took a bite, closing her eyes blissfully as the delicious, familiar flavours hit her tastebuds. 'What is it?' she said, realising Alex was watching her.

He laughed. 'I'm hoping I have the same to eat as you do.'

'Mum made the lunches and knows what I like,' she said, devouring the roll.

'Which is?'

She told him.

'That does sound good,' he grinned. After peering into his bag, he took out his own crispy roll and unwrapped the napkin. 'It looks like I have ham, lettuce, tomato and, yes, mayonnaise.'

'Is that a good thing?'

'Very good.' He took a bite and closed his eyes, groaning in exaggerated pleasure.

It dawned on Piper that he was teasing her and mimicking her reaction to her food. She nudged him, nearly knocking his food from his hand. 'Ooh, sorry. I didn't mean to do that quite so hard.'

'You're lucky I didn't drop it,' he said, pursing his lips theatrically. 'Otherwise I would have taken yours and eaten it.'

'Too late,' Piper said, licking her lips before taking a long drink of cold water.

They ate the remainder of their lunch in companionable silence. By the looks of things, Fliss and Phoebe were more interested in taking photos for their Instagram accounts than eating. Piper saw them strip off to their underwear and then help hold each other's towels while they changed into their bikinis. Then, dropping their towels, they ran into the clear turquoise sea, splashing each other and laughing.

'There's something wrong, but I'm not sure what it is,' Alex said, watching his sister.

Piper was surprised. Fliss seemed fine to her. 'Can't you ask her?'

'I would, but it probably wouldn't lead to any answers, only a quarrel.'

Piper was relieved for the first time that she didn't have a sister. She bit into the apple her mother had packed with her roll. 'She's got a lot of energy,' she said. 'I wish I had some of it. I'm always tired.'

Alex's head snapped round. 'You have two jobs,' he said. 'My sister barely gets out of bed before noon. There's no comparison.' He rubbed his face, looking suddenly tired.

'She doesn't have a job?'

He frowned. 'She's had quite a few, but can't seem to stick at anything for more than a few weeks. It drives my parents crazy, and now they're talking about cutting off their financial support, hoping to give her the incentive to find something and stick to it.'

Piper couldn't help thinking how Fliss might discover she was happier to be achieving something if she did find a job she enjoyed. 'Different lifestyles, I suppose.'

'She could learn a lot from you, Piper.' Alex glanced at her. 'Fliss's jobs only last a few months. I'm sure she'd be much happier if she found something worthwhile to fill her days, or even if she went travelling for a few months.'

Shielding her eyes with her hand, Piper looked at Fliss, posing for yet another photo in the water. She seemed happy enough, but you never knew what was going on in someone's mind. 'Maybe you're worrying too much,' she said to Alex.

At that moment, Fliss walked out of the water, grabbed her towel, roughly dried herself and came over to stand in front of them.

'Is the water as warm as it looks?' Piper asked in her friendliest voice.

Fliss looked at her from under her long eyelashes and gave a one-shouldered shrug. 'Does it look warm?'

'Don't be facetious, Fliss,' Alex said lightly. 'What's wrong with you today?'

Today? Piper wished his sister's high-handed attitude had only been aimed at her once.

Alex screwed up his paper napkin and dropped it into the empty lunch bag. 'Why were you acting so strangely at the dock today?'

She gave him a confused look, and then her eyebrows rose. 'Ah, you mean at St Catherine's.'

'You know exactly what I mean. Tell me what you were up to because I know it was something.'

Fliss gave a bored sigh. 'I was waiting for Naomi.'

'Naomi Giles?'

Piper couldn't miss the shock on Alex's face, swiftly followed by anger. Whoever this Naomi was, she'd caused quite a reaction and Piper was intrigued.

Fliss glanced at her, raising her eyebrows slightly. '*Your girlfriend*, Naomi,' she said with a triumphant smile. 'Honestly, Alex, don't act as if you haven't heard of her. You live together after all. You saw her when you left your flat the other day.'

'Hang on a second, Fliss. You know it's not—'

Fliss put her fingers in her ears. 'I'm not listening to you.'

A shockwave ran through Piper. *Alex had a girlfriend? A girlfriend he lived with?* Her mind raced. *How could he have kissed her so many times, said he loved spending time with her, when all the time he was living with a partner? And why was she so shocked?* It wasn't as if she hadn't been cheated on before. Clearly her taste in men hadn't improved since then.

'Why would Naomi be in Jersey?' Alex asked, shooting Piper a pleading look as she sat very still, not wanting Fliss to see how rattled she was.

'Because I invited her,' Fliss said, directing her words at Piper.

It was the last straw. She didn't want to hear whatever Fliss had to say, or listen to her discussing Alex's girlfriend with him. She picked up her lunch bag and stood.

'Please don't go, Piper,' Alex said, reaching for her hand.

She stepped away from him. 'You two obviously have things to talk about.'

Alex went to stand, but Piper waved for him to stay where he was. 'Please carry on. I want to have a chat with my cousin.'

'Piper, wait. I can explain everything.'

She noticed Phoebe, Jax and Dan, who was sitting on the boat reading, turn their heads to see what was going on. 'No, please don't. If you have anything to say to me, it can wait until another time. I don't want to put a dampener on anyone's day.'

She turned and walked away without giving him a second to reply. It stung to think she might have been wrong to trust her instincts where Alex was concerned, but she had managed to move on after her break-up with Rick and had no intention of feeling sorry for herself now.

Jax broke away from the others. 'Is everything all right?' he asked, falling into step beside her.

'It's fine,' she said, to reassure him. 'Just something Fliss and Alex need to discuss and I didn't think I should be sitting there listening into a private conversation.' She forced a smile, remembering the cake. 'Stay there for a minute, will you?' She tapped the side of her nose when Jax asked why. 'It's a surprise. But only a little one as we're out today.'

'What have you done?' He looked wary.

'Nothing horrible.' She mustered a smile. 'Maybe a little embarrassing, but that's too bad.'

'Urgh.'

Piper opened the cool box and carefully lifted out Jax's cake. After placing it carefully on the lid, she clapped her hands to get everyone's attention. She had no intention of letting Fliss's nastiness ruin Jax's birthday.

All eyes turned in her direction. 'If you wouldn't mind, I have a small announcement to make.' She noticed Alex's eyes widening and assumed he thought she was going to tell everyone about his girlfriend. 'Today is Jax's birthday and I've brought along a cake to celebrate the occasion.'

Everyone cheered, except Fliss who didn't seem very happy that the attention wasn't on her.

Alex was trying to catch her eye, but she looked away.

'Happy birthday, Jax,' Phoebe said, coming over to join them.

'I don't have any candles and Jax will hate it if we sing happy birthday, so I won't put him through that, but here's the knife to cut your cake and make a wish.' She handed it over, relieved her mother had remembered to put it into the cool box. 'Some traditions have to be followed.'

Jax stood and gave a theatrical bow. He caught Piper's eye and smiled. Despite his embarrassment, Piper saw how pleased he was that she had remembered and surprised him.

'Thanks,' he said. 'I'm glad you're all here to enjoy this with me and, knowing my cousin as I do, trust that this cake will be delicious. So,' he said, raising the knife. 'Here goes.'

Once he'd made a deep cut, to a round of applause, Piper cut enough slices and served them on paper plates. Phoebe made the most of the situation by flinging her arms around Jax's neck and planting a kiss on his lips. Jax glanced at Piper in shock and then said something to Phoebe before kissing her on the cheek.

They all settled down once more as they ate, Piper taking care to keep some distance from Alex and Fliss, and once she'd finished her cake announced she was going for a swim.

Jax stared at her, his mouth open in shock. 'Blimey, is this because it's my birthday?'

'Of course not,' she said. 'I just fancy a swim.'

He laughed. 'You, properly swimming. In the sea?'

She gave Jax a playful punch. She would rather have hugged him for cheering her up just when she needed it, but that might tip him off that something was wrong. She was surprised he hadn't noticed her avoiding Alex and Fliss.

'She's very pretty, don't you think?'

Piper hoped he was referring to Phoebe, but when she looked over her shoulder saw that he meant Fliss. Her mood dipped even further. Her cousin was a kind, thoughtful man and she didn't relish the thought of him getting involved with someone like Alex's sister.

'Piper?'

'Yes, I suppose she is.' She forced a smile. 'She's not really your type though.'

'What do you mean?' He seemed hurt that she wasn't being positive about someone he liked.

Piper knew she had to be careful. She didn't want to fall out with Jax. 'I just mean that she seems very worldly.'

He looked baffled. 'What is that supposed to mean? I've travelled all over the world.'

That was true. She also knew he had had quite a few girlfriends in his time, but doubted any of them were as cosmopolitan as Fliss. 'I just mean she's more of a city girl than the women you usually spend time with.'

* * *

Later, as Piper floated on her back in the sea, arms outstretched and staring up at the azure-blue sky, she thought about how perfect the day would have been if she hadn't discovered that Alex had been keeping a vital piece of information about himself from her.

She pushed the thought away and closed her eyes, relishing the refreshing shallow water as the sun warmed her body.

She heard Fliss chatting flirtatiously with someone a little further away, but didn't think anything of it until Jax replied.

'Any time you want me to take you out foraging or exploring the island, you let me know,' he said.

'I will.' She didn't sound very certain, Piper mused with relief. 'My brother was telling me about your adorable little dog,' Fliss added.

'I don't think everyone would agree with him about Seamus being adorable,' Jax laughed. 'He can be naughty sometimes.'

'A little like his owner, maybe?' she teased.

Piper's mood soured. Forgetting she was floating, she tried to stand and slipped under the surface for a second, swallowing a mouthful of salty water. Mortified, she kicked her feet until they found the seabed. Coughing until her throat hurt, she waded onto the island and went to grab her water.

Alex reached it first, unscrewed the lid and

handed it to her. 'Here you go.'

She took it and after several mouthfuls managed to get her coughing under control. 'Thank you,' she croaked, drinking a bit more. 'Bugger.'

Alex ran over to the cool box and brought her a fresh bottle out. 'Why don't you sit down?'

'I will, but I don't want to talk about Naomi.' She hoped her tone didn't invite an argument and was relieved when he simply smiled.

'Do you mind if I sit next to you?'

'No. Of course, I don't,' she said, making an effort to sound natural.

'I thought what you did for Jax was lovely.'

'We usually spend his birthday out and about, so I wanted to do something for him.'

Alex was silent for a few minutes. 'Can we speak properly when we get back?'

Piper was about to say something cutting about Naomi, but thought better of it. 'I don't know what there is to talk about. I just want to make the most of this blissful scenery and relax.'

Fliss shrieked with laughter and Piper and Alex turned to see what was going on.

'I have a suspicion she likes your cousin,' he said

quietly.

'I suspect he reciprocates those feelings.' Piper wished it wasn't the case. She really didn't want Fliss let loose on Jax.

As if reading her thoughts, Alex said, 'He'll be fine. I know you're protective of him and Fliss can be a little...' He stared at his sister thoughtfully. 'Dogmatic at times, but she's a sweetheart underneath.'

Piper supposed that Alex knew his sister far better than she did.

'I'm so sorry she invited Naomi to come over.'

Piper's stomach clenched. 'We agreed not to discuss this here.'

He nodded. 'I know. Sorry.' He gazed at her. 'I was hoping today would be perfect. And it could've been. I mean look at this place.' He opened his arms to encompass the beautiful scenery around them.

She stopped herself from saying that it would have been idyllic if she hadn't discovered he was involved with someone while pretending to be single.

'I'll just say one thing, if you don't mind.'

Piper sighed. 'Fine, go on then.'

'I know it looks as if I'm not, but I am single.'

Piper shook her head. 'That's not what your sister

said, and I didn't hear you correcting her.'

He took her hands in his. 'I was shocked that she invited Naomi over here. I promise you I'm not in a relationship with her.' He frowned. 'Not any more.'

'You're not?'

'No. I promise you that. But it is complicated.'

Of course it is, Piper thought. 'I want to believe you, Alex. Really, I do. But after my experience with Rick, I've been a lot more careful about trusting anyone else.' She slowly pulled her hands from his hold. 'Especially someone who appears to have a partner.'

'I will prove to you that this is all a horrible mis-understanding.'

She hoped he would do exactly that. 'Good.'

They tidied up their belongings and placed all their rubbish into bags before loading everything onto the craft. Then, taking their original seats, Dan took them back to St Catherine's.

* * *

Piper focused on enjoying every blissful moment of the boat ride. They stopped once again to watch several dolphins playing, leaping into the air and relishing their freedom. The scene made Piper smile and her heart soar. How could she worry about a new, fragile relationship when there was such magnificence to witness?

Dan passed the breakwater and then pushed the throttle forward and sped up, steering the boat in a large circle in the bay and making Piper, Fliss and Phoebe scream in fear and excitement.

Slowing down, he brought the RIB to the slipway and docked. Jax stepped out and helped them to disembark.

'Thank you for an amazing day,' Phoebe said, her nose pink from too much sun.

'Yes, thank you.' Piper hugged Jax and kissed Dan on the cheek before taking Jax's strong hand and stepping onto the slipway. Her legs felt wobbly, and her skin tingled after a day in the sun despite covering herself in factor thirty before leaving home and then applying it once more after her swim. 'It was the best fun I've had in ages.'

Alex handed Jax the rubbish bags and cool bags before getting off. He opened his mouth to speak and then noticed something above him and stopped, staring upward.

Piper and Jax followed his line of vision and she saw a beautiful, tall, blonde woman leaning over the white painted railings on the edge of the breakwater.

The woman waved at Fliss and then at Alex. 'I made it!' she announced as if expecting them to be delighted.

'I'll meet you up near the café,' Alex said to the woman. 'My bike's parked up there.' He thanked Jax and Dan. Fliss and Phoebe took it in turns to hug Jax and shout their thanks to Dan, before running up to greet the woman.

Alex turned to Piper, seemingly at a loss as to what to say next.

'Naomi?' she asked, unable to think how to react.

'Yes.' He took a deep breath. 'I'd better go. I'll call round later if that's all right?'

'It might be best if you leave it until tomorrow,' she said, not wanting to make it easy for him.

He opened his mouth to add something, but Piper shook her head and pointed towards the top of the slipway. 'I think you should get going. Naomi and your sister are waiting for you.'

27

Piper was determined to push Alex and his situation, whatever that might be, out of her mind. She had other worries to deal with. She drove back to the pier, parked, and decided to go in and check on her grandmother before going home, to let her know that Jax had enjoyed his birthday cake.

She knocked once and the door opened under the pressure. Hearing voices, she walked in to see Vivienne in the living room holding Colin's bag, and him standing next to her.

'What's going on?' she asked, deciding that if Gran didn't think it was her business then she would tell her soon enough.

Colin stepped forward on his crutches, looking apologetic. 'I was just thanking Margery for taking me in over the past couple of days.'

'You're leaving?' She looked from him to Vivienne. 'He's going to stay with you?'

'Yes,' Vivienne said. She raised her free hand. 'I didn't instigate him leaving, if that's what you're thinking, Piper.'

Vivienne seemed rather uncomfortable holding his case in her grandmother's home when only the other day she had been asked to leave.

'I don't understand.' Piper turned her attention to her grandmother. 'Gran? Are you all right with this?'

'I am, sweetheart.' She patted the sofa next to her. 'Come and sit here and I'll tell you all about it.' She looked over at Colin. 'Now, off you go, you two. We'll meet for that lunch when you're feeling steadier on your feet, Colin,' she said, obviously happy with the turn of events. 'Nice to see you again, Vivienne. I'll look forward to meeting you at that same lunch,' she grinned. 'Unless you both decide that you'd rather have a little time without the other one around.' She winked at them.

'Would you like me to carry that bag to your car,

Vivienne?' Piper asked, unable to let the fragile-looking older woman struggle with it alone.

'No, thank you, dear,' Vivienne replied, shifting the bag from one hand to the other. 'I can cope perfectly well.'

Piper raced to hold the front door open for Vivienne and Colin. 'Bye, then.'

She closed the door behind them, and turning to her grandmother raised her arms. 'Well? What's happened now?'

'Colin's gone to stay in Vivienne's bungalow,' Gran said, her eyes twinkling mischievously.

'I worked that much out for myself, thank you.' She looked at her grandmother suspiciously. 'You've been up to something, haven't you?'

Gran raised her eyebrows and tried to appear innocent. 'I'm sure I don't know what you mean.'

'Tell me.'

'Fine.' She sat back and folded her arms across her chest. 'First, I need you to make a fresh pot of tea. This one is cold.' She nodded at the coffee table, littered with empty cups and saucers. 'Oh, and bring a couple of those delicious butterfly sponge cakes your mum brought over this morning. Then I'll tell you everything.'

Piper knew there was no point in pleading with Gran to tell her what had happened until she did exactly as she asked.

* * *

Five minutes later, Piper sat waiting as Gran poured them both a cup of tea. Then, settling back in her seat, she pressed her hands together for a few seconds. 'While you were out earlier, Colin and I had a long talk about your grandfather, his late wife, Iris, and how they had all treated me. He admitted how he had believed your grandfather to be an honest and decent man and that it was only when Colin approached Peter to tell him that he wanted to part ways and set up on his own in business that he began to discover what a truly controlling, vindictive and nasty piece of work Peter was. It was also then that he and Iris talked and came to the conclusion that the things I had accused Peter of were most likely true.'

'Did it make you feel better to hear him tell you all that?'

Her gran reached forward to take her cup and saucer from the tray. 'It did. He said he had written to me, as had Iris.'

'You never mentioned getting letters from them.' Piper was confused.

'I didn't. Initially they didn't send them because they worried they had left it too long. Then, later, they realised they had no idea where to send them, so gave up any thought of trying. So I never heard from them and just buried my hurt deep inside.'

Piper reached out and rested her hand on her grandmother's arm. 'I'm so relieved you've finally heard what Colin had to say face to face. It might not have come across as well in a letter; you probably needed to see his face to truly understand how he felt about the whole horrible business.'

'Yes, you're right.'

'But are you happier about everything now you've had a long chat?'

'I am.' Gran took a sip of her tea. 'Eat one of those,' she instructed, pointing to one of the sponge cakes with the butterfly and buttercream top. 'You know how good they are.'

Piper picked one and took a bite. As she chewed, it dawned on her that Gran hadn't said anything about Vivienne. Swallowing, she took a drink from her cup. 'So how come Vivienne was here?'

Gran took her time finishing her cake. 'I called her.'

Piper gasped, spilling her tea. She let her grandmother take her cup from her as she pulled a clean tissue from her pocket and dabbed at the drops of liquid on her T-shirt.

'Gran! Why? What happened?'

Before her grandmother had a chance to answer, the front door opened, and Helen walked in. She blew a strand of hair from her face and lowered the full shopping bags she was carrying onto the wooden floor, looking flustered.

Piper stood and went to greet her. 'Are you OK, Mum?'

Helen motioned for her to sit back down. 'Yes, just hot. It's warmer than it usually is at this time of year,' she said, fanning her face.

'Do you need me to take the shopping next door

for you?' Piper knew something was amiss but had no idea what it could be.

'No, it's fine. I'll do it as soon as I find out why I've just seen Vivienne driving Colin away.' She looked at her mother. 'Mum? Please tell me you haven't quarrelled with him. I was hoping his stay with you had finally put the past to rest.'

She sat on the armchair opposite, looking deflated.

'Yes, Gran,' Piper said. 'You still haven't told me what happened. Why has he gone to stay with Vivienne?'

'Oh, calm down both of you. Everything's fine.'

Helen crossed her legs and visibly relaxed. 'It is?'

'Yes. We had a long chat last night.' She yawned as if to reiterate the fact. 'I'm still tired this morning. All that delving back to such a dark time. I didn't like going there, but I knew that you two were keen for me to sort this and so I forced myself.'

Piper rested a hand on her grandmother's. 'It was for your own benefit too.'

'I know. It was a bit of a struggle at first, but it wasn't easy for him either.' She patted Piper's hand, her own trembling slightly. 'But this has needed to happen for a long, long time and I think now the two of us can find some peace.'

'I'm so relieved,' Piper said, brushing away a tear with the back of a finger. 'I believe this business has haunted you far more than you ever let on.'

'It did.'

Piper wanted to be certain that everything had really been resolved. 'And you don't feel as much anger towards Colin and Iris now you've spoken to him and got his side of things?'

'I don't.' Gran sighed. 'After all, how can I hold it against them that they took Peter's word over mine when I trusted his honesty for so long? I think I was mostly hurt that they did, but then Peter was a cunning man and a liar and although Colin didn't tell me what he said about me, he intimated that Peter insinuated that I had been having an affair, which was his reason for slapping me.'

'The rotten sod.'

Piper felt sorry for her mother in that moment. Her own father wasn't the most perfect man, by a long shot, but he'd never been abusive in any way, just completely selfish. 'Gran, I'm so sorry that Iris didn't believe you. Or Colin.'

'Who knows what we would all do in their situation,' Gran said thoughtfully. 'I hope that I'd stand by my friend, but it was years ago, and we were very young and innocent.' She shook her head. 'I don't know. I'm just relieved now to have cleared the way between us so that we can have some sort of friendship.' She smiled. 'And that's why I phoned Vivienne and suggested she come and invite him to stay with her.'

Helen gasped. 'You called her?'

'But why?' Piper asked, confused. 'And where did you get her number from?'

Gran sat back in her chair and raised her hands. 'One question at a time, if you don't mind. Flippin' heck, this is like what those celebrities have to deal with in interviews.'

Gran was obviously happier if she was joking. She looked at Helen. 'I called Vivienne because I thought if Colin stayed here, we would feel we had to keep discussing what had happened. And I don't know about him, but I had said and heard all I needed to. I also wanted my house back and I could tell that he and Vivienne liked each other.' She turned to Piper. 'I got her number by phoning The

Cabbage Patch.'

Piper grinned. Of course she had. 'I'm glad you're happier now, Gran. And I'm pleased that he's spending some time with Vivienne if that's what they want. I felt a little mean when she was practically thrown out of here the other day.'

'So did I,' Gran said.

Helen stood and walked over to her mother, bending to hug her. 'Well done, Mum.' She stood up straight again. 'Right. Well, I have a date with Dave. We're going to meet friends for a few drinks later. So, I'll take this shopping home and go and have a shower to freshen up. I'll see you tomorrow.'

Realising her grandmother needed some time alone, Piper kissed her on the cheek, stood and went over to the shopping, picking up two of the four bags. 'Blimey, Mum, these are heavy. How did you carry all four of them?'

'Determination, love.'

'I'll see you tomorrow, Gran. If you need anything just call.'

'Will do. Now you two go and have fun. I've got a tapestry to finish.'

Helen left and as Piper reached the front door, Gran called to her.

'How's it going with that young man? Colin's grandson.' When Piper didn't reply immediately, Gran frowned. 'What's the matter? He hasn't done anything he shouldn't, has he?'

Piper didn't want to cause Gran any concern. She'd had enough to deal with emotionally over the past couple of days and she wasn't about to add to that. She fixed a smile on her face and shook her head. 'No, of course he hasn't. It's fine.' She raised the bags and puffed out her cheeks. 'Mum never did figure out how to keep her shopping light.'

'I heard that,' Helen said, popping her head around the door. 'Are you coming?'

'Yes.' Piper pulled a face at her Gran, making her smile. 'I'd better get going. I'll see you tomorrow.'

'Bye, love.'

* * *

Piper followed her mother into the guest house. She walked a few steps past the communal front room when it dawned on her that Alex was sitting in there. Going back, she peered in. 'It is you.'

Alex stood and rushed over to take one of the bags from her.

'Thanks,' she said, glad to have a few minutes to gather herself. The last time she had seen him he had been hurrying off to speak to his girlfriend. *What was he doing here?* Irritation rose. He had kissed her, for pity's sake. *How dare he do this to her? And to his girlfriend.*

She reached the kitchen and her mother looked up, then, noticing Alex over her shoulder, beamed at him. 'How lovely to see you here.'

Piper lifted the bag she was carrying onto the worktop to unpack. She gave him a sideways glare.

'Do you want to join Piper for something to eat a little later, Alex?' Helen asked as she helped Piper unpack the bags. 'I'm out with my friend, Dave, but I'm sure she won't mind cooking something for you when she makes her own supper.'

Piper gritted her teeth to stop from saying anything that might cause a scene.

'Thank you, Helen,' he said. 'But I've already got plans.'

I'll bet you have. Piper's heart pounded faster with anger. 'Don't let us keep you,' she said coolly.

'Piper?' She felt her mother's confused gaze. She was hardly ever rude to people and, as far as Helen was concerned, all Alex had done was help carry in the shopping.

'No, it's fine.' Alex gave Piper a sheepish look. 'Would you mind if I had a quick chat with you in private, Piper? I promise I won't keep you too long.'

'Sorry, I'm helping Mum with this lot.' She had no intention of giving him a moment of her time.

'Nonsense,' Helen said, taking a punnet of tomatoes from Piper's hand. 'You go with Alex and listen to what he has to say.'

Piper closed her eyes briefly to calm her rising temper. She was not going to argue with her mother and had no intention of telling her what had happened that afternoon at St Catherine's. 'If you're sure you don't need me to help you with anything.'

Helen shook her head. 'Now off you go and leave me to finish putting this lot away.' She looked at her watch. 'I must get a move on if I'm not going to be late. It'll be good to know that I don't have to worry about your grandfather and my mother getting along from now on.'

'Sorry?' Alex looked from Helen to Piper, and she realised he still expected his grandfather to be staying next door.

Piper took him by the elbow. 'I'll explain everything outside.' She glanced over her shoulder. 'Have a lovely time this evening, Mum, if I don't get to see you before you rush out.'

'Thanks, sweetheart.'

They stepped outside and Piper closed the door behind them.

'What's been going on?' Alex asked, concerned.

'I think I'm the one who should be asking that question,' Piper said. 'Don't you?'

28

'Is Grandad OK?' Alex asked, following Piper as she marched along the pier and up the few steps at the end of the row of houses before going down the uneven stairs to the small bay behind the pier.

She glanced around, relieved that they were the only people down there. 'Good. We can talk here.'

'Piper, will you tell me what's wrong?' Alex followed her as she made her way to the water's edge.

She took off her shoes and stepped into the water, sighing as some of the tension left her body, relishing the cool waves as they gently rolled over her hot feet. She turned to Alex. 'Firstly, Colin is fine. He and Gran have spoken at length and have smoothed over their differences.' She was rushing her words, wanting to confront him about Naomi and how he had been behaving behind his girlfriend's back, but felt he needed to know about their grandparents first. 'Gran phoned Vivienne and asked her to come and collect him.' She saw shock register on his face and raised a hand to calm him. 'It's fine. Gran has had enough of talking about the past and realised that Vivienne obviously likes Colin.'

'I'm pretty sure the feeling is mutual.'

'Exactly. Gran also felt bad about what happened with Vivienne the other day and so called her and asked her to invite Colin to stay at her bungalow.'

'And so he's gone, I take it?'

'Yes.' She turned her back on him and faced out to sea, at France in the distance, wishing she didn't like Alex nearly as much as she did. It would have made the conversation they were about to have far less painful. She braced herself, remembering his kisses and how betrayed she felt.

She turned back to him, hands clenched at her sides. 'How dare you kiss me when you have a girlfriend. Do you know how humiliated I feel? Do you know what it feels like to discover you are the other woman when you've been hurt by someone doing exactly that same thing to you?' Her cheeks flamed. 'How could you betray Naomi like that, Alex?' She was horrified to discover she was close to tears.

He tried to take her by the arms, but she twisted away. 'Don't you dare touch me.' She took a deep, calming breath. 'Do you have any clue how furious I am with you right now? With myself?'

'Why would you be angry with yourself? You've not done anything you shouldn't.'

'No, not knowingly, I haven't. Thanks to you.'

She walked further into the sea, not caring what she was doing, wanting to put some distance between them.

'Piper. Please,' he said, kicking off his trainers and following her into the water. 'Let me explain.'

'No.' She had listened to enough excuses over the years to invite more. Excuses from her father, from Rick as to why it was her fault he fell in love with Stacy, so very many of them. She hadn't worked this hard on her self-esteem these past eighteen months to give it away just because she had feelings for Alex. He might be different to any other man she had been involved with, more interesting and individual, but she was putting herself first now.

'But, Piper, please listen to me.'

She turned on him, incensed that he was still badgering her. 'I said no, Alex. I've had enough of being made to look foolish. You go back to Naomi. Your grandfather seems settled now and I should be working, not standing here listening to anything you have to say to me.'

She glared at him, determined to ignore the tiny sparks that pinched at her heart as he gazed back at her.

'I'll go then, but you're wrong about me. I wish you would, at least, let me explain.'

'I don't want to hear your excuses.' She pushed her hands deep into her jeans' pockets and turned back to stare out at the sea, wishing he would leave while she still had some semblance of control over her emotions.

Hearing his footsteps leaving, Piper looked back at him. His shoulders were stooped and when he reached the top of the steps he turned to look at her. For a second, her heart leaped when he seemed to be about to come back to her, but then he walked away.

'That's that, then,' she said, her voice tight. She reminded herself that she had done the right thing, as she pushed away her conflicting thoughts. *How could something that felt so right have turned out to be wrong?* Taking a deep breath, she slowly made her way off the beach and back to the pier in time to see him get on his bike and hear the roar as it took off up the hill.

* * *

'You sound as miserable as I feel,' Jax said, appearing from his mother's home with Seamus trotting next to him. 'Was that Alex's bike I just heard leaving?'

Unable to speak for a moment, Piper nodded.

He stopped and took her by the shoulders. 'What's happened?'

She shrugged hopelessly. 'Life.'

'Has this got anything to do with that woman he raced off to speak to at St Catherine's?'

'Yes. She's his girlfriend.' She looked up at Jax, wanting to gauge his reaction. He was scowling and she wondered if it was because he didn't trust Alex.

'He seemed like one of the good ones to me. Are you sure she's his girlfriend?'

'That's what his sister said and what reason would she have to lie about it?'

He gave her comment some thought. 'Maybe she's got it wrong.'

'And maybe she hasn't,' Piper replied miserably. 'He is a bloke after all and fully capable of lying.'

'We're not all like Rick,' Jax reminded her. He pulled her into a hug. 'Aw, I'm sorry things haven't worked out for you.'

She was relieved he didn't add that there were plenty of other men out there who were available. After battling to recover from Rick's betrayal, she had been determined not to get involved with another man unless she was completely sure of him. Unfortunately, the only man she completely trusted was Jax and there would never be anything between them other than being the closest of friends.

'Thanks.' She sniffed. 'I'll be fine. I've just had a

bit of a shock that's all and I'm feeling rather humiliated by the whole thing.'

'Why don't we go and treat ourselves to a drink in the pub.' He indicated a group of their friends laughing and teasing each other at the other end of the pier. 'Take our minds off things.'

They began walking towards the busy pub. 'Hang on a sec,' Piper said, grabbing his arm and stopping him. 'Why do you need something to distract you? What's happened?'

He waved at a couple of their friends and called out to them. 'We're on our way!' They cheered.

'Jax? Tell me.' She hurried to catch up with him.

He bent his head slightly, his voice low. 'After we've had our first drink.'

How long did he intend to be drinking? Piper wondered. Jax didn't often spend much time in the pub, preferring to be outdoors walking, foraging or simply contemplating the magnificence of the sea or a sunset. *Something was wrong.* Guilt coursed through her as she realised she had been so wrapped up in her own drama that she hadn't noticed her cousin was going through one of his own.

Aware that he wasn't ready to talk, she accompanied him to the pub.

'You grab us a seat,' he said, indicating the picnic tables either side of the front door. 'I'll fetch those drinks.'

'Just a soft drink for me. Surprise me.'

'Will do.' He stopped to say 'hello' to two women Piper vaguely recognised before going inside.

Half an hour later, the two women they'd sat next to were giving Seamus a quick cuddle before finally leaving to catch the bus that had arrived a little earlier. Piper waited for them to walk away.

'Are you ready to tell me what's upset you?' she asked hopefully.

Jax turned his glass around in a circle on the weathered table. 'You're going to think I'm getting ahead of myself.'

'You never do that.'

'It's Fliss.'

Her mood dipped further at the mention of Alex's unfriendly sister. 'Why? What's she done to you?'

'Nothing.'

Piper watched as Jax finished his drink and then it dawned on her. 'You like her, don't you?'

'Yes. Stupid of me, I know.'

'Why?'

'Because she's beautiful and I'm totally punching above my weight even dreaming someone like her would look at me.'

Infuriated, Piper glared at him. 'Don't you ever let me hear you talk about yourself in that way,' she said. 'You're handsome, clever and, according to the girls I know, hot. She'd be lucky to have someone like you, and don't you forget it.'

She heard a voice she recognised and looked up to see Fliss, Phoebe and a third taller woman she was sure she recognised as Naomi passing by. 'Well, look who it is.'

Jax did, his face lighting up when he noticed Fliss.

'Where are they off to, do you think?' Piper took a sip of her drink. They weren't visiting Colin now he was no longer at the pier, so maybe they were just having a walk, or going to spend some money in one of the shops.

When they stopped in front of her home, Piper

sat up a little straighter. She watched them have a quick chat about something and then Fliss knocked on the front door. Seconds later, Helen opened it, ready for her date with Dave, who had arrived in time to rescue her mother from the three enthusiastic women. If he hadn't, Piper's conscience wouldn't have let her stand by while the threesome questioned her mother, which they seemed to be doing now.

'I'm going to have to go and speak to them,' she said, finishing her drink. 'I think they're looking for me.'

'I'll come with you.'

She and Jax got up from their seats and together with Seamus hurried to where her mother was now waving to the girls and walking arm in arm with Dave to his car.

'Are you looking for me?' Piper asked, trying her best to sound friendly. She spotted Phoebe reddening when she saw that Jax was with her. Piper thought how typical it was that Jax liked Fliss – who Piper suspected was only interested in him because her friend was attracted to him – when it was Phoebe who liked her cousin.

'Yes, that's right.' Fliss seemed to be sneering, but Piper decided it might be a smile. 'Is there somewhere we could go and have a chat?'

'Sure. Let's go and sit in our backyard.' Piper looked at Jax. 'You coming?'

'If you'd like me to.'

'I would,' Phoebe said shyly.

Once settled in the backyard at the guest house and everyone had declined drinks, Piper sat in the last remaining chair. 'You wanted to speak to me about something?'

'It was me, actually,' Naomi said, speaking for the first time. 'Alex wanted me to come and explain our situation to you.'

Piper shook her head, confused. 'Why?'

Fliss groaned. 'Because he likes you, surely that's obvious?'

Ah, there was the Fliss Piper recognised. 'I think that's irrelevant if he has a girlfriend.'

Naomi stood. 'He doesn't. That's the whole point.'

Baffled by where the conversation was going and embarrassed to be at the centre of it, Piper sighed heavily. 'Fliss said that you lived together and had come over to be with him.'

'I know.' Naomi shot Fliss a furious glare. 'Which is why she's here to apologise. Both to you and to me.'

Piper glanced at Jax to see if he understood what was going on. He raised his eyebrows at her and shook his head. 'Don't look at me. I'm none the wiser. In fact, I'm not sure my presence here is helping. Do you mind if Seamus and I get going?'

Piper shook her head, happy for one of them to be able to escape. 'I'll catch up with you tomorrow.'

He walked into the house and Phoebe leaped up from her chair and raced after him. 'I'll come with you.'

Poor Jax. Piper gave him a sympathetic look, which he returned. She wasn't sure which one of them was better off, her being left with Naomi and Fliss, or him with a love-struck Phoebe in tow.

'You were saying something about apologies,' Piper said, still not sure what was going on.

'Yes,' Naomi said. 'Go on, Fliss. Get it over with.'

'All right, don't go on.' Fliss shrugged. 'I'm sorry. Really. When I told Naomi to come to the island, I led her to believe that Alex wanted to give their relationship another go.'

'Sorry, what?' Piper folded her arms. 'But don't the two of you live together?'

A pained expression flitted across Naomi's face before she closed her eyes briefly. 'I am living in his apartment, but only for the time being while my place is fixed.' She clasped her hands together. 'We never lived together when we were seeing each other.'

'Oh, I see.' Piper still didn't quite understand the dynamics of Naomi and Alex's relationship. 'But you are living with him now?'

'Only because he's helping me out,' Naomi said, an apology in her wide blue eyes. 'Recently, my up-stairs bathroom flooded, and I had to move out of my cottage. I needed somewhere to stay and can't afford to pay rent anywhere as well as paying my mortgage.' She frowned. 'My lousy insurance policy wasn't much use. So I asked Alex if I could stay with him until it was fixed.'

'And he said yes.' Piper was beginning to think she had been wrong about her initial dislike of Naomi. It embarrassed her to think that her feelings had been due to envy at Alex having a girlfriend when she had feelings for him.

'That's right,' Naomi continued. 'When his grandfather had his accident and he was going to be over here for longer than he had expected, he agreed.' She took a deep breath. 'As you've probably worked out, I'd happily get back with Alex. He's moved on though.' She picked at the side of her thumbnail. 'But he's a good man and, despite what you've been led to believe, certainly not someone given to being underhand. And I would hate for anyone to think badly of him, especially as he's been so kind to me.'

'Thank you for explaining everything to me.' Piper looked at Fliss, who she was surprised to note appeared embarrassed to be held to account. 'So, what you said was a lie?'

Her tanned cheeks reddened slightly. 'I am sorry, Piper.'

'But I don't understand why you would do something like that. It doesn't make any sense to me.'

'Or me,' Naomi said sternly. 'In fact, I'd go so far as to say it was cruel of you to give me hope where there was none and to let Piper assume that Alex had lied to her.'

'I know it was now,' Fliss said, close to tears. 'And

I feel horrible for being mean to the pair of you. Most of all, though, I wish I hadn't done this to Alex.'

Piper appreciated the apology, but couldn't quite let go. 'I still don't understand why you did it, Fliss.'

'I'm not sure.' Fliss flicked her long fair hair over her shoulder. 'Actually, that's not quite true. I picked up straight away that Alex liked you,' she said, giving Piper an accusatory look. 'He's never acted this way about a girl before. And he was enjoying being on the island a bit too much for my liking. Then Grandad got hurt and he came here again. I flew over to see Grandad and saw the way my brother was with you.'

'So?' Naomi shrugged. 'How does that affect you? You're independent and always doing your own thing. I don't understand.'

Fliss sighed. 'I admit I sound pretty pathetic, but I hated to think he'd fall for you properly and come to live here. Our parents are always away somewhere, and Alex is the closest person to me. I can trust him with anything.'

Piper felt a burst of pity for her. 'Couldn't you have spoken to him about your feelings?'

'I did. He told me I was being silly, but I knew I

wasn't.' She shrugged. 'I decided that if he wouldn't listen then I could hint to you that he was spoken for, and you would hopefully end whatever was going on between you. Then he would have no reason to stay here once Grandad came back to England.'

'And that's exactly what I did.' Piper realised she had played into Fliss' hands, not giving Alex a chance to explain.

Naomi shook her head. 'You had no way of knowing what she was doing.'

'I'm embarrassed,' Piper said. 'I should have listened to Alex instead of believing the worst of him.'

Fliss stood. 'I've said I'm sorry, and I really am. Can I pay for us all to go out for something to eat by way of an apology?'

Piper looked at her. She did seem sorry. And Alex must have been angry with her to persuade her to come to the house to apologise.

She nodded. 'I accept your apology, but you don't need to do anything. I'm just happy to know the truth.' *And that Alex hasn't lied to me.*

Someone's mobile buzzed and Naomi and Fliss immediately withdrew their phones from their pockets. After a quick check, Naomi pushed hers back into her trouser pocket.

Piper watched silently as Fliss read a message and then typed a reply.

'I think it's time we left,' Fliss said to Naomi. Then, addressing Piper, added, 'Alex is waiting outside and would like to see you.'

29

Piper's heart pounded so loudly she was surprised everyone couldn't hear it. She followed the women outside and waited while Alex spoke briefly to his sister and Naomi.

'Hi, Phoebe,' she said, finding herself standing next to her, a few feet away from Alex's bike. 'Jax not with you?'

'He had work to do,' she said miserably.

Piper noticed him in the distance on the beach. 'He's got a lot of work on at the moment,' she explained. 'It's a busy time of year for him.'

'I thought so,' Phoebe said, sounding a little placated.

'We're off now.' Naomi came over and gave Piper a hug. 'I hope I get to meet you again sometime,' she said. 'But in more amiable circumstances.'

'That would be very nice,' Piper said honestly. 'I'm glad it's all been sorted, finally.'

'So am I.'

Fliss rested a hand on Piper's shoulder. 'I truly am sorry for being such a mean cow.'

Piper smiled. 'Let's forget it ever happened, shall we?'

Fliss looked doubtful. 'Are you sure?'

'Absolutely certain.'

'That's a relief.' Fliss frowned. 'My brother was telling me he's thinking about relocating to the island, and I have a feeling it's because he'd like to spend more time with you.'

Piper opened her mouth to speak but was too stunned to find the words. It was the first she'd heard of him moving to the island for good.

Fliss winced. 'He hasn't spoken to you about it yet, has he?'

'No, he hasn't.'

'Bugger. Would you mind keeping this to ourselves until he does?'

Piper didn't mind at all. 'I promise I won't mention anything to him.'

'Thanks,' Fliss smiled. 'That's really good of you.'

She waited while the three women walked away, ready to face Alex. She might have thought that he had betrayed her, but she was the one who had been distrustful of him, not giving him a chance to explain. She braced herself and turned to him, unsure what to say.

'Hi,' he said, beaming at her. 'What do you say to us starting again?'

Piper nodded enthusiastically. 'I say that sounds like a great idea.' She walked up to him, still astride on his motorbike, and took his hand in hers.

'And don't forget you've promised to help me find a location for my friend, Matteo.'

Piper felt a sweep of excitement race through her at the thought of everything that lay ahead for them. Her life was finally getting to be much more interesting.

Alex raised her hand to his lips. 'Hi, my name is Alex.'

'Pleased to meet you, Alex. I'm Piper.'

He held out his spare helmet. 'Would you like to come to St Ouen's Bay and watch the sun go down?'

She took the helmet from him. 'I can't think of anything I'd rather do.'

ACKNOWLEDGMENTS

Firstly, I want to thank Joan Honeycombe, one of the honeymooners who spent her honeymoon with her late husband Gerald (Gerry) in Jersey in the late 1950s and whose reminiscences of that special time, I am most grateful for.

To Glynis Peters, Joan's daughter and one of my favourite authors who, when I told her about my inspiration for this series, mentioned that her parents were 'honeymooners'.

As ever, to my wonderful mum, Tess, my husband, Rob and my children, Saskia and James, who are my constant joy.

To the brilliant team at Boldwood Books, I'm so thrilled to be working with you all.

And especially to Claire Fenby and Tara Loder, my wonderful editor, as well as Camilla Lloyd for proofreading this book. I know *Finding Love on Sun-*

shine Island is much better thanks to your invaluable input.

And most of all to you, dear reader. I hope you enjoy this first instalment in the Sunshine Island series. If you did, please consider leaving a review on Amazon or anywhere else you fancy.

AUTHOR'S LETTER

Dear Reader,

Firstly, I'd like to thank you for choosing to read this first book in my new *Sunshine Island* series. I hope you've enjoyed it enough to want to read the second book in the series, and then the next one...

Jersey is the sunniest and, on average, warmest place in the British Isles. The Channel Islands are set in the Bay of St Malo and Jersey is the closest one to France and, therefore, slightly better protected by the Brittany Mountains in France than Guernsey, another beautiful place and the other large island in the Channel Islands.

I was born in Jersey and have spent most of my

life here. Although the island is only nine miles by five miles, almost one hundred thousand people live here. The island is known for its creamy Jersey Royal potatoes and its golden, sandy beaches. Tourism has always been a big draw to the island with many holidaymakers enjoying the delicious seafood and beautiful scenery. It's a very pretty place and, due to our connection with France, a lot of the roads have French names.

I hope that if you have visited Jersey and enjoyed it, this series will remind you of familiar places and if you haven't, that *Finding Love on Sunshine Island* gives you a taste of what it's like to live on this pretty island.

I share a lot of photos of the island on my Instagram page @AJerseyWriter should you wish to see more of the island and can't wait to share the next book in this series with you.

For now, though, I'd like to thank you again for reading this first book in my *Sunshine Island* series. If you enjoyed it, please tell your friends all about it and maybe write a brief review on Amazon for me. It can be as short as simply saying, 'I loved this book' or something like that. Reviews only have to be short, and in fact, now you can simply give a rating without having to review the book at all. Either way, it all helps other readers discover new books. If you do leave a rating/review, thank you in advance.

You can also keep up to date with all my writing news by subscribing to my monthly newsletter at https://deborahcarr.org/newsletter/
Follow me:
Facebook: https://www.
facebook.com/GeorginaTroyAuthor
Twitter: https://twitter.com/GeorginaTroy

MORE FROM GEORGINA TROY

We hope you enjoyed reading *Finding Love on Sunshine Island*. If you did, please leave a review.

If you'd like to gift a copy, this book is also available as an ebook, digital audio download and audiobook CD.

Sign up to Georgina Troy's mailing list for news, competitions and updates on future books.

https://bit.ly/GeorginaTroyNews

ABOUT THE AUTHOR

Georgina Troy writes bestselling uplifting romantic escapes and sets her novels on the island of Jersey where she was born and has lived for most of her life. She has done a twelve-book deal with Boldwood, including backlist titles, and the first book in her Sunshine Island series was published in May 2022.

Visit Georgina's website: https://deborahcarr.org/my-books/georgina-troy-books/

Follow Georgina on social media here:

[f] facebook.com/GeorginaTroyAuthor

[t] twitter.com/GeorginaTroy

[i] instagram.com/ajerseywriter

[BB] bookbub.com/authors/georgina-troy

Boldwood

Boldwood Books is an award-winning fiction publishing company seeking out the best stories from around the world.

Find out more at www.boldwoodbooks.com

Join our reader community for brilliant books, competitions and offers!

Follow us
@BoldwoodBooks
@BookandTonic

Sign up to our weekly
deals newsletter

https://bit.ly/BoldwoodBNewsletter